T0063914

DEFIANCE OF THE
REALM

DEFIANCE OF THE
REALM

M. W. KOHLER

DEFIANCE OF THE REALM

iUniverse books may be ordered through booksellers or by contacting:

iUniverse
1663 Liberty Drive
Bloomington, IN 47403
www.iuniverse.com
1-800-Authors (1-800-288-4677)

ISBN: 978-1-4917-5229-6 (sc)
ISBN: 978-1-4917-5230-2 (e)

Library of Congress Control Number: 2014919627

Printed in the United States of America.

iUniverse rev. date: 11/10/2014

NOTES FROM THE AUTHOR

Defiance of the Realm is the sixth book in *The Valley* series.

In the years following the defeat of Brandaro and the Domain Bandarson, the four young couples of Zentler had become parents. Those who had been injured in battle of Neponia healed and thrived. The Queen of the Southern Section had submitted to the will of the other two Queens, joining the alliance with the Realm and the Domains of Rightful Magic, but she developed resentment because she felt that they had forced her to do so. The citizens of Bandarson changed the name of their domain to Namsia, but not all of those of Bandarson City, which was now called Namsia City, or the outer provinces, agreed with the change. Namson and Glornina and all those of the Realm and the domains of Rightful Magic, settled into the daily lives of happiness. For the most part, the living of life seemed to come to a state of contentment. But, with all contentment, the Fates cannot allow it to last.

PROLOGUE

The Bandit ruler, Brandaro and those who followed his orders had been defeated. Namson, Overseer of the Realm, had led the forces of Rightful Magic to free the peoples of the Domain Bandarson. The majority of those newly freed peoples quickly began to realize the possibilities available to them. A new order was being established, as the responsibilities of their new freedoms were accepted. But, there was one woman, Cenlinas, who had been a bed slave to the bandit ruler when he was younger, was furious that the children she had birthed, the heirs to Brandaro's throne, were being denied their right to rule! She blamed the Overseer and all those of the domains who had obeyed him, for their conquering of Bandarson and the wrongful deprivation of her children, of their right to rule. She was not the only one of the domain to feel discontent, for there was still a great many that wanted the bandit life back and hated what was happening with the leadership of their domain. Cenlinas taught her children rebellion, as the others plotted to reclaim what had been.

In some of the domains of Rightful Magic and one not yet known to the alliance, there were those who plotted their own desires of contempt for the Overseer and the Domains of Rightful Magic.

On Natharia, the world of the huge, spider like creatures, who had helped those of Rightful Magic battle the forces of Dark Magic, Bistalan, the third son of Bleudarn, sought his father's power as the Ruler of that domain. He was convinced that the Realm should be held responsible to all Natharian's, especially himself, for what he saw as underpayment for all that the Natharian's had contributed to the wars with Dark Magic. He began to organize his revolution.

In Neponia, the Queen of the Central Section, Neponities, and the Queen of the Northern Section, Nepelia, convinced the Queen of the Southern Section, Nepolia, with means that were rather devious, to join the alliance with the Domains of Rightful Magic. The Southern Queen was becoming more and more dissatisfied with this joining and began to plot her own rebellion.

On a world that had not yet been introduced to the Domains of Rightful Magic, there were two domains, Gargoylia, and Weretoran. Both had listened as talkers had sought Daridar and the Bandits Domain. In one of these domains, Gargoylia, the most powerful Wizard had tried to join with Brandaro, to use the bandits to help destroy the Weretorians, but had been completely rejected, almost losing his life doing so. The now ruler, Garator, plotted to take control of their entire world and also, what he thought to be the wealth of the Realm.

The Gargoylians were a primitive race, not even speaking in complete sentences. The winged gargoyles, which were the only Gargoyles to possess horns and were the ruling class, were a race that could only envision gain, by taking it with brutality.

In the other domain, Weretoran, the Weretorians had discovered the previous attempt by the Wizard and had battled the Gargoylians to stop the joining and, their own destruction. They now sought to protect themselves from any further attempts by the Gargoylians. The King, Wereteran, was also considering joining in the alliance of the Rightful Magic of the Realm and other domains. Both of these races have had an association with humanity, from history long past.

———— ∿∿∿⊙∿⊙⊙⊙∿⊙∿∿∿ ————

Then there was Somora and those who had escaped Castope's Dark City with him and were plotting their way into the very core of the Domains of Rightful Magic, to defeat from within.

———— ∿∿∿⊙∿⊙⊙⊙∿⊙∿∿∿ ————

Cenlinas watched her biological twins, both now adults, as they walked towards the house. She smiled, but not too widely. They had learned the lessons she had taught them. She knew that both hated the Realm and the Overseer. They also hated what had become of their father's domain. She saw Brando, her son; speak to his sister and her nod of understanding. They had become quite secretive over the last year and there were times she worried of what they plotted. But, that worry was held in check by the knowledge that they plotted for the freedom from the Realms power over Bandarson.

She felt her anger as she thought of the name of Namsia, that the parsha dwarf had convinced the population to adopt. She was quite sure that her children would, in time, right these wrongs done to the domain Brandaro had made for them.

———

On Neponia, Neponities watched her daughter from the balcony of her room, as Nepanities practiced sword warfare with her Chosen Mate, Carsanac, in the rear yard of the palace. She smiled with pride as Nepanities parried the attack of her mate and then went on an attack of her own. Neponities frowned at the smile of the male, for she still found difficulty with his tendency to take an equals place when around Nepanities. She knew that somehow, Carsanac had instinctively known how to use the weapons of battle, which included the body itself and had patiently, taught Nepanities all that he knew. She was proud that he would love her daughter enough to want her protected with the abilities he had taught her. Neponities had insisted that he teach her armies the same battle tactics and she was amazed at the proficiency of her troops that had resulted from his efforts. She again felt the irritations as she looked to Carsanac's small smile. She was aware that with the new laws, that she herself had pushed through, that males now had more privilege and authority in Neponian society, but the old ways of thinking had not completely died away.

As she watched the mock battle, she remembered the last time her daughter had been forced to a meeting on a Challenge Field. The woman, who had forced that event, Nepodorsia, though older than her daughter, was a still young woman of power and was known to be a dangerous enemy. She had more than once proven her skills with weapons, especially swords. Nepanities had met her on that Challenge Field and seemed almost casual as she easily defeated the challenger. She had spared the woman's life in a very obvious display of ridicule for the reasons of the challenge. By doing so, Nepanities had made the woman's defeat even more of a humiliation. The resulting loss of standing in the social and business world of Neponia had caused the woman to hold a powerful, vengeful grudge against Nepanities and so, Neponities.

As these memories came to her, she could not help but think of the trip her daughter and her Chosen Mate, would be making soon. She would be sending them to the Southern Section, to bring Nepolia, the ruling Queen of that Section, the option of empowering the males of her Section. By doing so, what would be expected of a male in one section, would be the same as the other two, thereby standardizing the social levels to the same, in all three Sections. She was not sure that Nepolia would agree, knowing of Nepolia's contemptuous attitude concerning males in general!

On Natharia, Bistalan watched his father, Bleudarn, as he continued his plotting to take the position of Ruler from the one he saw as a weakling and betrayer of all Natharian's. He was enraged by the posturing he had convinced himself he saw from the Ruler of Natharia. He was absolutely sure that not only did the Domain of Natharia deserve a greater amount of compensation from the Realm, he was deserving of even more, for the shame his grandfather, and father, had forced upon him.

In the Domain Gargoylia, in the capital city of Gartisia; it was the time of sleep, but Gorastor, a young, but mature wingless girl, was awoken with the feeling of a hand moving up her leg. She did not need to open her eyes to know what was happening. In less time it would take to blink, she grabbed the hand, twisting it behind the back of her older brother, and flipping over on top of the one that would abuse her. "Do not think can," she whispered harshly, giving an extra twist to the wrist she held. Garteltor groaned, quietly.

"Alright," he whispered. "Let go." Gorastor chuckled.

"I lead, ladder," she hissed at him. "Sleep below."

"Alright," Garteltor said, too loudly. "Let go, leave." Gorastor chuckled again.

"Yes, help you," she snarled at him. She moved from his back and pulling harder on the arm she held, directed him to the ladder that led to the lower level. Once he was on it, she looked into his eyes. "Never again, or die," she whispered, and released his arm. He wouldn't even look at her as he climbed down the ladder.

In the Domain of Weretoran; Werelaran walked from his parent's tomb. His father had just been placed next to his mother and he was now King. His wife and new Queen, Wereselon; walked by his side, her belly just beginning to swell with the coming of their first children, for they already knew there would be twins. Many thoughts now raced through Werelaran's mind. The most prominent was the idea that somehow, the Gargoyles had been behind the unexpected death of his father. He was angered with that thought, even more so because he had not been able to find any proof that they had been.

He also sensed a hint of a strange danger. Again, he could find no proof of it, but he felt it none the less. Immediately after his father's death, but prior to the ceremony of his father's entombment, he had instructed the newly proclaimed, most powerful of witches, Weretilon, to monitor all communications to or from the yet unknown, but heard of, Realm. He felt that the time when Werewolves must again go among humans, was nearing.

CHAPTER ONE

As the sun began to rise in the eastern sky of the Realm, in the palace of the Overseer, Namson lay with Glornina held in his left arm. He had woken with a severe sense of something wrong. He wanted to return to sleep, but it was not to be. His thoughts fought for the right of supremacy and won. It had been five years since the rule of Brandaro had been defeated, yet, he still felt unrest. Something, somehow, somewhere, was not as it should be. He tried to ease his arm from under Glornina and she woke.

"What is it Namson?' she asked him with worry, after she had looked into his eyes. He shook his head, slightly.

"Couldn't sleep," he told her trying, but failing to smile; "thought I'd see if the coffee was ready yet. Sorry, I didn't mean to wake you." He rolled from bed and went to dress. "Do you want me to bring you some?" he asked, without looking at her. She got out of bed.

"No, I will come with you," she told him. She slipped on her robe as she joined him at the bedroom door. He again, almost made a smile as he opened the door. She took his arm with a very worried glance and they went silently to the dining room. They arrived just as the Melerets were setting the two large pots.

"Good morning Overseer, Mistress," Pelkraen said with a bow. "I had a feeling there would be early risings this morning, so I had the coffee and tea, started earlier than normal." Glornina smiled at Pelkraen. She was very fond of the weasel sized, cat faced creatures who had become so much a part of the lives of all those in the Domains of Rightful Magic.

As Namson began to fill his and Glornina's cups, Zachia and Emma walked into the dining room. Zachia, like his father, was dressed. Emma, like Glornina, was in her robe. Emma looked to Glornina with concern in her eyes. Glornina nodded her understanding as she followed Namson to the table. They sat at the head of the table, Glornina sitting to Namson's right. Zachia copied his father's actions and carried his and Emma's cups, to the table as well. They took their chairs, on the side of the table, to Namson's left, Zachia sitting the closest to his father. Silence sat with them all for several minutes. Zachia took several sips from his cup and made less than a happy face. A carafe of peach brandy appeared on the table in front of him. He picked it up and poured some into his cup. He took another sip and then nodded. They had all watched his actions and the women again looked to each other, their worries growing, as Namson reached for the container and poured some into his cup as well.

"Alright, what's going on?" Glornina asked with a trace of irritation in her voice. Both Namson and Zachia looked to her.

"Zachia, what is it?" Emma asked him quietly, looking at him with the worry she felt. Zachia looked to his wife, as Namson looked to his and both sighed.

"I don't know," Namson told Glornina softly.

"It's like there's something wrong, but I can't see it, or know what it means," Zachia added as he looked to Emma. Namson nodded, with a glance at his son. Emma and Glornina looked to each other, then back to their mates.

"Can you describe the feeling any more than that?" Glornina asked both Namson and Zachia. The two men looked to each other, then to Glornina. They both shrugged only slightly, as they slowly shook their heads. Pelkraen entered the room and walked up next to Namson.

"Overseer, the Keeper of all Magic of Vistalin, calls on the orb in your office. He says it is important." Namson nodded as he rose. He left the table for his office, not sure of the reason for the tightening of his stomach. He entered the room and turned to his left. He stopped in front of the orb. He looked to the confused, concerned face of Edward.

"Hello Edward, what can I do for you?" he asked. Edward tried to smile.

"My daughter Ventia woke me up saying that she has had a sensing, that there is trouble rising on Natharia," he told

Namson. "She doesn't know for sure what it is, but says it is serious." Namson stared at Edward for a few moments. He felt his stomach tighten more. He finally nodded.

"Alright, thank you. Zachia and I will check it out. We'll let you know what we find," he told him. Edward nodded and broke the connection. Namson returned to the dining table and sat again, reaching for his coffee. There was a strange look in his eyes when Zachia looked to him.

At an intersection, in one of the lower class neighborhoods that made up the outer fringes of Namsia City, a tall, skinny man came to a stop. He casually looked down each of the streets. "Has there been any more word?" Gentaring, one of the many illegitimate sons of Rentaring, one of those who had been part of the wrongs done to the peoples of the Domain Bandarson, asked in a whisper to the one he didn't need to look to.

"Not yet," replied the one who wouldn't come from the shadows. "But, the understanding has come to all who would fight to regain Bandarson and remove the dwarf from her stolen position that they are to unite and be ready." Gentaring gave only a hint of a nod and then walked away, towards the secret meeting he was to lead.

The female dwarf Daridar, the reelected Mayor of Namsia, which was not limited to Namsia City, but included all of the Domain Namsia, had been becoming more and more concerned about the slow, but steady increase of the civil unrest in Namsia City, as well as some of the closer Provinces. These happenings had become far more prevalent since her reelection.

Daridar was large for a dwarf, at well over five and a half feet tall. She was also blessed to have a less prominent dwarf appearance. She was sure that, that was probably why she had been more easily accepted by the most of the populace, who still held a less than equal's opinion of most dwarves. She was also aware that all of Namsia knew that in the days prior to the downfall of Bandarson and Brandaro's rule of this domain, that she had started the rebellion among female dwarfs, for the rejection of the male dwarf's absolute rule over them. She had also organized those who were called parsha's, for they gave their efforts for the pleasure of others'. She realized that as those she had organized were a very large portion of the populace of the city and the provinces. She was sure, that was why she had been so easily reelected Mayor.

The moment of unrest had not yet come to a point that could be considered truly dangerous, but the number and severity of these happenings had been rising for several months. She had decided to call for a special council meeting to address this troubling trend. She now looked around the large table, surrounded by the sitting council members of the four sections of Namsia City and the many provinces of the Domain Namsia, who had brought her shocking news. "Are you sure of this?" she asked them all. They all nodded their heads.

"Yes Mayor," Frintoran, councilman for the Southwest section of Namsia City told her. "There are reports from all over, that there are many who are not happy about what has happened to our domain. They blame you for the changing of the domains name, and are angry about your reelection." The last words were spoken in a very soft voice.

"I have heard rumors," Peligarn, councilwoman of one of the Southeast provinces said; "that these people are planning to rise up against you and are going to try to reclaim the domain as Bandarson again." Daridar looked to each, seeing the agreement in their eyes and knew what she had to do. She started to open her mind, but the abrupt entrance of one of her personal guards interrupted her.

"Mayor, the orb in your office, is gone!" the guard declared much too loudly as he stopped just feet from her. She stared at him as he continued to nod, even when quiet. Daridar looked around the room, seeing that all of the councilors were looking at her, wide eyed. She opened her mind, calling to the Realm and anyone who would answer her. Each of the council members nodded their approval of her obvious actions.

On the world called Earth, in the town of Zentler, which was less than five miles from the magical source called the Plain, on the south west end of town and at the garden four families shared; "Nathan, if you do that again, you know what I will do," Kris said sternly, after Ava's squeal had subsided. She hadn't needed to lift her head, or take her eyes from the weeds she was pulling, to know what her eldest had done. Isabella, pulling weeds on the opposite side of the garden, tried not to laugh. One and a half year old Geebee, whose full name was Gabriella and hung in the cradle of cloth beneath Kris and was supposed to be napping, giggled, her young eyes on her mother. "Don't you start," Kris said quietly to the girl and she giggled again.

"I wasn't doing nothing," Nathan said as he threw the lizard away. The four year old already showing the short, yet well muscled physical appearance of his father.

"Why you…," Ava cried out, with a hidden grin. She ran to her mother, and Isabella understood.

"He was just being a boy," she told her daughter quietly, still trying not to laugh. Ava smiled her little girl smile, and nodded.

"I know mama, but he can be a pain sometimes." The four year old girl began to twist from side to side, glaring at the four year old son of her mother's best friend, who had now found some other type of creature to play with. "In many ways, he takes after his father," she whispered. Her mother looked at her with concern.

—————

In the Domain Namsia, it was quite early in the morning, the bright sun was just clear of the horizon. On a small farm in the Province of Barlaro, near the town of Bentodon, about ninety miles north of Namsia City, Cenlinas watched her shirtless son, Brando, as he walked behind the plow being pulled by the large mule. *He has definitely taken after his father*, she thought. She smiled as she looked to the boy, who at eighteen was well over seven foot tall, very handsome, and extremely well muscled. She was proud of her children, even though her daughter, Brendo, was rumored to have earned a reputation with the boys of Bentodon. At least she wasn't pregnant, as far as Cenlinas knew anyway.

"Mama?" Brendo asked as she came from the house. "Do we have any more of that cream you got from Gensilia, at the market? I used the last of what we had this morning." Cenlinas turned, looked at her daughter and smiled. She could see why the boys of Bentodon wanted to be with her, just as she had understood why a young Brandaro had wanted her when even younger than her daughter; she had been brought to him as his bed slave.

"No honey," she told the very lovely and finely figured girl. It was at that moment, Cenlinas, for the first time, realized that Brendo, though taller than her own six foot height, wasn't as tall as her brother, at only about six and a half foot. Cenlinas knew the girl wasn't as physically strong as her brother, but was highly respected by most for the ferocity she had more than once proven. "I have to go to the market in Bentodon today and I'll see if she has any more. I'll be leaving in an hour or so if you would want to come with me?" Brendo nodded as she sat down in the chair next to Cenlinas, but at a right angle to her mother's chair. She looked to her brother as he plowed the small field next to their house.

"There are many women, young and old, who would gladly lay with him," Brendo said quietly, more to herself than talking to her mother; "if he didn't get so rough with them." Cenlinas chuckled softly.

"He has too much of his father in him. He couldn't change, even if he thought he should." Brendo joined in her chuckle, nodding. She knew that Brandaro was hers and her brother's, father. Cenlinas had repeatedly told them both of their lineage.

"Are you still going to Bandarson City in the next couple of weeks?" Brendo asked her mother.

"Yes," Cenlinas said, smiling; "and I'm pleased that you said it properly," Cenlinas smiled at her daughter. She turned back to watch the biological twin brother of Brendo. "I cannot believe those fools for changing the name. They would be nothing if it had not been for your father."

"I can't believe they actually elected that dwarf as Mayor, a second time!" Brendo said with contempt. Cenlinas actually growled.

"I don't want to talk about that parsha who thinks herself something valuable!" Cenlinas's rage exploded in her words. "She should have been put to death with the others' who were killed, trying to defile your father!"

"Mama, it is said that there were only a few who had died," Brendo said casually, not even looking to her mother. Cenlinas sprang from her chair, grabbing her daughter's arms fiercely, driving her backwards. This action causing the chair the girl had been sitting in to topple over backwards and Brendo landed on her back, her mother on top of her. Cenlinas's face red, her eyes bulging with the rage she felt.

"Take those words back!" she screamed at the girl. "There is no way that Brandaro would die without taking many of those bastards with him!" Brando, having heard his mother's first outcry about Daridar, had stopped the plow mule and came running to the porch. He easily pulled his raging mother from his surprised sister and forced her back to her chair. Brendo, still on her back, scrambled backwards from her mother until the railing around the end of the porch stopped her. Her now angry eyes locked on the raving woman, who was her mother, as she rose to her feet.

"Calm yourself," Brando said to his mother, as he held her easily. She looked to him and for a split second, she saw his father in his eyes. She smiled with the sight. "Like you, I think the reports of my father's affects on their forces, was a lie, meant to impress those of Bandarson, to convince them that their power was greater!" Cenlinas smiled, as her sons words and voice, reminded her of the only one she had ever loved. She calmed in his grip. "I have been talking with others' and I believe that there are many that feel as I do," he told her. "That is why we all are going to Bandarson City in the coming weeks. There will be many who will join us there!" Brando's voice had gotten very low, with a threatening tone to it. Cenlinas smiled wider as she nodded to her son.

Brendo looked from her brother, to her mother, and back. Both of her hands resting on the railing behind her, as she realized that she wasn't sure which of the two was the craziest, but, she was willing to put all of her money, on her mother.

∽∽·◦⬧◦◦◈◦◦⬧◦·∽∽

"My Queen," Calitoran said softly, interrupting Nepolia's continuing contemplations of what she was going to do about her forced acceptance to what she saw as the Overseer's rule. Her thoughts also included what Depelia, the one who possessed the second greatest level of magical power of her Section and was the strongest talker, had heard from the Mayor of Namsia. She turned her eyes to her Advisor, and occasional bed mate.

"What do you want Calitoran?" the Queen of the Southern Section asked, not hiding her irritation. The Advisor bowed.

"There is a messenger from Neponities, waiting," he told her, with a tremble in his voice.

"Let her wait," Nepolia said harshly.

"It is Carsanac, My Lady," Calitoran said softly, with fear. Nepolia sprang to her feet, her eyes blazing with rage.

"What!" Nepolia screamed. "How dare Neponities send the mere Chosen Mate of her daughter, as a messenger to me!" The Queens eyes bore into the now cowering Advisor. "This is the final insult I will take from that whore, who claims to be Leading Queen!" Nepolia came down the two steps of the raised platform that held her throne. "Tell that scum of a male that he can return to Neponities with the word that I will not tolerate this! That she has caused the war that now is to be for this insult!"

"Queen Nepolia," a baritone voice came to her. She looked from her Advisor and saw the surprisingly large, well muscled man standing fifteen feet inside the door of the large throne room. "I think you should hear Queen Neponities message, before you condemn your Section to a war it cannot win." His words were gentle, but there was a tone to his voice that enraged Nepolia even more, a tone of threatening equality. Nepolia started to walk towards the male, pulling the short sword from the scabbard that hung from her waist.

"Get out of my sight you low life male, or I will kill you myself!" she screamed at him. He didn't change expression as a dozen of Neponities soldiers came through the door, forming an arc, behind him. Following them came Nepanities and, she was smiling. She stopped next to her Chosen Mate. Nepolia froze, her eyes widening, as she saw that Nepanities was near the height of her mate.

"Do you really want me to return to my mother, and tell her of your opinion that she is a whore?" she asked quietly, her voice near the baritone of her mate as well; "and if you ever talk to my mate that way again, I will enjoy meeting you on a Challenge Field Nepolia." Her voice was still soft, but she was looking into Nepolia's eyes with an anger that carried power and, she had lost her smile. All knew of the finality of any that challenged Nepanities fighting skills, including Nepolia. They also knew that her Chosen Mate had taught her all she could do. Nepolia tried to regain her authority.

"What is Neponities message?" she demanded in a tone that did not carry the strength she had wanted.

"Queen Neponities...," Carsanac started.

"Not you male!" Nepolia interrupted with a yell, pointing the sword she still held at him. Nepanities put her hand on the hilt of her sword.

"Yes him!" she stated, taking a step towards Nepolia. Nepolia's eyes showed her rage as she looked to the daughter of Neponities.

"Then there will be no message," she said, her voice showing the intensity of the rage she felt. "Get out, all of you, now! Guards!" she screamed. The not so distant sounds of many feet were heard coming closer. Nepanities smiled again.

"I shall tell my mother of your refusal," she said, calmly. She turned, and started to leave the room. Carsanac turned, and walked by her side. The dozen followed them.

On Natharia, in a cave formed by the roots of one of the humongous trees; "The time has come," Bistalan said in a hissed growl. The bright morning sun could barely be seen through branches and leaves of the gigantic trees that grew to hundreds of feet in height. The four, who would lead the soldiers of Bistalan's cause, nodded. "My grandfather submitted to the lies of the Overseer. Settling for the trinkets offered for our webbing and battle." The other four growled with their understanding of the failure of Blidarn. "My father follows the foolishness of his father! He continues to offer our efforts and trials, for very little more than trinkets!" The growling grew louder and fiercer. "I say it is time that the Overseer and his blind and greedy minions, pay full price to the Natharian's!" A great roar erupted from those who thought Bistalan's words true. "Palitan, are your troops ready?" Bistalan looked to the Natharian to his far left. Palitan, who had been in a resting position, his underbelly resting on the ground, lifted to the full extension of his eight legs. His underbelly was now almost fourteen feet from the ground.

"Yes Lord Bistalan, we are ready!" Palitan replied. Bistalan shifted his sight, and body to the next one to the right.

Nasitan?"

"We are ready Lord Bistalan!" was the reply, as the named male rose to his full extension.

"Berotan?"

"We are ready Lord Bistalan!" The next called out his reply, as he too lifted to his full height.

"Mertilan?"

The fourth male rose. "We are more than ready," Mertilan answered with a growl. Bistalan nodded, as much as a Natharian can, as he swiveled, to look from one of his Generals, to the next.

"We start now!" The four Generals growled their acceptance of their order and left the meeting area, heading for those they would lead against the Natharian Ruler's forces. Bistalan smiled as he followed them out of the cave, and then turned for the Rulers web.

Zachia waited impatiently for his father to explain what he had heard from the Keeper of all Magic of Vistalin. "What did Edward want?" Zachia finally asked with a peculiar tone to his question. Both Emma and Glornina looked to him. Namson finished his coffee, but before he could tell of Edward's message, Tarson, General of the Realm Armies, and his wife Prelilian, a powerful talker, charged into the dining room.

"Overseer," Prelilian said loudly; "I have just received a message from Blirous, oldest daughter of Bleudarn. She says that her third brother, Bistalan, has killed her first brother, Bleulan, and their father, Bleudarn. She also says that his armies are fighting to take control of Natharia!" Namson and Zachia exchanged looks.

"I will gather the dragons," Zachia told Namson. He rose from his chair, turned, and grabbing Tarson's arm, left the room. They all knew that the dragons were the only ones that could battle the Natharian's in their own domain. Namson filled his cup half full of brandy and then drank the entire amount in one swallow. He kissed Glornina on the forehead and then followed his son. Glornina, Prelilian, and Emma, looked to each other with fearful looks.

"What are we to do?" Emma asked quietly, after some time. Glornina had stared at the door after her husband's and son's sudden departure. She looked to her daughter-in-law.

"Wish them well, and have hope," she told Emma with a worried sigh. They both rose, and with Prelilian, who had not yet sat, walked to the front door of the palace. When they stepped out on the front terrace, they were surprised to see the last few of a hastily formed army of dragons, plus those of magical power, who would be their riders, entering a portal. Just as the portal closed, Glorian, Namson and Glornina's oldest daughter, called to Glornina with her mind, from the Canyon.

"Mama, don't let Papa, or Cartile, go to Natharia!" she told her mother in a badly controlled scream. "Braxton say's they will die there!" Glornina, wide eyed, looked to Emma and Prelilian, who had also heard the message and then to where the portal had been. She was suddenly very, very, frightened. Pelkraen added to her fears, when at that same moment that Glornina had received Glorian's message, he came running from the palace, before she could call to her husband.

"Mistress Glornina, there is a strange call coming from a place called Weretoran. I have never heard of this place. They urgently ask to speak to the Overseer, immediately," he told her with worry. Glornina again looked to Emma, who now stared back, wide eyed, at her. Emma and Prelilian followed Glornina and Pelkraen, back into the palace. As they hurried to the orb in the Overseer's office, Jennifer came from the room that held the panel of talkers. She told Glornina of Daridar's message.

The panel of talkers had been reduced in number, now only three at a time, but had been kept to monitor all the domains communications and Jennifer had been the one who had received Daridar's worried message.

In the Domain of Gargoylia, in the Ruler's castle; there came a loud knocking on the door of the Rulers mud bath room. "Garator, need speak!" a voice announced. The Ruler of Gargoylia glared at the door as though his eyes were seeing the one outside. The two naked wingless females continued the slathering of mud on his body and then massaging it into his skin. His extremely large wings were spread and the females had to duck under them to do their job.

"You miss target," he told the one to his left, grinning. She grinned at the other female as her taloned left hand slid down the Ruler. "Ah, that better!" Garator said in a sigh. Both females giggled, as the one to his right, slid her hand down and aided in the firsts efforts, for it seemed, that it took two to handle the situation. The banging on the door returned.

"Garator, matters much!" the voice announced. Garator, Ruler of Gargoylia, roared with his rage. Both females withdrew in fear.

"Enter!" Garator, bellowed, as the females went to the back edge of the bath and held each other, trembling. Gartilan, Garator's Second, entered carefully.

"Regret Master," Gartilan said with a bow; "but voice speaks rulers," the Second said, trying not to look to the two naked wingless females.

"What voice say?" Garator asked, still enraged at the interruption.

"Says, there unhappy, outer provinces, rebellion coming," Gartilan told the ruler, still trying, but failing to not look to the naked females.

"Gather council," Garator ordered as he started up the steps, on the back side of the mud bath, towards the waterfall nearby. "Get out," he told his Second without looking to him. Gartilan turned and left the room. Garator pointed to the females. "Clean me." The two came up the stairs, following their master. They washed the mud from him and then satisfied his pleasures. After they had dressed him and he had left for the council chamber, they returned to the harem very tired and, very happy.

On the larger continent of Weretoran, which was on the opposite side of the planet from the Gargoylian continent, Werelaran, the King of Weretoran, walked casually through the capital city of Wereton, greeting all those he met with a respectful word, nod, and smile. They responded in kind, for Werelaran was well liked among all citizens of Weretoran. He was especially happy this morning, for his mate Wereselon, had just delivered twins, Wereperan, and Werenesilon. Both of the new born had changed to wolf with their first breaths, changing back to their human forms, minutes later. It concerned him that there were still those young who couldn't change. Their lack of ability to change to wolf form was the results of the return of the children of those who had ventured off planet and had mated with the inhabitants of a far planet. But, their numbers had been declining for many years now and that gave him hope. Abruptly, Peritor dropped down in front of him.

"Lord Werelaran," Peritor said quite loudly, forgetting to give the proper bow. "Weretilon asks that you come immediately. She has heard the voice from the once Bandarson again!" Werelaran looked to the messenger of their most powerful of witches.

Peritor was, as were all of the Weriron messengers, a female. The male Weriron had no wings and couldn't fly. The small creature had the body of a wolf, with four very sharp talons at the end of each of their four very powerful, wide paws that were very close to hands. The head of the creature was almost human like and the females had a very large pair of wings. They were slightly larger than the pigeon like birds that were their main food source. Though, they were known to eat anything they could catch. The males, who were larger than the females, would tend the live born young the females had birthed, plus do minor work in the homes and palaces of those they served. They were not used exclusively by the witches of Weretoran, as Werelaran had several in his service, but Weretilon had more than most.

"Tell her I'm coming," he told her. He changed to wolf form as Peritor sped off. Werelaran started towards the witch's castle with the fast lope of a huge beast. He had not thought about the changing of his clothes with his shape shift, for they actually became an extra part of his fur, in wolf form. When he arrived at the small, seemingly modest, white stoned castle, Weretilon's guards, who had been waiting for him, recognized the light streaks that ran through the dark coloring of his fur, opened the main gate as he neared. He changed back to human form, clothes and all, in the court yard. One of Weretilon's assistants led him to the witch's chambers. She looked up from her crystal as he entered.

"My Lord, the voice from Namsia speaks of unrest in her domain," Weretilon said as she rose, coming to him.

"What kind of unrest?" he asked.

"There would be those who would return to their evil ways and live the life that Brandaro had made for them," she answered. There was worry in her eyes. "Gorsentor says that she is sure that Garator has heard of this and he will surely try again to rally them to his side, as was tried with Brandaro. We may again need to fight to control the Gargoyles." Her quiet voice showed the fear she felt. Werelaran nodded as he thought, his head lowering.

The battle to stop the Gargoyles from joining with the Bandit leader had been bloody and costly, with a tremendous loss of lives on both sides. Though he knew they had killed the wizard who had managed to meet with Brandaro's forces, not knowing the lack of success of that meeting, and he did not want his race to go through that again. The only thing of value that had come of that war had been the establishing of a spy network of wingless Gargoyles, who wanted the freedom and joy that was known to all Werewolves. Werelaran finally lifted his head and looked to the witch.

"Can you beam a message to this Realm the voice calls to, without letting the Gargoylian's receive it?" he asked. "I think it is time they were told of what is going to be," he add.

"I will try My Lord," Weretilon said quietly, with fear in her eyes and concern in her voice. She returned to the large tear drop shaped crystal.

At the garden in the south west part of Zentler; "You two got here early," Penelopy said, as she and Terressa and their children, arrived at the hundred foot square garden that the families shared. Isabella and Kris looked to her, smiling.

"Not really," Kris said. "It's just we don't have to deal with the morning sickness." Penelope's oldest, Giorgio, named after her husband Marcus's father, ran off to join Nathan on the hunt for things that crawled, hopped, or slithered, and were an interest to four year old boys. Ava came to the two women and took the hands of the two, two year olds. Isabella, who was called Bella and was Penelope's second, and Benjamin, who was Terressa's first. She led them to a safer area to play, that was less populated with insect life. Penelopy looked at Kris with less than a happy look, but then had to smile, her hand settling on her slightly extended belly.

"Can I help it if Marcus is good at what he does?" she asked with a small shrug, beginning to chuckle. The others joined in her chuckle.

"No," Kris said; "I guess not." They all were grinning as they nodded. Terressa moved to the end of the rows Kris weeded, as Penelopy moved to join Isabella on her end. That's when Terressa saw the look on Isabella's face.

"You're pregnant aren't you?" she asked Isabella, keeping her voice low. Penelopy and Kris looked to Isabella with wide eyes. Isabella blushed and nodded.

"Really?" the other two asked at the same time. Isabella nodded again.

"The doctor says about two and a half months," she told them; "and I'm not the only one, am I?" she said with a accusing tone and a half grin, looking first to Terressa, then to Kris. The four exchanged looks and then smiles, along with hugs, sharing their pregnancies. Thankfully, for the two, Namson had dampened the jolting affect between Isabella and Kris, but could not stop Penelope's ability to see Isabella when they touched. That phenomenon had caused the beginning of the downfall of Brandaro.

It took a few minutes for them to return to their weeding. As they talked of the things mothers and friends talk about, they kept watchful eyes on the five children. The morning passed pleasantly, except for when Isabella had to go and take the small snake from the two older boys, who were fighting over whose turn it was to hold it. The boys hadn't wanted to give it up, so they were required to sit near the garden for a few minutes, as punishment. Ava giggled at the boys as she watched Nathan with a look her mother really wasn't too sure was proper for a four year old to use.

The husbands and fathers, Marcus, Melsikan, Carl, and Ben, joined them at lunch time. They completely surprised all, when they brought two large lunch baskets with them. Those baskets held enough for all four families. It was near the end of that lunch, that both Ava and Geebee screamed and began to cry.

"I'm sorry Brendo," Cenlinas said, as they walked towards the town of Bentodon. Cenlinas pulled a small, sided cart behind her, to carry the packages for the return to the farm. Cenlinas saw the look of distrust, when the girl looked to her, from the opposite side of the road. "I just get so mad when I think of the wrongs that have happened, that I reacted without thought. I am truly sorry."

"Okay," Brendo told her with a shrug. Cenlinas looked to her daughter and could easily see that the girl was thinking a different outcome if she was grabbed again. She also realized that she was not going to be forgiven too quickly. They traveled the rest of the way to Bentodon, in silence. As they neared the town, Brendo took off in a run. Her full, maroon colored dress billowing out behind her, saying that there was something she was going to do and was soon out of her mother's sight. Cenlinas sighed and walked into town alone. She was thinking that she would buy Brendo a pretty necklace and then maybe her daughter would forgive her. She entered the central market, stopping at several of the different shops and booths, to buy the needed, including a pretty and, expensive necklace, and a lot more of the cream that Brendo liked to use for her skin.

Neponities, Nepelia, Queen of the Northern Section and her daughter Nepeslia, as well as Cartope and her daughter Nepopea, sat in the meeting room of Neponities palace, talking about the adding of some new laws concerning the privileges of males. Neponities almost smiled as she remembered that it had been Michele, the youngest daughter of the Overseer, Namson, who had planted the original thought in Neponities mind, just before she had left Neponia with the last of the recovering wounded, from the battle with the bandit's.

"Is it possible that the men of your world have earned more rights than they now have?" Michele had asked the Queen. Neponities had looked to her Chosen Mate and saw him commanding some other men, as they made sure the last of the recovering wounded were in place for the portals openings. For some time after that, Neponities had watched the males of Capital City, as they went about their duties and continued the see the value they possessed. She had seen how the males handled many of the lesser troubles of everyday life, so the women would not be bothered by them. She had called for a meeting with Nepelia and had shown her what she had witnessed. The Queen of the Northern Section returned to the north and had watched the males of her Section. Seeing the same behavior in them, she had finally agreed with Neponities. They had talked with several of the prominent women of Capital City, as well as the Northern capital and Cartope, and new laws had been enacted in both the Central and Northern Sections, that gave males more privilege and, some power in Neponian society.

When Nepanities and Carsanac returned from the Southern Section, all five immediately saw the anger on Nepanities face.

"She was less than receptive to the idea, I see," Neponities said, with one brow higher than the other. Nepanities looked to her and angrily, shook her head once.

"She wouldn't even accept the message!" she told them. "She wouldn't allow Carsanac to speak to her and, she said that she considered this effort as a declaration of war!" she added with her anger taking control of her voice. Neponities and Nepelia exchanged looks and both looks told of their irritations.

"I do not think we can tolerate her attitude anymore," Nepelia said, her anger for the Southern Sections Queens attitude clearly present in her voice. All present nodded their heads in agreement.

"But what can we do about it?" Cartope asked.

"Close off her borders to anything that is not necessary," Neponities said quietly. They all looked to her. "Allow the trade of food goods and medicines, but nothing else.

It will not take long for her people to tire of not having the benefits of trade before they force her to agree!" Nepelia nodded her agreement; though no one was sure they liked the look in her eyes.

"I will send several battalions to help with your border patrols Neponities," Nepelia said with a determined voice. Neponities bowed her thanks.

None of them had considered that Nepolia might have plans of her own and the first of those was unfolding as they spoke. The guards at Neponities quarters never saw the woman who snuck in through the open balcony door of Nepolities private quarters and stole the orb.

~•~

Bistalan stood at his full extension as he looked around the open web at those who tried to hide behind each other. His father and older brother had not died easily and Bistalan still felt the pain of the wounds he had suffered in the battle. His yellowish blood still seeped from some of the larger of them, slowly crawling down his legs to the web. The sounds of the battles, that had been raging for hours, as his armies fought the armies of Bleudarn, were now being joined by the roars of dragons and the scent of burning webs and Natharian's, came on the breeze. He turned to his first sister, Blirous and approached her. "I know that you can talk to those of the Realm. You called them here, didn't you?" he growled as he neared her. She nodded her head as she rose to her full height and faced him directly. Although smaller than her younger brother, she stared into his eyes with defiance.

"You will not win in this rebellion Bistalan," she told him, with condemnation in her hissing voice.

"Yes I will!" he roared. With unimaginable speed, he lunged at her. His mandibles closed on her smaller head and tore it from her body, just as a blast of dragon fire burned through the webbing right behind him. The web started to collapse and Bistalan quickly grabbed on to the remaining web. Bistalan's lunge at his sister had saved him from being in the middle of the blast.

"You have lost Bistalan!" Namson yelled trying to aim at Bistalan's head with his blast spells, as Cartile flew closer, flaming again. From two of the trees that were part of the anchors of the web, on either side and above the dragon, two Natharian males leapt onto the dragon, their combined weight forcing Cartile to tear through the remainder of the webbing, towards the ground far below. Namson never felt his head being cut from his body when the mandibles of the closest Natharian bit down. The other one went to work on Cartile. The severing of the dragon's spinal cord, at the base of his neck, caused Cartile's death, just before his body had hit the ground, a hundred feet below the web.

Ava and Geebee, in Zentler, were not the only ones to scream when Namson died. There were many who screamed with his death, in all of the domains, especially Glornina and her daughters.

"Lord Garator, we nobody talk, since battle Werewolves, only hear," one of the councilors stated, almost pleadingly.

A murmur of voices followed his statement. Garator stopped his pacing, turned, glaring at them all.

"You quiet!" he ordered them all. Silence fell on the room.

Slowly, the rustling of folded wings was heard, as their regular behaviors took control of them. The number of Gargoylian's who had wings were the minority. They were also the largest in physical size and like their ruler, whose horns pointed two different directions, had a variety of shapes to their horns. They were considered the elite. The ruling class of their society, because they were also the ones with the higher level, though not by much, of magical talents. The annoying habit of constantly moving those folded wings was a normal and done without realization.

"I say quiet!" Garator bellowed. Total silence followed. Several of the council members actually held their wings to keep from moving them. Garator slowly went to his throne, his expression showing his thinking efforts. "We need talker," he finally said. Nodding heads were his only answer from the councilors. "Bring Garplasar," he told the soldier at the door. The soldier, with a very frightened expression, saluted, with his arm crossing his chest and left the room.

Worried and frightened looks were exchanged by the council members. Garplasar, who had been the under wizard of Garsalar, who had been the one to try to establish a connection with Brandaro and had been killed in the war with the Weretorians, was now the most powerful of all wizards in Gargoylia. They all knew that wizards, especially Garplasar, did not like to be ordered about.

They waited for the return of the soldier and hopefully, a calm Garplasar.

"Are you the one in Command of your domain?" Weretilon asked her crystal. Werelaran moved closer to the witch. Weretilon looked to her King. "She says she is the Mistress of the Realm. The Overseer is on a mission to a place called Natharia," the witch told Werelaran. He nodded.

"That will have to do," he told her and Weretilon turned back to the crystal.

"My King, Werelaran, wishes to speak with you," she told the one Werelaran couldn't see, for only Weretilon could see into the crystal. "She waits My King," Weretilon said without taking her eyes from the crystal.

"Mistress of the Realm, I am King Werelaran, of Weretoran, and we have heard the voice from the domain previously known as Bandarson, whom your forces had beaten, that there is unrest there. We wonder what your Overseer intends to do about this possible danger," Werelaran said loud enough for his voice to enter the crystal, through Weretilon. Silence followed his words, and then Weretilon spoke.

"She says that they have only just received the message themselves and have not yet had an opportunity to evaluate what is to be done," the witch said without any emotion to her voice, because she was now part of the crystals powers. Werelaran nodded.

"Mistress of the Realm, please try to understand," Werelaran said as calmly as he could. "There are two races of our world. We are called Weretorians and the other race is called Gargoylian's. The Gargoylian's have tried before, to unite with Brandaro, to overtake our race and gain in their greed. If this unrest is to be a real thing, the Gargoylian's will again try to unite with the revolutionary forces, to try and take control of our entire world. We must act quickly to stop them, or we could be in danger. Please tell us as soon as you can, what the intents of the Overseer are to be,"

"She guarantees she will," Weretilon said. "She asked who she is to contact when that time comes."

"She is to contact you Weretilon," Werelaran said softy. The witch nodded and told the crystal her Kings words. Weretilon turned to the King after the connection with the Realm had been broken and there was worry in her eyes.

"Can we trust them, My King?' she asked quietly. "They are humans!" Werelaran tried to smile.

"We have no choice Weretilon, no choice," he said with a sigh. He turned to leave the witch's castle. "Tell me as soon as you are contacted," he told her as he passed through the door.

"Yes, My King," Weretilon answered, but not loud enough for the King to hear, for he was already in the court yard and had changed to wolf form. He left the witches castle, heading for the Central Community Chambers of his palace.

———— ~•~•~•~ ————

Glornina turned from the orb and looked into the worried eyes of Emma, Prelilian, and Jennifer. "What am I to tell Daridar?" Jennifer asked before Glornina could call to her husband with Glorian's warning. Glornina held up her hands to the others' and called to her husband. Namson had to be warned of his daughter's message, before anything else!

"It is going to take more time," he answered her. "Bistalan has a greater force than I thought, and they are determined."

"No Namson, Glorian's warning was clear, you and Cartile must return immediately!" she yelled with her mind.

"I can't now," he told her. "Bleudarn's government must continue. Bistalan cannot be allowed to rule, or we will lose the Natharian alliance!"

"Please my husband, come home, now," she begged.

"I'm sorry my love, but this is too important. Don't worry, I'll be alright," he tried to comfort her. She knew the meaning of his words. He would fight to the death, to keep the alliances of the Domains of Rightful Magic. Those were the last words she ever heard from him. It was only a few minutes later that she felt him die, as did all of her children and the grandchildren. Ava and Geebee in Zentler, and many, many, others', felt the same horror.

Glornina's heart and voice, screamed with her pain of loss. She fainted.

———ᴡ——ᴏ✦✧◯✧✦ᴏ——ᴡ———

On Natharia; "Merlintile, we must withdraw," Zachia yelled to the dragon he rode. "We are far too outnumbered. This is their world and they know the terrain better than we do!" The dragon nodded and called to the dragons who could talk, as Zachia passed the word to the humans that rode the other dragons. Zachia called to his father and received no answer. He called again and still no answer came back to him. That was when he and the rest of the forces of the Realm heard the screaming call from Jerimal, who rode the dragon Platile. They had just seen Namson and Cartile killed by two Natharian's as they went after Bistalan directly. A part of Zachia's heart died at that moment. Quickly realizing his responsibilities, he knew what he had to do. He put out a call to all, to gather for a portal back to the Realm. All replied that they were on the way. There were fewer returning to the Realm, than had left.

CHAPTER TWO

Daridar was worried. It had been hours since she had sent her request to the Realm and she hadn't received a reply yet. She now sat alone in the council chamber, slumped in her chair. She had sent all of the council members to their city sections and Province offices, to try and prepare their police and Guard, to try and form a plan for what they would be facing. Her assistant, a dwarf female named Drendar, brought her some hot tea that had brandy added to it.

"Daridar?" Drendar asked quietly. "What is the matter?" Drendar did not like the look on Daridar's face. Daridar looked to her for a moment, then straightened in her chair and took the offered tea.

"I don't know, but I'm going to find out," she said with a determined voice and again called to the Realm. That's when she learned of Namson's death and fear came to her. "What are we to do now?" she asked herself, out loud. Drendar looked at her with an expression that was very confused and, very frightened.

Nepolia lay on the lounger, in the living section of her chambers. Her male attendants moved about with their duties, quietly. They knew what would happen if they disturbed her at the wrong time, so they were being very careful. It really didn't matter, for Nepolia was completely lost in her thoughts. She was waiting to receive the orb that one of her most trusted personal Guard was to bring her, as she continued to work on the next phase of her plans. She knew that there was unrest in Namsia. Depelia, the only one who could hear Daridar when she talked to the Realm, had told her so. She had to somehow make contact with those who were going to revolt and make an alliance with them. Although her mines of the Power Stones, were far fewer and much smaller than the other two Sections, she knew she could convince the rebels to join her, by offering her Power Stones to them. She was convinced that, with the offered stones, they would help her overthrow the two other Queens, especially Neponities. She would then rule all of Neponia! She could then rid herself of the yoke of the Realm and she could do as she pleased.

Bistalan had managed to hold on to what was left of the web. Then using his extruded web, he quickly rebuilt enough of the webbing so that he was quite secure by the time the body of Cartile hit the ground, far below. The first thing he realized was that there were no longer the sounds of the dragons. His self elected aide, Castilan, who had managed to leap to a nearby tree when the attack had come, came to him, as some of Bistalan's guards quickly began to rebuild the rest of the web.

"What are your orders Lord Bistalan?" he asked. Bistalan looked to him and came close to a smile.

"Find out what is happening with the Generals and the status of our victory," he told the smaller male. Castilan nodded quickly and scurried away. Bistalan pivoted, looking around and could see that all those of his father's council had fled. That enhanced his grin. His messenger quickly returned, being followed by the four messengers from his Generals.

"Lord Bistalan," the first of the four said quickly. "General Mertilan says that the forces of the Realm have fled and we are quickly defeating the few still resisting, of Bleudarn's forces!" The other three nodded.

"General Berotan states the same," another said.

"So does General Nasitan," the next stated.

"As does General Palitan," the last one said. "We have won Lord Bistalan!" he added. Bistalan nodded.

"Tell the generals to gather here as soon as they can," Bistalan ordered and the four scurried away.

───────

Garplasar entered the Council Chamber, followed by the very frightened soldier. All of the council members could see the angry look of the wizard and they began to feel fear. Garplasar stopped, still ten feet from the oval central table. "Lord Garator, not like this," the wizard growled. Garator frightened the council members even more, when he waved down the wizard's growl.

"We need talker," he told the wizard. "One talk voice," Garator stated, looking into the wizard's eyes. "You find one, bring me!" The wizards head lowered, but not his eyes. An even harder and angrier expression came to his face.

"You order me?" Garplasar growled deeply. Garator rose, walked the short distance to the wizard and put his face within inches of the wizard's face.

"Yes," he growled even deeper than the wizard had. The entire council had started to slump lower in their chairs as they looked back and forth between their Ruler and the wizard. They all were very close to bolting for the other door of the chamber and the soldier was easing back towards the door he had entered, for they were all quite sure that the wizard was going to do something that was to be painful for them all. Silence crowded the room as wizard and Ruler stared at each other, each with a low growl. Abruptly, the wizard nodded.

"Need go off world, "Garplasar said in his growl. "Very hard."

"Do," Garator told him with his growl. Seconds ticked by before the wizard again nodded, but only once. The wizard turned and left the chambers. Garator returned to his throne at the head of the table. All of the councilor's eyes followed him, as they all started to breathe again. "You work plan, tell me," he told them, waving his hand in dismissal." The Councilors quickly fled the room, leaving Garator alone with his thoughts and, his growing grin.

Werelaran changed to his human form as he came to his palace. The guards at the gate came to attention as they opened the gate for him. He told Wereperan, his aide, who had met him at the gate, to summon the council to the meeting hall. Wereperan bowed and hurried off. Werelaran then went to check on the status of his wife and new children.

"What is it?" Wereselon asked quietly, as soon as she saw his face. She turned back to the two sleeping babies, continuing a mother's care with coverings and love.

"I have had Weretilon make contact with the Realm," he told her just as quietly, coming to her side and looking to his new children. Her eyes snapped to him, wider that normal.

"Was that wise?" she asked in a whisper, slowly straightening. "Does the Council know?" she added. He looked from the children, to her and the smile he had found looking to the children changed slightly.

"They will shortly," he told her. He leaned to her and kissed her gently. "You should rest now my love, let the nurse tend to the babies," he told her softly, leading her back to the bed. She was forced to keep her human form and thusly needed to use a regular bed, until her body had recovered from trials of birth. He smiled a confident smile at her, turned from his family and went to the Council Hall.

In that Hall, there was a rather loud buzz of concerned voices, wondering of the reason for this unscheduled meeting. When Werelaran entered the hall, it silenced immediately. The fifteen council members, representatives from each of the fifteen Havens of Weretoran, went to their chairs and sat, all watching their King with wonder in their eyes. He arrived at his place, which was the point of the large tear drop shaped table. He did not sit in his throne, but stood between it and the table.

"Council members of Weretoran," he began, his voice strong, but all heard an undercurrent of concern. "I have learned that there is unrest in the domain once called Bandarson and there is the threat of revolution." There were shared looks of worry among the Councilors. "I regret to have to tell you, but again, we must face the threat that the Gargoylian's may attempt to join forces with those who would cause this revolt!" he announced. The eruption of questions, statements and outright fear, echoed in the hall, as many of the council members stood with their statements. He waited until the first wave of outbursts had settled, slightly.

"Please, give me your attention," he called out over the few still active voices of some of the Council members. Silence came and those who had stood with their outbursts, returned to their seats, their eyes locked on their King.

"Why is this to be?" Werementran, the representative from Haven Weresola, asked as soon as he had sat. Werelaran almost smiled as he lifted his hand to the Councilman.

"Weretilon has heard from the voice from Namsia and it seems that there are many of that domain, who are not happy with the new Government or the name change and, that there are rumors of the possibility of rebellion," he told the Council, and there were exchanged worried looks. "If Garator learns of this and there is little doubt he will, or already has, he will again try to join with those rebels and using that alliance, try to conquer Weretoran." Again the voices of the Council members took over. Werelaran slowly sat and waited. As he sat back in his throne, his eyes looked from one, to the next, at the council members around the table. When the voices had silenced and most eyes had turned back to him, Werelaran continued. "I have had discussions with each of you privately, about Garator and the greed and brutality of the creature," he said. There were nods of agreement all around. Werelaran sighed. "I do not think that there are any who want to battle the Gargoyles again, or the horrors that battle would bring, so I have had Weretilon contact the Realm, and I have asked them to help us," he told them, There were wide eyes and, absolute silence, staring back at him.

The Elder of the Guardians of the Realm, Drandysee, stood next to Emma, who was holding her children to her. Glorian and her husband Braxton, each holding their children and Michele and her husband Crendoran, holding their children, stood just outside of the gate to the palace. The dragons, Jastile, mate of Cartile and her daughter Semitile, mate of Merlintile and their children and their mates, stood with the humans. The portal opened and those who had gone to Natharia, returned. Many were wounded, some seriously. Healers came and led the wounded to the enormous park across from the gate and began their work. Zachia and Merlintile came to those who waited. The tears in their eyes told all the truth of the deaths. Zachia came to his sisters, Emma, and his children, as Merlintile went to Jastile, his mate Semitile and their children. There were no words as arms encircled and necks were crossed. The pain of their losses held their voices prisoners, as portals and appearances were occurring around them. Zachia broke the silence of the group as those from the many domains joined them.

"Mama?" he asked his sisters softly.

"She is being taken care of by Pelidora and her maids," Glorian told him softly as tears formed in her eyes. "She fainted when she felt papa's death and hasn't woke yet.

"What happened?" Michele asked in a whisper, fighting her tears. Zachia looked to her, as the rest looked between him and Merlintile. Other dragons began to land and approach.

"Platile and his rider Jerimal, who is young, but a strong magical talent and both of them are strong talkers, were the ones to actually see it happen and they told everyone,"

Zachia's voice was affected by his pain. "Papa and Cartile went after Bistalan at the Councilors web. Bistalan must have thought of that possibility, because there were warriors waiting in the trees around the web. When Papa and Cartile attacked, two leapt from the trees, landing on Cartile, killing papa, and driving Cartile to the ground, killing him." Zachia's voice cracking with his telling, as again, tears came to his eyes. Emma came to him. Mike, the oldest of Zachia and Emma's children, now eleven and already showing the power that he would be, held his younger sisters, as Glorian put her arm around his shoulders. Emma put her arms around Zachia and they joined all the others with their tears of pain and loss. Minutes passed with only the sounds of sobbing to fill the air. Finally, Emma pulled back from Zachia slightly and looked to his tear reddened eyes.

"You are now Overseer," she said loud enough for all around them to hear. The word spread as an explosion. He stared at her for a few moments and lifted his eyes, first to Drandysee, Elder of the Guardians, who nodded his validation. He then looked to those who surrounded them. He looked from one to the next and each pair of eyes he met looked to him with the shared feelings of loss, as well as hope and nodding agreement. Time passed slowly as Zachia looked to the gathered. Then Edward stepped forward, his arm around his wife Carla's shoulders.

"What are your orders, Overseer?" he asked. Zachia looked into the eyes of the Keeper of all Magic for Vistalin. He slowly straightened and squared his shoulders. He again scanned all those around him. He returned his eyes to

Edward and nodded. He shifted his eyes to Carla, who still commanded the talker's panel.

"Call all those of the panel and try to establish a connection with any of the contacts we have on Natharia and try to find out what is happening there," he told her. She nodded and turned her thoughts to those of the panel. He glanced at Emma, seeing her pride and love of him. He looked to Braxton. "Unite all seers and sensitive's and try to find out anything you can." Braxton nodded and looked to Glorian. She smiled as she nodded. The two started to talk with all of the seers, as well as try to comfort their children. Heather, the oldest of their children, was doing her own talking, with all of the very young seers and sensitives. Tarson, with Prelilian at his side, came from the park where the wounded were being tended. The large bandage on his left arm told all of the battle. "Prepare the Armies and keep connected with all the domains Generals," he told him. Tarson nodded and turned to his Commanders and the gathered races, including Merlintile. The largest of all dragons had been named second in command of the Realm dragons by Cartile, many years earlier and now, with Cartile's death, had become the leader of the dragons of the Realm. Tarson beckoned that they all follow him. Merlintile looked to his father Crastamor, with a nod. Crastamor accepted his son's decree and went with Tarson.

"Zachia," Emma interrupted his thoughts; "there was a message from a domain named Weretoran, just before we all felt Namson's death. The ruler of that Domain seeks a conference with the Overseer and I cannot help but feel there is importance to that conference." Zachia saw Prelilian's nod of agreement and then again looked to Emma, waiting. "Just before we heard the Weretorians request," Emma continued; "Jennifer had come to your mother and said that Daridar was worried of rebellion on Namsia." Zachia's eyes were opening slightly wider with each of Emma's words. "The message from this Weretoran said that the other race of that domain, called Gargoylian's, would try to make an alliance with the rebels of Namsia, to try and take over the Weretorians." When she had finished, he stared at her a moment, as his eyes returned to normal. They all saw the determined expression that had come over Zachia's face. He nodded.

"Tell Jennifer to get as much information from Daridar as she can and, who do we contact in this Weretoran?" he told and asked. In the background, leaders of all domains and races were giving instructions to those who had come with them. Those instructed, traveled where they must, to follow the orders they had been given.

"A female, at least it sounded female, for there had not been any visual with the message, named Weretilon," Emma told him. Zachia nodded and turned to the others that stood near.

"The leaders of all domains and races come with me. I do not yet know all we face, but as soon as I have an idea, I will tell what must be done," he told all and turned back to Emma. "Let's go call to this Weretilon," he said, and looked Merlintile. "I will make sure that the window is open my friend," he told the dragon who was the largest of the dragons of the Realm and who was much too big to enter the Palace proper. Merlintile nodded and started around the Palace to said window, so he could be part of what happened in the Overseer's office. Zachia led the rest, who were to be part of this meeting, into the Palace.

———

Glornina came back to consciousness, as the meeting in the very crowded office was begun. The word of Zachia's acceptance to the position of Overseer had passed quickly through the Palace. Glornina was told as soon as she was fully awake. She closed her eyes, as her tears continued to come from her. A hint of a smile, for the pride of her son, came to her lips as she nodded slowly to the news.

———

In Zentler, Isabella was trying to calm her sobbing daughter, as Kris tried to calm Geebee. No one could understand the young girls jumbled words they heard between the girl's sobs. Gordon, the Mayor of Zentler, and his wife Xanaporia, a strong magical talent, as well as a talker, came to the garden area. They stopped at the edge of the garden and looked to the eyes of those who looked to them. They all could see the sadness in the Mayors and his wives eyes. "Namson, the Overseer of the Realm, has been killed in the battle of Natharia," Gordon told them, his voice cracking. They all stared at him, not willing to accept his words. They all turned to Ava as she then clearly said five words.

"Zachia is now the Overseer," the girl announced. None saw the slightly lifted right brow of Ben, or his expression of concentration immediately afterwards.

Cenlinas searched the town for Brendo, but she couldn't find her daughter anywhere. She finally shrugged, figuring that Brendo was still mad enough that she didn't want to be found. She left the town of Bentodon for her small farm, with her many packages in the cart behind her. It took several hours to reach the farm and Cenlinas was very shocked to find her front yard crowded with carriages and horses. As she neared the house, she heard the strong voice of her son and she smiled as she stepped onto the porch. She left her cart of packages on the porch, next to her chair and looked into the very crowded room. Brando was easily seen, as he stood taller than any other. She smiled wider as she listened.

"It was bad enough that they called those monsters of the Realm here, but to add to the insult, they put that dwarf Daridar, on the council they had formed and then forced their pollution into the minds of those of Bandarson City enough, that they then elect that thing as Mayor. Then they insulted all of Bandarson even more, by reelecting that parsha dwarf!" Brando roared to the gathered and they returned his roar with their shared anger. "The time of reclaiming is coming!" Brando continued and again the crowd roared. Brando waited until all were quiet and all those gathered were beginning to look to each other with confusion. Brando's sneer caused most to grin. "As you all are aware, there has been a secretive efforts, by those who would remove the dwarf and return to the bandit's way and, I have been leading those efforts. You all will now spread out through the Provinces, telling those that feel as we do, that they are to meet me," Brando's sneer turned a smirking grin; "in Bandarson City, three weeks hence. We will join with and lead those who would rebel against what has come of our world, we will take back what has been defiled. We will return to the life that my grandfather and father have proven to be the best!" Brando yelled the last of his statement, lifting his fist high over his head. The entire gathered crowd roared their agreement. Cenlinas had to move quickly to keep from being trampled as the crowd poured out of the door, heading for their rides and the goal their leader had given them. Each and every one of them thinking of the value of the position they would receive, for their support of young Brando, when he was Ruler of Bandarson!

Cenlinas watch her son, as he followed the mob out onto the porch, her eyes wide with pride. She listened to the words of the followers as they swore their allegiance to Brando, as they left the yard. When the yard was completely empty and the dust had begun to resettle to the ground, he turned to her with a smile that would have scared anyone, but her. "You will rule Bandarson as you were meant to," she said to him, as her tears of pride and joy fell from her eyes. He nodded and came to her, pulling her into his arms.

"Yes, I will mama." Brando chuckled softly, his voice low. "I will have a stronger rule than any before me," he told her in a voice so empowered that she felt a tremor of unexpected fear.

———

Calitoran stood near Nepolia as she watched from the balcony, as the two squads left for the northern borders.

He and the few male's who spied on the Queen for him, had been learning of the many plans the Queen was creating. He knew that these were the very best of her soldiers and that she had given them very clear instructions. Calitoran and Nepolia both knew that there were still almost a hundred of the Bandarson bandits who had been captured, being held in the quickly made jail on the north side of Capital City and he knew that these troops were to free them. He also knew that the Queen wanted them to gather all of the amulets that could absorb cast spells, that Nepolia was convinced Neponities hid in her palace. Calitoran was aware that she did not believe the stories that all of those amulets with the Milky Crystals, had been taken back by those of the Realm. He watched as she turned from the balcony and ignoring him, quickly passed through the throne room, into the doorway of the small room just off from the throne room. He followed her, staying just out of her range of vision. He watched Nepolia as the Queen looked to Depelia. They both could see that Depelia stared at the orb and she was scratching her head.

"Have you made it work yet?" Calitoran heard Nepolia ask. Depelia looked to the Queen and Calitoran could see the woman's frustrations, in her eyes. She angrily shook her head once.

"I don't understand what I am to do," she told the Queen, turning back to the orb. "If those bitches in the Central Section can work it, I should be able to do it easily, but it resists my efforts!" Calitoran almost laughed as Nepolia glared at the woman.

"You had better figure it out soon," Nepolia threatened, which the advisor saw added to Depelia's anger. "We will need that orb!" Depelia turned to the Queen.

"I know that, My Queen," she said, badly hiding the frustrated anger she felt. "I will figure it out soon, I swear, but I need time." Nepolia looked to the next most powerful of magical strength of her Section and took a slow breath. Again, Calitoran almost laughed.

"Good, but try to make it quick," she said, turning from the woman and left the room. The Advisor could see that she fumed as she went to her quarters.

Calitoran knew better than to bother her and quickly found some other place to be, but he was amused that Nepolia had been told off, even if only slightly.

<hr/>

Bistalan looked over the members of his father's council, who had again been gathered by his soldiers. He knew that he needed their support, for they had strong connections with many of the tribal leaders of their provinces. They had all been forced to a resting position and all were cowering, but one. "I will give you the chance to join with me and assist me to rule Natharia, or," his posture and expression turned threatening; "I will have you killed in the most horrible of ways!" Several of the largest, of the surrounding soldiers moved closer, drooling. Bistalan saw Bremtilan, the eldest of the councilors and the only one not to cower to him, slowly rise from the forced resting position. Bistalan knew that the councilor did not do this in caution, but simply because his great age wouldn't let him move any quicker. When Bremtilan had reached his full height, he looked calmly into Bistalan's angry eyes. Bistalan signaled the soldiers not to attack. He was curious what the elder council member would say. The words he heard, enraged him.

"Bistalan, your greed for power has been known to many, for a long time. Even your father knew that someday, you would try to take that power." Bistalan began to grin with the oldest councilors words, but quickly lost it with Bremtilan's next statement. "Your father planned a defense against your actions, if ever you were to try what you have. Your seat of power will not last long for those plans and, for the plots of others', who would try to take that power from you with their own greed." Bistalan moved closer to the councilor and Bremtilan did not flinch from the threat. "You threaten death to those who will not concede to your will. I have lived a very long and contented life and I fear no death, for I know that your life will be much shorter and your reign as Ruler, even shorter! So go ahead and kill me, if you are truly as stupid as you show!" Bistalan charged in and quickly tore the elder apart. The others turned from the gore of Bremtilan's death.

"What say the rest of you?" he asked in a roar, slowly turning, looking to the eyes of each of the councilors. "Do you join that old fool, or do you live under my rule?" The mumbled voices of the councilors told of their acceptance of his rule, but not all of those voices spoke with truth.

A mile away, in a cave formed by the roots of one of the gargantuan trees that covered eighty percent of the land of Natharia, six Natharian's met. They had to whisper for all of the patrols of Bistalan's soldiers.

"Bleudarn's instructions are clear," Dasilan said to those gathered and they all nodded their agreement. "We all know what we are to do," he said and again there was nodding. "Then let us begin. We meet again, here, in one week. Do not fail, or there will be hell in Natharia!" The rest whispered their understanding and one by one, carefully snuck from the cave.

—

Gorastor ran down the dim and dirty alleyway. The news she carried, which she had been told by one of the young slaves of Garator's castle, had to be given to her mother. She was panting hard from her running and the tight wrappings on her body, under her clothes. As Gargoylian females were basically the same physical design as human females, those wrappings were trying to hide her maturity from Garator's spotters. Those spotters were always patrolling the capital city for young, well formed wingless females, for the Rulers pleasures, though she was convinced that the Rulers desires could be no worse than those of her older brother, when he had tried to get at her. She all but ran her father down, as he stepped from a crossing alley.

"Gorastor?" Garpartor yelled in a whispered surprise. His gnarled hands grasping his daughter's shoulders and spinning with her impact, he somehow managed not to allow either of them to fall. She looked to him, her eyes quite wide.

"Garator talk Garplasar, seek talker," she whispered with fear. Her father's eyes joined hers in width.

"Garplasar seek talker?" he asked. Gorastor nodded rapidly. Her father hurried them both down the alley that ran between the two long buildings. They hurried into the apartment, that consisted of two large rooms and loft that was their home. Gorsentor, Gorastor's mother, opened her eyes wide to the girl's news, as Garpartor closed the door. She went to the fire place and began to work one of the larger stones from it, as Gorastor closed the shutters of the one window, shutting off most of the dim light that came from the alley. Gorsentor double checked to make sure the door and window were closed, as Gorastor lit a candle. She then pulled the small tear drop shaped crystal from the hole behind the stone she had removed. She made the sign and spoke the words she had been taught, many years before and told Weretilon the news Gorastor had told her.

***

Werelaran sat on his throne, which was nothing more than a larger chair then those of the council members and watched the members as they talked among themselves, concerning his announcement of contacting the Realm. There were many that did not appear to be pleased with the news. He knew that this would be, for they all remembered the old stories told by the returning of their race from the world of humans. The fear and hatred those early travelers had faced. The killings without, as the

Werefolk saw it, reason, had caused the laws to be passed, in both Weretoran and Gargoylia, for the Gargoyles had centuries before, made that same trip and returned for the attacks they had suffered from the primitive ones they had met, that never again would they associate with humans. A young female page entered the chamber and went straight to Werelaran. Voices quieted as she came to the Kings throne. She gave a short curtsy and then whispered to the King. Werelaran nodded. The page curtsied again and left the chamber. All the councilors looked to the King as he stood.

"I have just received word that the Realm has made contact with Weretilon," he told all. "I shall return shortly and inform you of what has been decided." All eyes followed him as he left the chamber. The muted sounds of conversations were heard as he changed to wolf and quickly traveled to the witches' castle. He changed back to human in Weretilon's court yard and was quickly led to Weretilon's chamber. The witch looked worried when he entered.

"My King, there are troubles in the Realm," she told him.

"What troubles?" he asked with concern in his voice.

"It would seem that the Overseer was killed on Natharia and his son Zachia, has assumed his father's place as Overseer," she told him, her voice not much more than a whisper. He looked at her and nodded.

"Then I will talk with him," Werelaran said calmly. Weretilon stared at him. He could clearly see her fear in her eyes. "There is no choice Weretilon, we must have their help," he told her softly. She finally nodded and faced the crystal.

"Lord Overseer, My King is here and is ready to talk with you." Her head began to nod slowly as she received the message. "I will tell him," she said and turned to Werelaran. "He asks for a more complete description of Weretoran and Gargoylia, My King," she said. Werelaran nodded, and pointing Weretilon back to her crystal, he began giving a description of their domain and the domain of the Gargoyles. He included the attempt of Gargoylia to make an alliance with Brandaro and the battle that resulted from that attempt. It had taken quite a bit of time for the telling. When he had finished, he watched Weretilon as she received the reply.

"He asks if it would be permitted for an envoy to come to Weretoran and speak with you directly." Weretilon's voice was unemotional. Werelaran hesitated only slightly.

"Yes, it would be allowed," he said and Weretilon glanced quickly at him, a small amount of anger in her eyes and then relayed his words. She nodded and turned to the King.

"When he has formed the envoy, he will let us know," she told him and there was still fear in her eyes and that fear was now heard in her voice. He nodded, turned, and returned to the council chambers, where there was quite a varied response to his news.

Two abreast, the thirty Natharian's of the Realm tribe marched into City Realm. People turned to the synchronized cadence of the huge creatures. The females, smaller and with only six legs, set a softer simpatico rhythm with their steps, for it took four of the females steps to three of the males, creating a combined rhythm, that could quickly become pleasant to hear. The strange cadence was actually causing the ground to tremble. All eyes turned and watched as they passed. The peoples of the city were in mourning of their lost Namson and many of those eyes turned angry, as they knew that Namson had been killed by Natharian's. The people of the city fell in behind the Natharian's as they neared the turn onto the street that fronted the palace, though there were four who followed with an almost amused look on their faces. The Guardians at the gate of the palace notified Zachia as soon as the leaders of the parade turn onto the street. Zachia, with Emma at his side, rushed from the palace to meet the advancing Natharian's. The Keepers of Magic of the different domains and the leaders of the many races of the Realm followed them, as Merlintile came running around the palace.

Zachia and Emma stopped in the middle of the street. The rest formed two rows behind them, as wide as the street. Balsarlan, leader of the tribe of Natharian's in the Realm and his mate, Slirous, led the Natharian's. Slirous was the talker, who as a child, had come to the Realm with the Natharian's who joined in the battle against Palakrine. The Natharian's stopped ten feet from Zachia and the rest of the tribe spread out in offset rows behind their leader. There were several minutes of shared looks between the two lines, as murmurs spread through the people of Realm

City, behind the Natharian's, as well as those behind Zachia and Emma. The murmurs of the people suddenly changed tone, as did those of the ones behind Zachia, as they looked to the palace. Finally, Zachia turned to where the rest looked and saw his mother, Glornina, standing on the terrace. Glornina started for the gate and the guardians all bowed deeply to her as she passed them. She stopped next to Zachia, taking his left arm. All of the Natharian's lowered in a bow to her, their eyes closed, as did all that were present.

"Lady Glornina," Balsarlan said, lifting only slightly from his bow, his hiss based voice carrying over all present. "We come to offer solace and to share in your mourning for your great husband."

"Balsarlan," Glornina stated as she released Zachia's arm and walked towards the huge creature. "I and my son are proud that you have come. I am sure that Namson can feel the honor you give to him." She stopped just short of the Natharian leader, who still held his bow. Glornina reached out her hands and placed them gently on Balsarlan's and Slirous's heads. "Thank you my friends," she said softly. Balsarlan and Slirous both lifted until their eyes were even with Glornina's, as Zachia and Emma walked up next to her.

"We can never repay Mike for the honor he gave to those Natharian's who had asked to stay here in the Realm, or the continued honor and support given by Namson," Balsarlan said loud enough for all to hear. "We have come as representatives for all Natharian's who have been welcomed into all of the Domains of Rightful Magic. We have talked among ourselves and we now swear our service and dedication, as we had for Mike and Namson, to Zachia, Overseer of the Realm and to each of the domains we have been welcomed." A great roar from the gathered crowd erupted. "We also speak for all Natharian's of the Rightful Domains, that we condemn the actions of Bistalan and the traitors who have followed his horrible commands. We willingly commit to the destruction of their wrongs!" Another cheer erupted among the gathered. "We await your commands, Overseer," Balsarlan said. Again, the entire tribe bowed, this time, to Zachia. He returned the bow as the Natharian's lifted from their bow.

"I feel that I speak for the entire Realm and all of the Domains of Rightful Magic, when I say that we are proud to have your race among us and the felt truth of the commitment you have made," Zachia stated and the ever growing crowd gave a cheer of their agreement. "I also feel that the honor you have shown for my father is known and accepted by his spirit!" Again, the huge creatures bowed. Zachia glanced to Belserlan, first son of Balsarlan and Slirous and shared a smile with his friend. Salerous, the mate of Belserlan, matched the smile of Emma, as they too shared a look. The two groups dissolved and all melded into one large crowd. The Natharian's lowering to the resting position so the others' didn't have to look up so high and they all talked of what the future held for them. Balsarlan, Slirous, Belserlan, and Salerous, joined Zachia, Emma, Glornina, and the leaders of the domains and races, on the grass, just inside the gate. Chairs were brought from the palace for the humans and any that could use them. The rest found a comfortable position.

"What are your plans for Natharia?" Balsarlan asked first. Zachia looked to him and almost managed a smile.

"Unfortunately, the revolution on Natharia is not the only troubles we now face Balsarlan," Zachia told him and the Natharian looked surprised. Zachia went on to explain about the message from Daridar and the contact with Weretoran.

"What was learned when you called to them?" Glornina asked Zachia, as soon as Zachia had finished his outline of their current situations. Both Emma and Glornina saw the strange look that came to Zachia's face. Zachia looked to each who were sitting in the circle of leaders, but before he could say anything, Pelkraen came running from the Palace and his excitement caused him to forget Zachia's new title.

"Zachia," the Melerets voice was panicking. "We have overheard two orb transmissions." Pelkraen was panting as he stopped in front of Zachia. "Both transmissions were obviously made by ones not familiar with an orb, for they were general broadcasts, not sent to one target and they were both calling, not to Namsia, but to Bandarson!" Silence washed over all, including many outside of the fence who had heard Pelkraen's yelling.

"Where were they sent from?" Zachia asked, taking the Melerets shoulders.

"One came from Natharia, the other from Neponia!" Pelkraen told him. Zachia stared at the Meleret for a few seconds. He turned back to the fearful eyes of those around him. His peripheral vision, without actually consciously realizing the event, saw the four unknown citizens of City Realm, who had managed to get close to the fence, suddenly straighten and look to the window of the palace. The four nodded to the face they saw there and then slipped away. Zachia's mind stored that seeing, without him even knowing he had.

―――――◦◦◦◦◦―――――

Cenlinas stood on the porch, her arms folded in front of her, looking at the idle plow, now standing alone in the half-plowed garden. She looked over her right shoulder, into the house where her two children sat on the couch talking quietly. She watched as they drank from their mugs of recently brewed generas, an ale like drink that most of the farmers brewed for themselves, and wondered if it was really a good thing that her son was to rule Bandarson after all. She also worried about what role his sister would take in his plans. She saw Brando stand, setting his mug on the side table and go into his room. He quickly reappeared, carrying a rather large bundle. Brendo had stood. She drained her mug and set it down. She was showing a very evil grin as she took the bundle from her brother and went to her room. Part of the covering slipped and Cenlinas saw a clear, round glass shape, beneath the covering. *I wonder what that was*, she thought. A noise turned her attention back to the outdoors. She looked to the north west, and saw two riders approaching. She went into the house and to her son. "There are riders coming from the north," she told him. She picked up the two mugs and went into the kitchen, as Brando started for the door. Brando met the riders as they dismounted. She heard their laughter as they came into the house. She walked by them and went back out onto the porch and sat in her chair. She heard their voices as she sat.

"There are many of the northwestern towns who would join with us Brando," one said.

"They prepare, and should be here within a few days," the other said laughing, which Brando and the first joined. More sounds came to her and she could see riders approaching from all directions. As they stopped and dismounted, and entered the open door of the house, Cenlinas thought of the many possibilities that could be. The voices of the gathered men grew louder as the numbers of those coming, grew. Cenlinas stood and went to the door and looked to the young men who would join her son, to correct the wrongs done to Brandaro. She entered and went to the table the young men gathered around. They made way for her to near the large pitcher. Her grin grew wider as she poured herself a mug full of generas and joined in their celebration of the coming revolt.

In Namsia City, Daridar looked out of the window of her office, wondering what was to become of them all without Namson to lead them. She had no confidence in the young son.

Nepolia was concerned when she entered the throne room. Her attendant had told her that a messenger had returned from her troops. *Why would there be one this quickly? They could only be just over the border by now?* She wondered. When she entered the room, the messenger bowed.

"Queen Nepolia, Central and Northern troops patrol the border in force. We cannot cross. They have blocked the roads and are not allowing anything but food or medicinal roots to pass!" the fearful woman announced. Nepolia stared at her for a moment and then went to her throne, her hand gently stroking her chin in thought. As she sat, an idea came to her. When she looked to the messenger, she had developed a small grin.

"All roads are being blocked?" she asked and the messenger nodded. "The patrols of the borders have increased?" Again the messenger nodded. Nepolia's smile grew more. "Go back to your squads and tell them to return immediately, I have another idea," she told the messenger. The woman bowed and ran from the room. "Calitoran," Nepolia called and he came to her quickly.

"Yes Mistress?" he asked in a fearful voice.

"Bring Pelinon to me," she told him, sitting back in her throne. Calitoran bowed and hurried from the room, hiding his small smile. He returned quickly with the castle seamstress. Pelinon looked to her Queen questioningly. "Pelinon," Nepolia asked sitting forward, her forearms going to the armrests of her throne; "are you familiar with the uniforms of Neponities soldiers?" The Seamstress smiled with her nod. "Good," Nepolia said smiling with her. "Have your seamstresses begin making twenty four

of them, immediately." The head Seamstress bowed with
a knowing look in her eye.

Pelinon returned to her work shop and set the men and
the few women there, to making the new uniforms. Those
uniforms were designed to be basically a short vest, with
the wide open front and a very, very, short skirt. She then
went to a young girl who was sitting, reading a book in the
very back of the room.

"Benilon," she whispered to the girl. "Can you still talk
secretly with Seastaria?" she asked her daughter.

"Yes mama," Benilon answered in a whisper.

"Tell her to inform Queen Neponities that Nepolia intends
to sneak two squadrons of her soldiers across the border,
wearing Central Section uniforms. Also tell her that I will
make a small change in the uniform so the intruders can
be spotted easily." The girl nodded and closed her eyes for
a few moments.

"She asks what difference," Benilon told her. Pelinon
smiled.

"The Section patch will be on the wrong shoulder," she
told her daughter. Benilon smiled as she passed on the
information. Seastaria didn't have far to go to inform the
Queen, because Neponities, Nepelia and her daughter
Nepeslia, as well as Seastaria's grandmother, Cartope,

were standing right beside her, by the side of Nepelia's carriage. Both Queens took the news badly.

———

"What can she be plotting now?" Nepelia angrily asked anyone. They all shrugged. "I will send another battalion for whatever she plans," the Queen of the Northern Section said to Neponities, as she and her daughter, climbed into her carriage.

"Thank you Nepelia," Neponities said. She then looked to and beckoned Nepanities to her. Her daughter stopped besides Neponities, as the Northern Queens carriage pulled away.

"What is it mama?" Nepanities asked, waving to the departing Queen and Princess. Neponities turned and started back for her palace and her daughter followed.

"Has your rather unique Chosen Mate had any ideas about Nepolia?" the Queen asked quietly. Nepanities smiled and shook her head slightly.

"Nothing definite, but I'm sure Carsanac is working on it," she told her mother. "He's still angry about the way she treated him."

"Good," Neponities said softly, causing Nepanities eyes to open wider as she looked to her mother. "Please let me know immediately, if he does come up with something," she added with a small grin.

"Yes mama," Nepanities answered, now with a curious look to her mother.

———

Bistalan left the meeting with his Generals feeling the power of his success. Immediately after the Realm forces had left Natharia, he had started a work force to building his new web palace, with very specific design orders.

Staying to the trees, the new Ruler of Natharia circled the new palace. He smiled as he looked at the structure, which was much larger than any other web building. It was so large in fact, that several trees were used, in the center, to support the great weight of it. The residences of the Natharian's were not just a flat, open web. Those were used for meeting places and for the gathering of food.

He smiled with his realization that this was to be his grand web and it contained many rooms he was sure he would not use. He stepped onto the web landing, which circled the entire palace, very happy to feel very little sway. Bistalan entered his new palace, with Castilan right behind him.

"Lord Bistalan," Castilan's voice was soft, but carried worry. "What of Bremtilan's words?

"What of them?" Bistalan responded as he looked over the entrance hall, his smile growing.

"What if Bleudarn had indeed set up a plan to defeat you?" the aide almost whispered his question. Bistalan lost his smile as he swiveled around abruptly and faced the frightened aide. His words were a hissing growl.

"I am Ruler of Natharia! I don't care what Bremtilan said! There is no one, or thing, that can take that rule from me. I had foreseen the possibility of such a ridiculous plot and have my Generals fully prepared to defeat any that may arise. Bremtilan was an old fool and another example of Bleudarn's stupidity, as a wasted Ruler!" Bistalan pivoted again and returned to the reviewing of his palace. Eventually, he climbed the web ramp that led to his sleeping quarters. He chuckled as he looked to the bed. He eased himself onto the padded platform that was designed to support his entire body. The central post that held the bed, allowed the sleeping pad to sway as wind, or movement of any kind, demanded. He allowed his eight legs to completely relax and sighed, as his head settled to the raised padding. "I am now, the Ruler of Natharia Castilan and I will be for a long time to come," he told his aide. "Now leave me, I am tired and wish to sleep." Castilan bowed, backing down the ramp. He didn't let the new Ruler see the fear that would not leave his eyes, or his thoughts.

Dasilan, leader of the resistance fighters, moved among the gathered Natharian's that were involved with his cell of the resistance forces. "I have shown you the plan that Bleudarn had made and have given each of you your specific areas and duties to work." Heads bobbed all around him. "We cannot allow Bistalan to gain to large amount of a control over Natharia, or he will be harder to remove. We cannot allow Bistalan access to all of the resources of Natharia!" His voice couldn't echo in the soft webbing of the secret web hidden in the densest part of this section of forest, but the voice was definitely strong enough that it should have. In a quieter tone he continued. "You each have responsibilities to your part of the plan and for those you command." Again, heads bobbed. Dasilan looked around at the gathered. "Now go do what is best for all of Natharia!" Hushed whispers were heard, as they all slipped cautiously out of the web and went to their assignments.

Garplasar, having left the Rulers castle, now flew towards his castle and he plotted. He landed in the court yard and sent word that Garpilar should join him in the wizard's magic chamber, immediately. He had just settled into the plush chair before his desk, when there came a loud knocking on the door of the large room. "Enter!" Garplasar called. The door opened and in walked the ugliest of all creatures in Gargoylia. Garpilar was much shorter than any other winged Gargoyle; he was even shorter than most wingless Gargoyles. He slouched as he walked with a shuffle, more than a step. His face was so distorted that it was difficult to pick out any distinct feature and, he sniffled almost constantly. All those of Gargoylia hated and feared this creature, because he was horribly mean and more powerful in strength, than any Gargoyle. Garplasar smiled as he thought that the rest of Gargoylia didn't know that he had a rather large army of these creatures. He called them Gaspilarians.

"Master," Garpilar sniffled as he stopped next to Garplasar. The wizard turned to the hideous creature and a larger grin came to the corners of his mouth.

"I want you to pick out five of your most powerful soldiers and return to me," the wizard told him. "I will explain your duties when you return." With the education he had received from his teacher Garsalar, Garplasar spoke to his minion with complete sentences. He was the only Gargoyle, in all of Gargoylia that knew how. Garpilar looked to his master, nodded, and left the chamber. Garplasar watched the creature until it had closed the door and then turned back to his desk. A full smile came to his mouth. "Garator wants a talker, to try and rally Bandarson to his side, and overthrow Weretoran," he said softly to himself and then chuckled. "By the time the Ruler thinks he has made his alliance, I will already control Bandarson, Weretoran, and the Realm! Then, Garator will be my servant!" The wizard's chuckle turned to a deep, roaring laughter that raised the few hairs on the back of the neck of the guard who stood watch outside his door.

At the Rulers castle, Garator left the council chamber and went to his dining room, for he had missed his breakfast and lunch and was very hungry. The two servers of his meal suffered, or enjoyed, his groping, for both were young wingless females. In different parts of the castle and other places, Council members gathered to talk of Garator's plots. When he had finished his meal Garator headed for the harem, for the groping had awoken another hunger in him.

Werelaran was finally able to return to his family as the sun began to settle for the night. Wereselon served her husband his evening meal as the nanny, who was a lesser witch, watched over the new babies their mother had settled for the night. Wereselon didn't interrupt her husband's concentration as he mulled over the events of the day. Silence and worry, ate her meal with her. After they had finished, Wereselon went with her husband, to the living area. She accepted the glass of wine Werelaran brought her and watched as he sat on the sofa next to her.

"Are you sure of your choice to involve the humans?" she finally asked, quietly. "What of the laws?" she added. He didn't answer and she was about to ask again, when he looked to her, trying to smile.

"Those laws were enacted in a time when Werewolves were not much more civilized then the Gargoyles," he said softly. "No one has forgotten the stories told by those who returned, but that was a very long time ago and changes have affected our race, as well as the humans." He took a sip of wine, looking to his glass after. She copied his moves, but continued to watch him. "The Gargoyles have maintained their society of cruelty and desires for powers, but the Werewolves have evolved to a more peaceful and caring way of life and, so have the humans." He turned his eyes to her. "I cannot help but feel that the time of our races joining, to stop all domains that thrive on the same cruelty and greed of the Gargoyles, has come." He found a smile, though it was not very large and appeared worried. "Yes my love, I am sure of my decision." She looked into his eyes and saw more than just their shared worries; she saw a truth that she could believe. She nodded, joining in his smile. He drank the remainder of his wine and stood, holding out his hand to her. She drank her wine and took his hand, standing. They went hand and hand to their sleeping chamber, where they removed their clothes. Then, in the manner of their kind, changed to wolf form and curled up on the straw bed.

"I pray that you are correct my love," Wereselon whispered, as they went to sleep.

Zachia lay listening to the night's sounds that came through the open balcony door. His thoughts returned to the entombment of his father's body. Namson had ordered, with the death of Mike, that only Mike and Gloreana's tomb, would stand on the palace grounds. Those two had established the basis for all of Rightful Magic and they were to be honored by all who followed, for their truths and, their sacrifices. All tombs of future Overseers and their wives, including his own and Emma's, would be placed in the park, across from the palace. Each new Overseer would select the location for their tombs, as one of the first duties they assumed as Overseer. Namson and Glornina had selected their site immediately after Namson had made this proclamation. Zachia had honored his father's order and placed his tomb in that selected spot.

His mother had turned from the tomb, after his father's body had been interred and looked to him. "You will swear that I am to lay with him, when it is my time," she had told him. Zachia made his vow to her, though his heart screamed its pain to do so. "It is now time that you select yours and Emma's place," she had added. He had taken Emma's trembling hand and together, they selected the placement of their final resting spot. Emma had wept through it all.

He turned his head and looked to Emma, laying on her right side, facing him, seemingly asleep. He eased from the bed and taking his robe, walked to the balcony. He didn't see Emma's eyes open as she turned her head, to follow his travel to the balcony. She watched as he donned his robe and then, placing his hands on the railing, leaned on it. She turned over and got out of bed. She picked up her robe and put it on as she came to him.

"Zachia?" she asked softly as she stopped next to him. He looked to her and smiled.

"I'm sorry, I didn't mean to wake you," he told her putting his right arm around her shoulder. She smiled back at him.

"I wasn't really sleeping dear," she told him with a quiet chuckle. "I knew something has been worrying you and I was waiting for you to go to sleep." He sighed and looked out over Realm City. "What are you thinking about Zachia?" she asked, moving closer into his side, her arms encircling his waist. He chuckled this time.

"Everything," he told her. "Papa's death, mama, what's going to happen on Natharia and Namsia, but what seems to have captured most of my thoughts, for some reason, is this new Domain of Weretoran." She looked up to him.

"Why is that?" she asked. He shrugged and sighed again.

"I don't know for sure, but it's like I've heard of those races before, but I can't remember where I heard it," he told her. Silence came to them both for several minutes.

"Can you remember any part of what it is that you heard?" Emma asked, breaking the silence. He shook his head a couple of times. He again looked around the city and then looked to the rising moon and tensed. Feeling the sudden tensing of his body, she looked to him in alarm.

"Zachia?" she whispered. Zachia lifted his left hand and pointed to the rising full moon.

"That's it," he said and she looked to the moon.

"The moon?" she asked, beginning to be concerned about her husband's sanity. "What about it?" He rapidly shook his head, as though to clear his thoughts and turned to her, taking her shoulders in his hands.

"Do you remember when we all went to Gordon's, for Xanaporia's birthday, about three months before the bandits attacked?" he asked, his voice becoming excited. She stared at him for a few moments, in thought and then nodded. He nodded with her. "There was a full moon that night, and while we were outside, having brandy, there was a distant wolf howl?" She nodded and smiled.

"Yes, Gordon said that the Werewolves were out and…." Emma's eyes opened wide. "He said the Werewolves were hunting and laughed. He then told us of the folk tales about humans who would turn to wolves with the full moon and hunted human prey!" Zachia was nodding faster with her words, tightening his grip on her shoulders slightly.

"Maybe, those weren't just folk tales. What if there really were werewolves and the humans just added their fears to their telling?" he whispered. She stared back at him. "I think," Zachia said softly, looking again to the moon and then back to her; "that maybe I should go to Zentler tomorrow morning and have a little talk with Gordon." Emma looked to the moon and then to him.

"I'm coming with you!" she told him, and they both started to laugh.

CHAPTER THREE

Daridar had spent the remainder of the day talking with different people of the Realm, concerning Namsia's situation and preparations. She had then gone to her home and had had a night of only occasional sleep. The couple of brandies she had drunk before going to bed hadn't helped her sleep at all. She was not in the best of moods when her personal guards showed up to bring her to the Town Hall and her office. It did not help her mood in the slightest, when Parsony, the Commander of her personal guard, started insisting that the Guard find her a more secure place to work and for living.

In a small house, on the outer edge of the town of Bentodon, Tarington, and his brother Trenlor, smiled at each other as Tarington relayed what Brando and his followers were up to, to Kenyea and her mate Promlur, who was part of Daridar's guards. Kenyea passed that information on to Somora, as well as what the Commander of the Mayors Guard was trying to get Daridar to do. Somora smiled as his various spies reported to him.

Nepolia smiled as her two squads again left for the Center Section. She thought the uniforms were perfect and she was sure that soon, she would have the means to begin the next stage of her plan.

At the same time as Nepolia watched her departing troops, on the border of the Central and Southern Sections, directly south of Capital City, Nepanities, followed by Carsanac, walked into the tent of the Commander for the battalion that guarded that part of the border. The Commander stood, coming to attention, though her eyes did travel over Carsanac quickly. Nepanities felt no insult or anger for the Commanders eyes. In fact, she felt pride that her mate would attract the attention of the Commander. "Commander Carsonties, have you alerted all of your patrols about the southern soldiers and what they are to look for?" she asked the Commander.

"Yes Mistress," the commander stated, still at attention. Nepanities waved her to sit and took the chair in front of the desk. Carsanac stood to her side, his hand resting on the back of the chair. Carsonties sat, meshing her fingers and placing her hands and forearms, on the small desk. She looked to Nepanities and waited, though her eyes did stray to Carsanac's lower anatomy, a few times.

"I will be joining with your patrols and my Chosen Mate will be coming with me. Please have a tent set for us,"

Nepanities said softly. The Commanders eyes opened wider and then she nodded.

"Yes Mistress," she said. She called the soldier at the entrance of her tent and ordered a tent for the Princess and her mate. When she returned her attention to Nepanities, there were questions in her eyes. "Is there a special reason for this Mistress, or am I and my troops, under inspection?" There was a tone poorly hidden, that showed the Commanders concerns and irritation. Nepanities smiled and shook her head.

"There is no inspection, nor any doubt of yours, or your troop's capabilities Commander," she said. "It is just that Nepolia is trying to send troops into our section, secretly, and my mother and I are sure that they are, for whatever reason, headed for Capital City. We are quite sure they will try to come through this area." Nepanities smiled at Carsonties and the Commander returned the smile, with a nod. Nepanities sat forward. "Now show me the layouts of your patrols," she said. Carsonties went to the large board that held the map of the area she had been assigned to patrol. She pointed out the patterns of the patrols and the time changes, so that there seemed there was no regularity to them and how the patrols over lapped each other at various places and times. Both Nepanities and Carsanac nodded their approval of the presentation. Nepanities stood and looked to the Commander. "Please make sure that your troops know that we are not here to judge their performances and that we will be walking different patrols, at different times, with them." The Commander nodded as Nepanities turned and left the tent, Carsanac right behind her. They went to the tent shown to them, and rested. They joined the midnight patrol, that very night.

There was a gentle rain falling on the far tops of the huge trees of Natharia and the slow, caressing drippings, found their way down to Bistalan as he walked onto the Councilors web. The Councilors all went to a bow, recognizing his rule, but there were more than a few who watched him carefully and not with obedience in their eyes. Bistalan settled on the Rulers pedestal and the councilors settled to theirs. Bistalan had seen that there was no replacement for Bremtilan as yet and he whispered to Castilan to have General Mertilan find out why, because his troops had taken that province. He turned back to the councilors and a snarling growl issued from him.

"I will now tell you of my reasons for this takeover and what I expect from the Natharian's of your provinces," he told them, as his sight passed over each. "For far too long, the Overseer and those of the other domains have used the Natharian's as slaves for their greedy desires!" The power of his voice causing echo's from the surrounding trees. "They have given mere trinkets for our webbings and our labors. This will stop, and Natharian's will be paid properly for what they have been robbed of!" He again allowed his sight to pass over the half circle of Councilors before him. He saw all of the attempts to hide the shared glances that showed the varied thoughts of the councilors. He wore an angry smile as he rose from his pedestal. "We will punish those of the Realm and the domains and collect what we are due!" he roared at them and many cringed as they looked to each other with fear.

⸙

Garteltor lay in his bed, thinking. That bed was the long, raised sitting pad, in the center of the large main room. He knew what Gorastor would do if he tried to sleep in his bed, in the loft, with her. He had come home shortly after his mother's message to Weretilon. He had walked in on the conversation of his parents and his sister, as they talked of what Garator was attempting. He quickly realized what was going to happen if the Ruler accomplished his goal and he did not want what he had heard about the war between the Weretorians and Gargoyles, to happen again. He had been very young when that war had erupted, and he really didn't remember much of it, other than the fear his parents had felt and shown. He had later learned about the reasons for those fears and the horrible loss of lives, because of that war. He thought that tomorrow, he would meet with the other members of the gang he had formed, which did what they could to disrupt any of Garator's soldiers, or spotters. He was now thinking of things the young males could do to stop Garator from creating another nightmare for Gargoylia.

⸙

Werelaran lay listening to the gentle breathing of his sleeping mate. They had been awoken by their twins, very early in the morning and they both had risen to attend them. The nanny, who was a lesser witch and had helped Wereselon with the birth, had not been surprised when the parents walked into the nursery as she tended the babies. The King and Queen had returned to their sleeping chamber when the babies had gone back to sleep, after a change of diapers and a feeding from their mother. Werelaran had heard that his mate had quickly gone back to sleep, but sleep was denied him. His thoughts, about the joining with the Realm and the news Weretilon had passed to him concerning Garator's efforts to find a talker, kept sleep from him. He rose quietly and changed back to human form. Putting his robe on, he went to his office. He went to the cart that held several different containers of liquor and poured a small glass one third full, with burtanlias, a brandy like liquor. He went to the window and looked out at the dark court yard and the city beyond. He slowly took a sip from the glass. "Am I truly doing right?" he quietly asked the city. It did not know and so, did not answer him.

Zachia and Emma were up very early and were very surprised when they walked into the dining room and found Glornina already there. She looked up and smiled at them, as they got their cups of coffee. They both had seen that she did not sit in the chair she had always taken, the chair to the right of the Overseer's. She now sat in the chair, on the side of the table, to the left of the Overseer's chair that Zachia had used before.

"Mama," Zachia asked; "why are you up so early?" Zachia was hesitant about the chair he knew he was to use, as they approached the table. Glornina smiled as she saw his hesitation.

"You are now the Overseer, you sit there," she said to her son, pointing to the chair Namson had used. "And, you are Mistress of the Realm," she told Emma; "you sit there." She pointed to the chair she had used before. Zachia and Emma exchanged looks, which showed their sadness. Zachia finally nodded and pulled the Mistress of the Realm's chair back for Emma. She hesitated, looking to Glornina, tears coming to her eyes. Glornina smiled as she rose and came around the table to Emma. She took the young woman into her arms as she looked to her son. "The title and privilege of Overseer is now yours," she told him softly; "and so is the responsibility and, the debt." She smiled at him, then to Emma, and then back to him. "Do not worry about me, for your father is with me. He comforts me and I know that he feels pride in you and has faith in what you do," she told Zachia. "And you Emma," Glornina turned back to her daughter-in-law; "must be his strength, when doubts come to him." She smiled and gave a final and gentle squeeze to her hug. "Now, sit to his right hand and be the Mistress of the Realm that I know you can be!" Emma returned the hug, and then looked to Zachia. He held the back of the chair as Emma sat and then he sat next to her, at the head of the table. Glornina returned to the chair she had been sitting in, to Zachia's left. "What do you have planned for this day?" she asked as she picked up her cup. Zachia and Emma, quickly overcoming their hesitations about the seating arrangements, smiled at her and told them of their revelation, the night before. "Can I come with you?" she asked, looking to her son, her eyes brighter than before and a small grin on her lips, for she too remembered the evening of the party and all Gordon had told them. Zachia grinned as he nodded.

"I also think that we should send some people to Namsia, to find out for sure, what is happening there, as well as an envoy to this Weretoran," Zachia said, sobering the moment. Glornina nodded her agreement.

"Who do you think should go to which?" Emma asked. Zachia looked to her and then his mother.

"Melsikan and Isabella, plus a small army to Namsia, and Gordon and Xanaporia to Weretoran," he said quietly. The other two nodded their agreement. Baldor slipped away from the kitchen door, to send his two part message to Somora.

Cenlinas had watched two of those who supposedly had spread Brando's call for followers. She had seen that they really didn't talk all that much, but had been very busy listening to all who did speak, especially Brando and Brendo. She could not help but feel that they were not what they pretended to be. When Cenlinas told Brando of her concerns, after the others' had all left, he smiled and nodded, for it turned out that Brando had been doing his own watching. He told her he had seen the same as she had. Cenlinas heard her daughter behind her.

"I did some asking around and there were none that knew what section, or province, they had traveled to," Brendo said, as she joined them.

"Did you find out their names?" Brando asked her. His sister nodded. When Cenlinas looked to her daughter, she did not like the hard look in the girl's eyes.

"The taller one is called Tarington and the other one is called Trenlor," she told him. Cenlinas heard that her voice, though hushed, carried her anger easily. Brando nodded, as he beckoned to someone that Cenlinas had not seen standing nearby. A large man, much older than Brando, stepped closer to the three. Cenlinas saw that the huge man was almost as big as her son and was older than she. She also felt something familiar with his face. It was when Brando said his name that she recognized him completely. She stared at the man as she heard Brando's voice.

"Barkoor," Brando said to the man, his voice getting a very hard edge to it. "Find out what you can of them and then I will decide what is to be done with them." The big man nodded and left the house. Cenlinas watched him go as the memories of her induction as a bed slave to Brandaro, came back to her. Barkoor had been the personal guard for the young Brandaro, going wherever Brandaro went, including the bedroom. She could remember the times that she had been taken by Brandaro, seeing the big man standing or sitting nearby. Sometimes watching, but never showing interest. She had learned much later, after Brandaro had found out she was pregnant and she had been sent away, that Barkoor, when very young, had been castrated by Bandaro, Brandaro's father, because of crimes committed by the boy's father. The boy was then trained in the many facets of military combat. When he had become proficient enough, he was assigned to guard the young Brandaro.

When Brandaro had found Telposar, Barkoor had been reassigned and all seemed to lose track of him.

"Where did you find him?" she asked Brando, in a surprised voice. "I thought him dead." Brando smiled at her as he slowly shook his head.

"He had been assigned by father, to search out the targets for the bandits to attack. With father's death, he came to me, swearing his service," he told her. Brendo looked as wide eyed as her mother, as they looked to Brando. Cenlinas remained quiet, listening, as Brando turned to his sister. "Have you succeeded with your working of the orb?" he asked Brendo quietly and she smiled.

"Yes," she told him, with a nod. "I have received messages from two domains that say they are interested in joining with us, to aid in our rebellion and of course, they ask for us to help them in their yearning for power and to punish the Realm and, destroy the Overseer!" Cenlinas could not stop the small smile from forming.

"Where and who, are those of these domains?" Cenlinas heard. Brendo's smile grew and Cenlinas feared the vicious gleam that came to her daughters eyes.

"One is the race of creatures that aided the Overseer's forces that took Bandarson City," she said, her eyes turning to slits. "The ones with many legs and were very large. The other is from one of the Queens, of one of Sections of the domain that our father had tried to raid and, where he met his death!" Brando almost smiled with her words. Cenlinas was thinking as she looked back and forth between her children. A smile began to form on her lips.

Nepanities and Carsanac had been walking with the patrol for less than an hour, when Carsanac leaned to her. "Signal silently, that they should stop where they are," Carsanac whispered to Nepanities. She didn't hesitate and signals were quickly passed. Within a few seconds of Carsanac's warning, not one of the patrol moved.

"What is it my mate?" Nepanities asked in a whisper, as she looked around and then to him. He slowly lifted his finger, pointing. She looked to where he was pointing, but could only see trees. Then a movement, but she wasn't sure what had caused it. The moon light, sifting through the breeze stirred trees, could have created the effect.

"Do not look directly at it, look slightly above it," he whispered. When she adjusted her sight, she saw them with surprising ease.

"How many?" she asked, as she tried to count them herself.

"Twenty four," Carsanac said. He saw her nod her agreement as she reached that same number in her mind. She turned to the closest scout and signaled her instructions. Very quickly, the scouting party had formed their defensive line. One of them had started back to main camp, to bring the rest of the troops. The remainder awaited the oncoming shadows that were the two squads from the Southern Section.

"There are only ten of us left," Nepanities whispered. Her Chosen Mate smiled and nodded.

"Put the best five over there," he whispered to her, pointing to the best position. She nodded. "And you and the other four, over there." She again nodded. "When I stop them, they will try to overpower me," he said. "When that happens, I will call the word "now". When you hear that word, attack loudly, making as much noise as you can. Rattle bushes and change your voice tones. They will think there are more of you than there are and quickly surrender." Carsanac was sure she didn't like the idea of using him as bait, but he felt she knew him well enough and hoped she would trust his judgment. Signals passed on the instructions and they silently moved to their position.

In Neponia, males were not allowed to carry weapons, except for registered hunters. Carsanac waited until all were positioned. He then slipped a quiver and bow over his head and shoulder. He casually walked into an open area, in clear sight of the leaders of the Southern Sections troops. The moon gave more than enough light for the troops to see him and he was challenged immediately.

"Hold male," a voice said. A soldier stepped into sight, twenty feet from Carsanac. "What are you doing out at this hour and what makes you think you can carry a bow?" Other soldiers joined the first. In just seconds, all twenty four of the enemy stood in a semicircle, twenty feet from Carsanac.

"Drop that quiver and bow male," another one said as she stepped in front of the rest. Carsanac smiled as he turned to face the soldiers. He slowly lifted the bow from his shoulder and held it as he pulled the quiver of arrows over his head, with his other hand, but he didn't drop them as ordered. His smile widened as he faced the women. He then said one word, loudly.

"Now!" he yelled. He then notched an arrow so quickly that the women couldn't comprehend that he had. Nepanities and the four with her charged out, yelling at different volumes and tones, as the other five copied their actions from the other side. Most of the surprised invaders were so shaken by the trap, that they immediately dropped their weapons and raised their hands. There were three that didn't and they tried to bluff their authority. Carsanac smiled as he heard the woman who had stepped forward.

"What is the meaning of this," one of them, wearing the insignia of a lieutenant and still holding her sword, yelled. "We are on Queen Neponities business. How dare you attack?" she roared. Nepanities walked slowly to her, wearing a small smile and pulling her sword from its scabbard. Carsanac couldn't stop the wink at Nepanities, when she glanced at him.

"You say you are on the business of my mother?" she asked, turning back to the woman. Some of those of the enemy troops recognized her. They gasped and whispered her name loud enough for the lieutenant to hear. The woman opened her eyes in fear and dropped the sword she held. It was then that the reinforcements arrived. They quickly gathered the enemy into a secured line, three abreast.

"How did you know?" the lieutenant asked the guard closest to her. The guard smiled and beckoned Nepanities over. She whispered to the Princess and Nepanities grinned, again glancing at Carsanac before she answered. She looked back to the captured woman. Carsanac almost laughed out loud with Nepanities words.

"There are many spies in Nepolia's castle," she said and signaled the Commander to lead the captured away. Carsanac and Nepanities chuckled as they followed the parade of captured Southern soldiers.

———

Dasilan, the leader of the resistances forces, moved carefully from the Council Web. He had listened to Bistalan from a place of hiding, high in the trees and he knew that they had to speed up the efforts of the resistance. Dasilan, once a safe distance from Bistalan, raced through the trees, towards the meeting place. He had to tell all division leaders to intensify the efforts of their divisions. He also knew that he had to have the talkers, who were in constant contact with the Realm, to pass on that the Overseer must stop the efforts of Bistalan, quickly.

———

Garator woke slowly. He didn't open his eyes immediately, for he sensed danger near. He could feel the presence of the five females who had shared his bed the night before. He almost smiled for the remembered pleasures. He felt a gentle movement in the bed. He allowed his eyes to open to slits and looked around without moving his head. He saw the naked female reaching for something behind the headboard of the huge bed. He knew that she was new to the harem. Although she had done all he had demanded, he had felt that she truly did not want his attentions. But, he had been so involved with them all; he had ignored her actions as first time fears. He watched as she drew her hand from behind the headboard, and slowly turn to him. The sun was just lighting the room as she faced the Ruler, with a large dagger in her hand. Just as she lunged at him, Garator reached out with both hands. One went to the hand that was plunging the dagger, and the other went to her throat. This action caused the two females between them to wake. The other females screamed for the horror, as he ripped the throat from the attacking one. His laughter echoed off the walls.

In the Wizards castle, Garplasar had already sent Garpilar, and his hideous force, to the Realm, to find a talker they could kidnap. He had sent a communication crystal with his minion. He had told Garpilar that when they had captured a talker, he would spell them back to him. He, and a dozen Gaspilarians, now prepared to travel to Bandarson. He was sure that he would be done with his business on Bandarson by then. He had no idea how wrong he was on both counts.

In a shadowed part of the capital city of Gartisia, Garteltor met with the members of his gang. He began to tell them of horrors he had felt, and seen, during the war with the

Weretorians. He then told them of his plans concerning Garator. They had, at first, looked to him as though he had no sense, until he told them of Garator's motives. They had looked to each other with fear, and then listened much more closely. Garteltor's sister and parent's were trying to make their own plans, not knowing of his efforts. When they did finally manage to tell each other of their efforts, they found a great similarity in the plots, but Garteltor's was much more intense and, much more deadly.

———————

Wereselon woke with the morning sun, and immediately knew her mate was not with her. She stood, changed to her human form, and donned her robe, as she went in search of him. She stopped the first servant she met, and asked the location of the King. The girl seemed hesitant to tell her. "Where is Werelaran?" she softly asked again, placing her hands on the girl's shoulders. The girl glanced at her, shyly.

"He is in his office, with burtanlias, and stands looking out over the city," the girl told her softly. Wereselon looked at her for just a moment, sensing the girls concerns.

"Do not be worried, little one," she said, for the girl was only sixteen, and had only been in service, in the castle for a month. "The King has many thoughts, and cares deeply for all of Weretoran. It is a passing moment that will be alright in the end." The girl looked to the Queen and nodded, as she almost smiled. She had heard the rumors that were rampaging through the palace and she was old enough to know the Queen had seriously understated the situation. "Would you please ask the kitchen to send some tea, and morning cakes, to the Kings office?" she asked the girl. The girl nodded and hurried off to tell the kitchen of the Queens request. Wereselon hurried to Werelaran's office. She hesitated at the door, and then knocked.

"Enter," her husband's voice called out. She worried for the tired tone she heard. She opened the door and saw that Werelaran had not turned from the window. She closed the door softly, and then neared her husband.

"Werelaran?" she asked, her worries clear in her voice. He turned at the waist, and looked to her. He tried to smile as he turned completely, coming to her. He placed the glass he had been holding, on the desk as he passed it. He took her into his arms, and she came willingly. "What has caused this?" she asked his cheek. He pulled back from her slightly and looked into her eyes. She clearly heard the worry in his voice as he answered her.

"Garator is searching for a talker, to make an alliance with Bandarson," he told her. She searched his eyes, looking for any sign that this was not the truth, but only found that it was indeed, the truth.

"What are we to do?" she asked, coming back into his arms. She was surprised as he chuckled softly. She pulled back and looked to him. He wore a small, strange smile, as he returned her look.

"The only thing we can do. Hope that the Realm, and the Overseer, will move quickly my wife," he said softly as there came a knock on the door. A voice announced that their tea and morning cakes, had arrived.

Zachia, Emma, and Glornina, appeared in the special room of the court house of Zentler. The peoples of Zentler, with the return of Isabella from the terrors of her captivity in Brandaro's castle, had told those of magic that they knew of their powers, and had said that they were quite comfortable with them, but they didn't want to share that information with any that might be visiting the town. So, special places were designated, throughout the town, so those who could magically teleport, could disappear, or appear, without any strangers witnessing the event. Zachia led the three as they stepped from the room, into a silent and completely empty building. "What day is it?" Glornina immediately asked with a chuckle. Emma looked to the calendar kept on the Mayors secretaries' desk. She followed the crossed out dates.

"Sunday," she said with a grin matching Glornina's. They both looked to Zachia and he joined their grins, with a nod.

"Gordon's," he said, and they appeared in Gordon's office, at his home. They turned to the door and Zachia reached for the door knob, just as the knob turned and the door swung open quickly. Gordon and Zachia both jumped at the sight of each other. The three started to chuckle, but the tone of Gordon's voice quickly stopped that.

"You're here, good," Gordon said much too loudly. He grabbed Zachia's arm and pulled him towards the living room. "I was going for the orb in my office, to tell you that Ava and GeeBee have had a seeing and there is danger for the Realm!" he told them. They entered the living room and those of the Realm saw that Melsikan, Isabella, and their children, Carl and Kris, and their children, Penelopy, Marcus, and their children, and Terressa, Ben, and their child, were sitting, talking quietly to each other. Emma and Glornina saw that Ava and GeeBee were being held, and comforted, by their mothers, and that Kris's eyes were wider than normal, as she looked to her small child. But, the thing that drew Zachia's attention was the strange look on Ben's face. It was then that Glorian's, Prelilian's, and many other voices blared into their heads.

"There are invaders in the Realm!" There were gasps, and everyone looked to each other. Zachia called to his sister.

"Who?" He asked.

"I don't know," Glorian said; "but Braxton says that they've come to take someone!"

"Tell Tarson to assemble the army and begin searches," he told Emma, and she nodded, sending the order.

"He already is doing so. Prelilian told him," Emma said, and Zachia nodded. He turned to the rest.

"Everybody that can teleport, pick someone who can't. I want everybody in the Realm, now," he said. Nods matched exchanged looks as they grouped up. Zachia waited just a minute and then gave a nod of his head and they all stood in the entrance hall of the palace. For no reason he could explain, Zachia looked to Ben and saw him look surprised, then turn his eyes from someone. Zachia looked to where

Ben had been looking and saw one of the male servants entering the hallway between the two meeting rooms that led to the western wing of the palace. He felt a strong sense of familiarity with the one who had went down the hall. He sent a silent message to Pelkraen, one of the few that he could talk with, to follow that servant and find out what purpose he had. Pelkraen said he would and Zachia turned back to the others'. "Does anyone know who these invaders are?" he asked. All shook their heads.

"Gargoyles, six of them!" Ava suddenly said, loudly. There was not a sound for several seconds, but Isabella's eyes were very wide as she looked to her daughter.

"The message from Weretoran said that they were afraid that Gargoyle's, would try to make an alliance with Bandarson," Emma said, looking to Zachia. Zachia nodded, as he wondered how the girl could know what a Gargoyle was.

"What the hell are you talking about?" Gordon asked in a whisper. "Gargoyle's don't exist." Zachia smiled, or tried to.

"Well, it seems that they do and, so do werewolves! I've talked with them," he told the wide eyed Mayor and the rest. "Everybody but Emma, mama, and Melsikan, please wait in the reading room," Zachia said. They all looked at Zachia and then to each other. Hesitantly they started to move towards the reading room. "Ben," Zachia said suddenly; "why don't you join us in my office?" There was a hard look in Zachia's eyes when Ben looked at him. Fear showed in Ben's.

"Why can't I wait in the reading room?" Ben asked. "I don't have any magical powers."

"Really?" Zachia asked, his voice soft, but it held an edge that frightened Terressa, as she looked to her husband. Zachia saw Terressa give Benjamin's hand to Isabella, who looked to her with surprise.

"I think I should come as well," Terressa told Zachia, her eyes searching her husband's. The Overseer saw her look and nodded.

"Come on then. Ben come with me," he said and there was no doubt of his meaning. Ben looked around quickly, his eyes showing his growing panic. He turned and ran for the door. Zachia caught him in a holding spell and then pulled him to the office, as the rest followed.

"What do you think that's all about?" Isabella asked Melsikan quietly, before they started for their assigned destinations. Ava took Benjamin's hand, and led him, with the other children, to the toys that were always kept in the reading room, after a hard look at her father. He nodded to her and looked to his wife. As Zachia stood to the side, letting the others enter the office ahead of him, he saw Isabella look to Melsikan and then heard his badly controlled whisper.

"Something Ava brought to my attention some months ago," Melsikan answered, almost as quietly. She looked to him, confused. "She told me that she was getting a strange feeling around Ben, as though he was not who he acted to be," Melsikan said. Zachia glanced at the one standing next to him, locked in his spell.

"What?" Isabella whispered her surprise as she looked to her daughter. She knew that Ava was already very powerful in magic, but she hadn't thought the girl could also be a sensitive, until today. Melsikan nodded as Isabella turned back to him.

"So, I've been watching Ben since, and he has been doing some strange things. I don't know the all of it, but I think there is a chance that he is a danger to us all." He turned and followed the Overseer to the office. She had seen the truth of his concerns, in his eyes. She again looked to her daughter and worried what was coming for them all, as she followed the others' to the reading room.

Zachia, after removing the holding spell, put Ben in the chair that was directly in front of the desk. He then sat his right hip on the front edge of the desk. Terressa sat in the chair next to her husband, her eyes going from him, to Zachia, and back, rapidly. "Alright Ben," Zachia said softly. "What's going on? Why did you try to run and, who is that servant you didn't want to look at?" They all saw Ben clench his jaws for a moment, then he looked to Zachia in anger.

"I don't know what you're talking about," he said angrily. "I ran because the look you gave me, scared me. I didn't know why you were angry and I was frightened that you might do something crazy. I don't know nothing about no servant, and I don't know what you're talking about!" Out of the corner of his eye, Zachia saw Terressa's brows lifted slightly and Glornina, who had been watching her, also saw her reaction.

"What is it Terressa?" Glornina asked quietly, just before Zachia could. The woman looked to her. She then looked to Zachia, back to Glornina and, finally her husband.

"Why were you sneaking out at night, so many times?" she asked him. "Were you seeing another woman, or was there another reason?" Zachia and the rest saw Ben look from her, to Zachia and then around the room. All could see his nervousness.

"No honey, I was just walking. I couldn't sleep, so I would go for a walk, and that's all." His voice was very shaky. Terressa's eyes filled with tears as she slowly shook her head.

"You are lying," she said softly, as those tears started down her cheeks. "I know your voice and you are lying!" Ben shook his head, and she could now see the fear in his eyes. "What were you doing?" Terressa yelled and stood, her fists clenched. Glornina and Emma quickly got to her and grabbed her before she could advance on Ben. "Tell me, what you were doing when you snuck out!" she screamed at him. Ben coward in his chair from the power of the rage in her eyes and her screams.

"Ben," Zachia said, his voice louder than normal. He had suddenly remembered the scene he had witnessed, on the lawn of the palace and the ones he had seen look to the window. That is where he had seen the servant before. He came off the desk, getting very close to Ben's face, his hands gripping the arms of the chair. "Answer her! What were you doing?" Zachia's voice was almost as loud as Terressa's. Ben's eyes were wide and he was looking rapidly back and forth between Zachia and Terressa, when, without any warning, the door of the office burst open and the servant that Zachia had seen Ben turn from, charged into the room. He raised a dart gun and shot Ben in the back of the head. Before anyone could stop him, Baldor turned the gun on himself and pulled the trigger a second time. His dead body fell to the floor. No one had had time to scream before it was all over. Terressa didn't make a sound a she fell to her knees, grasping Ben's body, weeping. The rest could only look wide eyed at each other.

It was several hours later, after Terressa had been put to bed, with a spell to help her sleep, and Benjamin was being cared for by the other adults, that Zachia, Emma, and Glornina, came into the reading room. He could see that all were shocked and very upset about all that had happened. Zachia knew that he had to calm them. He was just about to begin to speak, when a messenger from Tarson was shown into the room by a Guardian.

"Overseer, the invaders have been captured," he said. "Tarson says that he needs you right away!"

"Where are they?" Zachia asked.

"West of the city, near the lake. I am to guide you," the messenger said with a bow. Zachia nodded and looked to his wife and mother.

"Do what you can to calm them. I will be right back," he told them, and followed the messenger. As soon as he had left the room, all in the room looked to Emma and Glornina. Emma, without hesitation, began to tell them what had happened, choosing her words carefully, for the sake of the children in the room. Glornina smiled at her, nodding. She saw that her daughter-in-law was already becoming the Mistress of the Realm.

———

On the west side of the city, Tarson was leaning against a large tree, staring at the enclosed creatures, slowly shaking his head when Zachia walked up to him. "What have you got?" Zachia asked, causing Tarson to jerk with his surprise.

"Six of the ugliest and strongest things you can imagine," he answered, pointing to the creatures that were screaming and beating on the sealed enclosure they were in, except for the one in the center of that enclosure. He stood, staring at them, holding an amulet. "As soon as we closed on them, that one in the middle grabbed that amulet and I sealed them magically, so they couldn't send any signal," Tarson told him, as he and Zachia neared the enclosure. Zachia nodded.

"When I tell you, drop your shielding and I will spell them to cells. Maybe I can get that amulet before a message can be sent, while I'm at it." Tarson grinned and nodded his understanding. "Now," Zachia said, and Tarson dropped the shielding and the creatures disappeared. When Tarson turned to Zachia, he saw the amulet in the Overseer's hand.

"I've got some wounded I need to get taken care of," he told Zachia. The Overseer's brows lifted in surprise. "I said they were strong," Tarson said with a small grin. "I am willing to bet that each of those things, are near as strong as an ogre!" Zachia's brows went higher and Tarson nodded, then turned and went to his troops. Zachia sent a message to Tremliteen and then spelled himself back to the reading room. Everyone jumped when he appeared. Zachia's voice told of an intensity of purpose when he spoke to those in the reading room.

"Melsikan, Isabella, Gordon, Xanaporia, mama, Emma, would you come with me please. Tremliteen showed up, as they all entered the office. All were very happy that Ben's body had been removed and the remnants of his death had cleaned up. Zachia went to his chair behind the desk and sat. The rest found seats where they could, Emma coming to his side.

"What's happening Zachia?' she asked. He looked to her.

"I've just received confirmation concerning the message we received from Weretoran," he told her. He then turned to the others' in the room. Emma's eyes were not the only ones to widen with his announcement. Everyone looked to him, but those from Zentler were confused. He looked around the room and settled his eyes on the faxlie. "Tremliteen, I would ask that you travel to Grrale. Ask him if he, and his mate, would come as quickly as they can," he said. The faxlie nodded, and flew out the window, turning towards the wolves grounds, southeast of the city. He again looked around the room. "Several days ago, just before my father's death, a message was received from a Domain that called itself Weretoran." He was speaking mostly to those from Zentler. "The King of that Domain, one called Werelaran, said that a Domain that shared their world was going to try and make an alliance with the rebels on Namsia and he was sure that with that alliance, the other Domain, called Gargoylia, would try to conquer them."

"Gargoyles and werewolves," Gordon whispered his eyes quite wide. Zachia nodded to him.

"I had asked for, and received, permission to send an envoy to their Domain and look into this further," Zachia went on. "Well, if what I have just seen is any indicator, their message was the truth!" There were concerned looks exchanged through the room.

"What have you seen?" Melsikan asked, and all looked to Zachia.

"Six of the ugliest things you can imagine, and Tarson told me that each were near as strong as an ogre," Zachia told him and the room. Silence grabbed them all for a moment. "The leader of the six was wearing this," Zachia held up the amulet he had taken from the leader, as he had spelled them to their cells. Melsikan rose from the couch and came and looked at the amulet.

"It's a communication crystal," was all he said and returned to the couch. Zachia nodded.

"But who does it communicate with?" Zachia asked. "Glorian told me that the invaders were here to take someone, but whom?" They looked at him and then each other. "Most importantly, why," Zachia said quietly.

"What are you going to do son?" Glornina asked. He looked to her and then to all in the room.

"I'm going to send that envoy, to find out all they can about these two races, and the purpose of both!" he said with feeling. Gordon and Xanaporia exchanged quick glances. Tremliteen came in the window and landed on the desk.

"Grrale, Terryle, and their pup Crrale, and his mate Serryle, are coming," he announced. Zachia nodded and thanked the faxlie.

"Are they to be part of the envoy?" Xanaporia asked. Zachia nodded and looked to Gordon.

"Do you remember what you told us about werewolves and the legend of gargoyles, that day at Xanaporia's birthday party, three months before the bandit's raid on Zentler?" he asked the Mayor. Gordon nodded, after a few moments of thinking. "Well, you may have been misinformed," Zachia said with a chuckle. "It would seem that the werewolves were the good guys." He turned to Emma. "Please tell Jennifer that I would like her, and her husband Alan, to come here as soon as they can," he told her. Emma nodded and concentrated.

"I hope Isabella and I are going to be part of this envoy as well," Melsikan asked. Isabella looked at him in surprise.

Zachia smiled, and shook his head. Isabella sighed, quietly. Zachia called to his youngest sister, Michele, with a brief message, and then looked to Gordon. Michele and her husband Crendoran appeared, as Jennifer and Alan came into the room. They were followed almost immediately by the four wolves'. It took a few moments for everyone to find a place to sit. When they had and silence had settled, Zachia stood and looked to each.

"We are facing four separate and yet, connected situations," he told them all. "First, we have a report of a rebellion on Namsia. Second we have the message sent by orb, from Nepolia to Namsia, using the name Bandarson, which we don't know what that's about, but I have some concerns. Thirdly, there is a Domain called Gargoylia that is going to try and make an alliance with the rebels of Namsia and try to conquer another Domain called Weretoran. Fourthly, we also have the revolution on Natharia, and, there has been a message sent from there, to Namsia, also using the name Bandarson." There were nodding heads all around. "I'm going to address each situation. First, Melsikan, Isabella, Jennifer, Alan, I would ask that you to travel to Namsia and find out what the hell is happening there, because that seems to be the center of all the activity. Melsikan, I want you to take at least a dozen of the best soldiers with you. Talk with Tarson; he will know who would be best." Melsikan nodded, but Isabella looked at Zachia with less than a happy look. Zachia ignored her and went on. "I need to know what exactly is happening there." Melsikan again nodded. "Second, Gordon, I want you and Xanaporia, and the wolves, to go to Weretoran and find out all you can about the situation there. Zachia almost laughed as Gordon nodded slowly, rather wide eyed, obviously trying to find an understanding of what was happening.

"Gordon," Emma interrupted; "I think you should take my younger brother Cartland, and Xanaleria as well. He inherited great Grampa Beltyne's ability to shape shift and she has a powerful magical ability." All there saw Gordon as he again nodded, but all saw the stunned look in his eyes. Xanaporia nodded as well, with a small grin, for she had not seen her daughter in some time.

"Michele, Crendoran, you have been to Nepolia and know the Queen," Zachia continued. They both nodded. "I need you to go and find out what is happening there and where the orb message came from and if possible, what it said." Again, the two nodded.

"What about Natharia?" Glornina asked. Her son looked at her and then his desk. He lifted his eyes again, and tried to smile.

"I'm going to ask Belserlan to form a small force. I'm going to send them there to find out where the message came from, what the message is all about and hopefully, recover the orb that was used for that message," he told her. She looked to him for a moment and then nodded. "Alright, everyone, find any others' you feel can best help in your assignments and be ready first thing in the morning," Zachia looked to them, his eyes telling each of his worry and, his determination.

Isabella, after leaving the palace of the Overseer and returning to Zentler, to prepare for her journey to Namsia, had gone to City Hall and told Dolores, Gordon's secretary, that the Mayor and his wife would be out of town for a while. Dolores had simply nodded, with a knowing look. When Isabella had left, Dolores went into the Mayor's office and passed the word to Somora. Later, when she found out that Ben had not returned with the others', she started to worry, for none of the magical ones would tell her why. She called to her King for instructions. Carl and Marcus returned to their jobs and the ladies did what they could for Terressa and Benjamin.

CHAPTER FOUR

Beling, the Chief of the Namsia City Protective Force, walked down the hall of the court house, towards the Councilor's Chambers. Everyone knew that he was the oldest of the many illegitimate sons of Porkligor and looked remarkably like him, especially in size. There had been many who had questioned the Mayors selection of him for the post of Chief. What Daridar knew, that they did not, was that Beling had hated his father with a passion unmatched by anyone. He entered the large room and was shocked by the number of people that filled the room. Not only was the Mayor there, so was Parsony, the head of the Mayors private Guard. He looked around the room, seeing that all of the Councilor's were there as well. There were also many other people and Beling had no idea who any of them were. With his arrival, Beling heard the Mayor speak.

"Everybody, find your seats," Daridar commanded. The Councilors went to their chairs. She beckoned Beling and Parsony to come to her side. When all was settled, she indicated the four strangers near her. "These people are from the Realm and they have come to learn what is happening here," she said loudly, making sure all heard her. The councilors looked to the four, and then the twenty who stood further back. "I have already given them all of the information I have and now they would like to ask questions of you all. You all will be free to walk about, but do not leave this room and please, answer whatever questions that are asked of you, as completely as you can." There were exchanged looks throughout the councilors. "The one standing next to me is Melsikan, the leader of this investigation." Daridar continued, drawing the councilor's attention. "He was part of the Realm forces that captured Brandaro's castle." There were nods and smiles directed to him, and he returned them. "Beside him is Isabella, his wife. She is the one that Brandaro had captured and then lost. She is the one to call the Overseer to us." There were lifted brows from the women of the council and not very well hidden leers from the men. Isabella was surprised that she didn't blush. "Next to her is Jennifer. She is one of those of the Realm I had talked with, prior to their arrival." Again there were nods and smiles given, as well as some leers. She returned the smiles and nods. "Last is Alan. He is Jennifer's husband and a strong magical power." This time there were just lifted brows with concerned eyes below them. Daridar saw that Alan had an amused, yet intense look to his eyes and, did not smile at the councilors.

Out of the corner of her eye, Daridar saw that Melsikan watched four councilors who repeatedly looked to each other.

In a farm house, about four miles north of the town of Bentodon, eighty five miles north of Namsia City, rebels met. Brando, with his sister at his side, and his mother behind him, listened to Barkoor's report without interrupting. "They went to a small hut, just inside Bentodon city limits. When I looked in the window, they were just sitting at the table, staring off at nothing. It was very strange, for they made no sound, yet both nodded several times, as though they were told something, and they understood. I then went to the Inn that was nearest the hut and was told that the two came every night, to drink and eat. They always stayed to themselves, in the corner booth. No one seemed to know a lot about them and none could remember seeing either of them before two months ago. Also, they don't seem to have work, but always have plenty of money. That is all I have been able to find so far," Barkoor said, sitting back in his chair. Brando nodded as he also sat back, in thought.

"I don't like this Brando," Brendo said softly. "They have got to be spies, but for who?" She looked to her brother. "Could that dwarf have sent spies among us, but if she did, how did she know where to send them?" He looked to her for several seconds and then slowly shook his head.

"I do not think these are spies from the dwarf. Remember how she made such a big affair of how she could talk with those of the Realm, with just her thoughts?" Brendo nodded, her eyes opening wider.

"Do you think they are from the Realm?" she asked quietly. Again he looked to her for a few moments and then shook his head.

"How would they know where to send them either?" he asked, more to himself then to her. "No, I think these two are from someplace else. Someplace that has an interest in what is happening here. This means, they are planning to either help us, or to conquer us." Brendo's eyes opened wider, as Brando's face darkened with the beginnings of anger. He looked to Barkoor. "I think it best, that you bring these two to me and we will find out their intent!" Barkoor nodded as he stood and left for Bentodon.

With the received message, through Cartope, which only a certain number of people were to know about and which had been passed on to the Northern Queen as well, Neponities, Nepanities, Nepelia, Nepeslia, and Cartope, were waiting on the rear terrace of the palace when Michele and Crendoran appeared. The old friends were welcomed and then introduced to the Northern Section royals. Immediately after the introductions, they all went into the palace. Refreshments were served as the Neponian's told Michele of their sorrow for the loss of Namson. Michele thanked her and told them of her brother's acceptance as the new Overseer of the Realm. The Neponian's acknowledged the new Overseer with a bow. Finally, after a few minutes of talk, about many things, Neponities asked the reason for this visit, that was not to be spoken of to others'. Michele got a concerned look on her face.

"There was an orb message sent from Neponia, to Namsia, using the name Bandarson. The Overseer wants to know what that message was and, who sent it," she told the

Center Section Queen. Neponities and Nepelia looked to each other with concern. Michele saw that Nepanities, Nepeslia and Cartope were worried about something as well. Neponities straightened her back and looked to Michele. Michele did not like the look in Neponities eyes as she spoke.

"The orb that had been left here at the palace was stolen. Nepelia and I think that Nepolia has taken it," she said. "She has also sent two squadrons of her troops, wearing our uniforms, to infiltrate this section. We have not yet had a chance to find out their purpose, but it is clear that the Southern Queen has plans that do not bode well for the rest of Neponia." Nepelia, Nepanities, Nepeslia and Cartope were nodding their agreement to Neponities telling. Michele and Crendoran exchanged quick looks. Michele looked back to Neponities and told her of the rumors of a rebellion on Namsia, the contact with Weretoran and the threats there. She also told them of the rebellion on Natharia that had cost her father's life. She then heard the Princesses question.

"Could Nepolia be planning to aid in the rebellion on Namsia?" Nepanities asked her mother.

"If she is, I'm willing to bet that she would try to use those forces to try and take over us!" Nepelia said with anger. All those gathered nodded. Michele was considering sending a message to her brother, when the Princess of the Northern Section spoke.

"She could supply them with Power Stones and they would be hard to defeat then," Nepeslia said softly. They all looked to her and realized the dangers that now faced them. Michele then told them that there had also been a message sent from Natharia to Namsia, and that message, had also used the name Bandarson. They all stared at her, wide eyed.

"If the Natharian's join in the battle," Neponities whispered; "it is probable that we would be defeated."

"Not all of Natharia and none of the Natharian's in any of the other domains are with the rebels of Natharia," Michele told them all. Michele was not the only one surprised when Carsanac stepped into the doorway.

"I am sorry to interrupt My Ladies," Carsanac said. They all looked to him and saw the small smile he wore comfortably. "I might just have an idea of what can be done," he said with a bow. Nepelia, Nepeslia, and Cartope, looked to Neponities, with surprise. Neponities looked to her daughter, who looked to her mate. It only took a moment or two before they all wore the same grin as Carsanac. Michele glanced to Crendoran and saw that he was as confused as she was.

~~•◦❖◦•~~

"What do you mean you don't know where it is?" Bistalan roared at Castilan. The aide cowered from the larger Bistalan.

"It was knocked from the stand, in Bleudarn's web, as you battled with Bleudarn and your first brother, My Lord, and I have not seen it since," Castilan said.

"Get me my Generals, immediately! I want that orb found, do you hear me?" he roared again. Castilan nodded as he started to scurried away.

"Yes, Lord Bistalan," the aide said and made it out of the room. He passed Bistalan's orders to messengers, as he tried to think of some safe place to hide.

In a secluded collection of trees, not that far from Bistalan's new palace, in a large, well hidden web house, another group met. "You have made contact?" Pastilan asked. Daralan nodded with a smile and then frowned.

"I have not yet received an answer though, Lord Pastilan," Daralan said. Pastilan looked at him for a moment and then turned to his General.

"Are you ready to take control Mertilan?" he asked. Bistalan's renegade General grinned and bowed.

"Yes, My Lord, as you have designed," Mertilan said with a bow. "My warriors are in position to kill the other generals of Bistalan. We will then control the Armies!"

"Good," Pastilan said with a nod and a smile. "That arrogant Bistalan has unknowingly opened the door for me and he is going to be very surprised when I come through it!" The other two nodded with grins of their own. "Make it happen Mertilan, take Bistalan's armies from him. I will then rule Natharia!" The General nodded and scurried from the room. "Let me know as soon as you receive an answer from Bandarson, Daralan," Pastilan said. Daralan nodded with his bow. Pastilan went into his private chambers. He made sure that no one could see, or hear him and then, with his thoughts, called to Somora, to tell of the success of Somora's plan, so far.

Based on what he had learned from his mentor, Garplasar, with the twelve Gaspilarians, appeared in the empty court yard of the deserted castle. He looked around in confusion. There still should be those of Brandaro's forces here. He then saw that the gate had been destroyed and he could see humans walking around outside of the castle. He realized that he had assumed too much, concerning the rebels.

"Master?" one of the Gaspilarians asked.

"Get out of sight," Garplasar hissed and lead them to the first doorway he saw. Once hidden, Garplasar thought. How was he to find the rebels now? They couldn't just walk into the city. He was thinking of what he could do when he saw the small human, playing at the destroyed gate. He smiled and pulled one of the Gaspilarians to him. "Bring that to me, without a sound," he whispered and the creature nodded and snuck out. It did not take long and the twelve year old boy was being held in front of the wizard, his mouth covered with a bony hand and his eyes opened wide with terror. Garplasar smiled as he put his hand on the boys head and began his incantation. He quickly found out that this little one didn't know what he needed, but he quickly found that the small one did know where he could find the information that would tell him how to find the rebels he sought. In just minutes, the boy's eyes closed as his heart slowed and then stop. The Gaspilarian threw the body down when Garplasar beckoned them further into the castle, away from the doorway. There, he told them to rest, for they must wait for the night.

King Werelaran, Queen Wereselon, the witch Weretilon, and Weretustran, the General of the Armies, waited in the court yard of Werelaran's palace. The portal formed and Gordon and Xanaporia led the envoy into Weretilon. When all had passed through, the portal closed and a moment of awkward silence settled on all. Xanaporia stood to Gordon's right. Her daughter, Xanaleria, stood next to her and Cartland stood at the end of the line. Grrale, Terryle, Crrale, and Serryle, took position to Gordon's left. Gordon bowed.

"I would address King Werelaran," he said when he had straightened. The Weretorians bowed together.

"I am Werelaran," the King said, when they had all straightened. "This is my Queen, Wereselon," he said, his hand indicating the woman beside him. All those from the Realm bowed. "Our most powerful witch, Weretilon." His hand pointed to the woman who stood to the right of the Queen. "Weretustran, the General of our Armies." He indicated the man standing to his left. Again all from the Realm bowed.

"My name is Gordon," Gordon said, then indicated the woman next to him; "my wife, Xanaporia. Her daughter,

Xanaleria and her husband Cartland." He pointed to the two beside Xanaporia. "The wolves', Grrale, his mate Terryle, his son Crrale and mate Serryle." He pointed to the four to his left. Those of Weretoran bowed, but their eyes were locked on the wolves'. "We were sent by the Overseer of the Realm, to find out all we can of your concerns. I should tell you all that what we think a band of raiding Gargoyles, has been sent to the Realm for reasons we do not know yet." The Weretorians exchanged worried looks.

"Come," Werelaran said; "we have a place we can talk. I have called the Council together." He turned, and lifted his hand towards the door of the castle. Gordon nodded and they all followed the Weretorians into the castle.

"Mama," Benjamin asked between mouthfuls of cereal; "where's daddy?" All those at the table looked to the boy and then to Terressa.

"He won't be with us anymore honey," Terressa said, fighting her tears. Benjamin looked to her, confused.

"Why?" he asked. Terressa couldn't look at her son.

"Because he is on a very important trip, for the Overseer," Emma said, trying to help. Everyone looked to her, their eyes wider than should be. "It will take a very long time to complete," Emma added. The boy looked at her for a moment and then to his mother. Terressa nodded, trying to smile.

"Oh, okay," Benjamin said and went back to his hot cereal. None at the table could talk. Terressa looked to Emma and mouthed the words, *Thank you.* Emma smiled and nodded, but the smile was mournful.

On a special platform, in the web of the Natharian leader, Zachia was meeting with Balsarlan, and his first son, Belserlan.

In the very large pasture behind the Elders house, Merlintile, the leader of the dragons of the Realm, was meeting with the races of the Realm. He was establishing patrols for the protection of the Realm City. He didn't think they should just depend on the alerts of the seers and sensitive's.

In the Council chamber of the City Hall of Namsia City, Melsikan was getting irritated that the four he wanted to question were avoiding him. He saw them rapidly heading for the door. He put a holding spell on them and they froze.

"What are you doing?" Daridar asked in a loud, angry voice. Melsikan looked to her and he wasn't smiling.

"They were trying to run out and I want to know why," he told her calmly. Taking Isabella's arm he went to the four, Daridar was right behind him. He moved in front of the four and saw the fear in their eyes. So did Daridar. "I am going to release you one at a time and you are going to tell me why you were trying to run away," he told them. Daridar beckoned Beling and Parsony to her. The first of the four fell to the floor when Melsikan freed him. His eyes were wide with fear as he looked to Melsikan.

"I don't know anything about the rebellion," he said in a high voice, as he rose to his feet. Melsikan took a step closer to him and the man tried to back up, but Beling was standing behind him and he couldn't. He straightened and got an angry look on his face. "I am a member of this council and you can't treat me like this. Now get out of my way!" Melsikan smiled and closed on the man even more.

"Why were you trying to run away?" he asked calmly.

"I know why," Isabella said angrily, as she stared at the man. He wouldn't meet her stare. Melsikan looked at her and he saw the rage that had come to her. "He was one of the guard leaders at the castle. He was one of Brandaro's men." Her voice had turned very hard.

"I don't know anything," the man cried and tried to run again. Melsikan put a holding spell on him, again. Daridar was looking between Isabella and the man.

"Do you remember his name?" Melsikan asked softly. Isabella shook her head.

"Beling, put that man under arrest," Daridar said, having seen Isabella's clenched fists.

"Get his name and find out which province he represented," Melsikan told Beling. He then turned to his wife, taking her shoulders with his hands, he looked into her eyes. "Are you alright?" he asked her softly. She looked to him, and he could see her battle to remain calm. She finally nodded, with a deep breath. "Would you look at the others and see if any of them look familiar?" he asked. She looked at him. Her painful memories showed clearly in her eyes. She took another breath and turned to face the other three. She looked them over carefully and then turned to Daridar.

"You should remember this one," she said, pointing to one of the men. Daridar came to her side and stared at the man. Her eyes narrowed as she nodded slowly.

"You were also one of Brandaro's guards and, you and Pinsikar tried to rape me in that cell," she said, her voice a snarled whisper. She kicked him in the groin, as hard as she could. Isabella nodded as she turned to Melsikan.

"So are these two," she told him, pointing to the other two men. Parsony came to the group with several of the Mayors guards.

"If you would release them, we will gladly place them all in a cell," he said to Melsikan.

"Make sure they are placed in private cells, far from each other and any others'. I need to know which province they represent, plus anything else you can learn from them," Melsikan said calmly and Parsony smiled, nodding.

"I assure you, we can get all the information you want." Melsikan believed the man completely, releasing the four. The guards quickly grabbed the four and hauled them away. Isabella looked to Daridar and smiled. The dwarf returned the smile. Her face sobered as she turned to the silent, wide eyed people still in the room.

"The questioning will continue," Daridar told them, as Melsikan and Isabella joined Jennifer and Alan, and they again, began their interrogations. With little surprise, everyone was very cooperative.

———

In a small farm house, Brando closed on the two, their hands bound behind them and held at their tip toes by Barkoor's two hands. "Who do you work for?" Brando asked, his voice low, threatening. The two glanced quickly to each other and then back to the face that was not getting any happier for their silence. Barkoor shook them rather severely. "I asked who you work for," Brando repeated and he glared with his words.

"We are with you Lord Brando," the larger one, Tarington said, but his voice trembled with his fear. Brando's hand lashed out and slapped him, hard.

"I asked you who you work for and you had better tell me the truth, or you will be screaming for a lot longer than you can imagine!"

"We work for your victory, Lord Brando," the smaller one, Trenlor, said in a whine that was close to tears. Brando looked to Barkoor.

"See if you can get the truth from them," he growled. Barkoor smiled as he nodded, dragging the two from the house, heading for the barn. Their voices were already beginning to sound as screams.

———

Nepolia sat on her throne, her head down, her eyes looking through her brows, as she watched the entrance of the General of her armies and her aide. The two stopped in front of the throne, and bowed.

"Your Majesty," General Folisia said with her straightening. She hope the nervousness she felt, was not portrayed in her voice.

"Why have I not received word of our success?" Nepolia's voice was very close to a growl. Folisia swallowed, but not near as hard as the aide did.

"I do not know My Queen," the General said nervously. Nepolia lifted her head and all could see the anger in her eyes.

"Then perhaps, you should find out," Nepolia said. Her voice low and her anger could be heard easily. The General and the aide bowed again.

"Yes My Queen," Folisia said in her bow. With the aide so close they almost were one, they beat a hasty retreat from the throne room. Calitoran, standing next to the throne, could easily hear the harsh breathing of Nepolia and, was wishing he was someplace else, when Depelia rushed into the throne room.

"My Queen, Bandarson has answered and they want to speak with you!" she yelled. Nepolia all but leapt from her throne and followed the woman back into the orb room.

The Natharian General, Mertilan, following his new ruler's orders, met with his division Commanders and carefully explained what he wanted of them. They willing agreed to his orders, because, although they all had agreed that Bleudarn needed to be removed as Ruler, they did not think Bistalan the best choice to replace the old Ruler. They all knew that the most of the Commanders of the other Generals armies felt the same and they quickly made connection with them. It did not take much effort and the other three Generals were killed, and Mertilan controlled all of the armies.

"Lord Pastilan, I have command of the Armies," Mertilan reported. Pastilan smiled as much as a Natharian could, slowly nodding. He had received Somora's orders as to the next stage of his plan and Pastilan told Mertilan what he wanted done. Very quickly, Bistalan's new palace web was surrounded. What outer guards did not quickly agree, were quietly killed. Mertilan surveyed the squad that had very carefully moved into position to charge the entrance.

They had moved carefully for they did not want to cause any movement to the web that would alert those inside. Once he was sure all were ready, he gave the signal and the squad charged. Those inside were totally surprised, especially Bistalan. He quickly realized that he had made a serious mistake, not having a rear entrance included in his building plans. He did not die easily, taking many of the invading squad with him, but in less than fifteen minutes, Pastilan ruled Natharia. In an hour, the council was called together and informed of the change of Command. Many were very relieved, but those same many, feared that they now just had a different threat to the lives of all Natharian's.

It was during that council meeting, in a different part of Natharia, that Dasilan was informed of Bistalan's death and the one that now claimed to be Ruler. Ten minutes later, Belserlan and a few of those from the Realm Tribe, appeared at the designated place. Dasilan informed them of the new Ruler and his concerns that they had only traded one devil, for another.

Belserlan quickly informed Dasilan, of the rebellion that was coming to Namsia. "There was an orb message sent from here, to Namsia. Zachia wants to know who sent it and what that message was," Belserlan said quietly to Dasilan. Dasilan looked to the newcomer for a minute, with rather wide eyes.

"Do you think that Bistalan was trying to make an alliance with the rebels there?" he asked.

"We do not know," Belserlan said; "but we must find the orb and those who are using it and learn what is being planned," Belserlan told him. Dasilan nodded and called several of his best scouts. He quickly assigned them to the job of finding the orb and who held it.

The spotter elbowed the one next to him. He pointed and his partner looked that way. "She small," the elbowed one said. The first one nodded.

"Young, grow," he told the second. The second one nodded and they closed in.

"Bindings loose," Gorastor frantically whispered to her mother, as they shopped in the small market. Gorsentor looked to her with concern and looked around for a place of privacy where they could rewrap her daughter. That's when she saw the two spotters closing in on them. Gorastor saw them at the same time and emitted a gasp of fear.

"Run," Gorsentor whispered harshly. "I block," she added. Gorastor turned and started to run. The two spotters chased after her. Gorsentor's efforts to block their way proved quite futile. She was savagely thrown down, breaking her arm. The spotters caught Gorastor within two blocks and they quickly learned that she was stronger than she appeared. Their efforts to tie her proved far more difficult than they had expected. When they were finally able to get her tied, gaining several injuries in the process, they carried her off, towards Garator's castle. Several other females aided Gorsentor from the ground, being careful of her arm that the spotters had broken. Gorsentor's tears, from seeing her daughter being carried off, stole her vision of everything else.

———————

They entered the Council hall and every council member stood and bowed to the visitors, but they all were staring at the four wolves'. "Just what we need," Grrale whispered to the other three; "to be the center of attention." The other three chuckled, as did their human friends, for they had heard Grrale's growled words. As Werelaran neared the table, he saw the first problem. There was no place for the wolves to sit at the table. He stopped and looked to Weretilon.

"We will need a bench large enough for our four footed visitors to sit comfortably," he told her and turned to the wolves'. "I am sorry, but we were not aware that wolves' were to be part of the envoy." He told them as Weretilon began her incantation. Grrale started to smile.

"You cannot change?" Wereselon asked in surprised, as she looked wide eyed to the wolves'. Werelaran touched her arm as all four wolves' shook their heads, grinning. "I meant no insult," Wereselon added quickly, blushing.

"We are not insulted, Your Majesty," Terryle told the Queen. "No, we cannot change to human form, and in our own way, that is the way we like it." She chuckled with her words. Wereselon smiled and gave a small nod to the mate of Grrale. Wereselon thought that she liked this female wolf, and then looked to other female, seeing the grin on her muzzle as well.

"That does not mean that we do not hold respect for your ability to do so," Serryle said softly with a slight bow. Crrale nodded and smiled, with his pride of his mate. Wereselon looked to her King and smiled. Werelaran returned her smile and then looked to the humans. He lifted his hand to the four chairs and new wide bench that took up almost one complete side of the table.

"Please, be seated," he invited. The Council members had been forced to squeeze close together around the rest of the table, but none seemed to mind as they fought not to stare. Those of the envoy could plainly see the questions in the council member's eyes and, in some, the fear. When all had found their places and had sat, Gordon looked around to those around the table. When his sight had returned to the King, he spoke.

"Your Majesties, Zachia, the Overseer of the Realm, has sent us here to find out all we can about your Domain and your concerns," he started his opening. "I have been instructed to inform you that the Gargoyles have tried to send invaders to the Realm and as yet, we are not sure of their intentions. Zachia has asked if there would be a chance that you might know what that purpose might have been." The murmurs of the council members, accompanied the shared glance between the King and Queen. Werelaran quickly looked to each of the envoy. When he looked to Gordon again, he took a breath.

"Garator, the Ruler of Gargoylia, is trying to find a talker. Someone he can use, to try and form an alliance with the rebels of Namsia, in hopes that they would aide him in the conquering of Weretoran." Werelaran had kept his voice calm, but with the last, he could not hide his anger.

"So you think that the invaders were sent to find a talker?" Xanaporia asked. Every Weretorian at the table nodded. Three of the envoy looked to Xanaleria and she passed on to the talker's panel, what she had been told.

"Are you one of these talkers?" Werelaran asked, seeing the look of concentration on Xanaleria's face.

"Both my daughter and I are talkers," Xanaporia said quietly; "but she is stronger than I" There were many exchanged looks among the Weretorians.

"What if Garator learns of them, here in Weretoran?" Wereselon asked fearfully of her husband. He looked to the visitors and was surprised to see small smiles on each and every one of them. He was confused at first, until he realized that they must have very strong magical powers. He thought the Gargoyles would have a great deal of trouble trying to take them. Gordon confirmed his thoughts.

"You need not be worried your Majesty," he told the Queen. "My son-in-law is powerful in magic and my wife and her daughter are very powerful in magic. Even the wolves have some power." Those from the Realm had to chuckle at the wide eyes that surrounded them, but Gordon was not the only one to see the worried look of the one called Weretilon, the witch.

———

In the Realm, Zachia was receiving messages from all those he had sent. He and Emma had tried to question the captive Gargoyles, but they refused to answer any questions. They would just jump around in their cells and scream names at their interrogators. Zachia alerted the other domains to be on the lookout for spies in their domains, not knowing the complete truth concerning Ben and Baldor; he could not help but feel danger for their actions.

CHAPTER FIVE

After the questioning of the remaining council members had been completed, Melsikan instructed those members not to discuss what had happened, or what they had been asked, with anyone. That included aides, secretaries, or even mates. Daridar had added that to violate these instructions would result in severe punishment. The Council members had left the room with deep worries and, confusion. Parsony returned to the chamber shortly after Daridar, Melsikan, Isabella, Jennifer, and Alan, had sat down at the table, all at one end. He informed them all that Melsikan's instructions had been followed. He was wearing a small grin as he told them the results of the interrogation of the four.

"One was the representative from the province that included the town of Bentodon. The other three represented the three northern provinces, around the first province," he told them. "They all admit that there are activities in their provinces. With a little persuasion, they admitted that they knew of the rebellion and, they all had an idea of who is leading it." Parsony looked to each of the Realm. His eyes settled on Melsikan. "They all told me that the children of Brandaro would be leading the revolt, Brando and his twin sister, Brendo. Those children were already teenagers, when the Realm defeated Brandaro, and freed the Domain Bandarson."

"That bastard had children?" Isabella asked in a whisper, her eyes wide. Parsony nodded back at her. They all looked to her and then to Melsikan.

"Parsony, do you know where this Brando and Brendo can be found?" Melsikan asked. Parsony nodded, his grin growing wider. Jennifer passed the information to the talker's panel in the Overseers palace.

"There is more, Lord Melsikan," Parsony said angrily. They all looked to him. "It would seem that the Mayor of Bentodon, which is the town nearest the farm of Brando and Brendo, is newly elected, after the sudden and unexplained death of the previous Mayor and, no one seems to know where he came from!"

In the farm house, Brando watched as Barkoor hauled the two spies into the barn. He did not like the feeling that was coming to him. He abruptly turned to his mother and sister. "Get packed," he told them. "Don't forget the orb," he told Brendo.

"What is it?" Cenlinas asked with fear in her voice, as Brendo nodded and started for her room. He turned to his mother and his eyes had turned very angry.

"Those two have been talking with someone and they now know where we are," he told her, pushing her towards her room. "It will not take long for them to come here and my gut tells me that it will not be good if we were still here when they do. Now pack, I will hitch up the wagon. Move," he added loudly. He turned, and leaving the house, went to the corral. He led the mule to the nearby wagon. As soon as he had finished hitching the mule, he looked to the barn, realizing he had not heard any sound from it since Barkoor had first took the spies there. He walked to it and opened the door. He was shocked to see Barkoor's twisted body lying on the dirt floor, the prisoners bindings lay beside the body and, there was no evidence of the two spies. He raced back to the corral and quickly saddled his and Brendo's horses. He led the two horses and wagon, to the front of the house, just as his sister came out with the first load, dressed in breeches, shirt and vest. He helped load the wagon and very quickly, all were ready to go. Brando looked to his sister. "Take mama to Corlaar's, wait for me there," he told her. She nodded. "Get set up as quickly as you can and listen." Again Brendo nodded and looked to her mother in the seat of the wagon.

"Come on mama," she said and started her horse out of the yard. Cenlinas looked once to her son and then, snapping the reins, followed Brendo. Brando made sure they were well on their way before he turned his horse towards Bentodon. He knew who he wanted to talk to and he was angry!

Neponities had beckoned Carsanac into the room. He entered, stopping a few feet from them and bowed to them all. Carsanac saw that the women could see Wenzorn, the leader of the Mearlies, Wanlizorn, Wenzorn's son, and Phelton, the elf that had taken the elder Phelilon's place, were standing in the doorway. He saw Neponities beckon that they should enter as well. When all stood before the women, he watched as Neponities looked to him. "What is your idea Carsanac?" she asked calmly, catching Carsanac's contagious smile. Carsanac bowed again and began.

"Let me start by saying that I had no intention of snooping into the business of you Ladies," he told them. Queen and daughter exchanged knowing smiles; "but I could not help but hear Lady Michele's words."

"And what have you thought since?" Neponities pushed her question. The smile on Carsanac's face grew slightly.

"I believe that I know what Queen Nepolia's intentions were, when she sent her troops to the Central Section," he told all before him. They looked to him with a mixture of surprise and confusion. His grin stayed in place, but his eyes hardened. "I believe that she intended to free the captive bandits held in the prison, north of Capital City." There were quickly exchanged looks among all present.

"That would make sense if she was plotting to join the rebels of Namsia," Carsanac heard his mates voice, as he watched the faces of the others' in the room. He saw Neponities join the other women and Crendoran with nods for their agreement of that thought. Carsanac nodded as well and his eyes brightened.

"My idea, in part, is that we give her exactly what she wants," Carsanac said calmly. Carsanac was not surprised when Nepanities joined in the unified outcry of all those who looked to him; "*What?*" they screamed. Carsanac held up his hands and they all quieted, but there was anger in Nepelia's eyes.

"Why should we give her what she can use against us?" Nepelia asked, her anger coming with her question. Carsanac bowed, still holding the small smile.

"Please Your Majesty; let me tell of my thoughts. It will be your right and privilege, to deem its worthiness," he told her in his bow. Carsanac did not miss seeing Neponities place her hand gently on Nepelia's arm. The two Queens shared a look and then Nepelia nodded slowly. She slowly sat back, looking to Carsanac.

"Tell your thoughts," she told Carsanac with a voice that held her anger in reserve. He bowed again.

"Thank you Queen Nepelia," Carsanac said and his grin returned as he glanced quickly at Nepanities. "There are many facets to my thought and this will take some time to explain. I ask your patience, My Ladies." Neponities nodded and looked to her daughter as the small grin returned to her.

"Go ahead Carsanac. We are listening," she said, as she returned her eyes to him. Michele and Crendoran were looking to each other in complete confusion, but that quickly changed as Carsanac explained his ideas.

"As I said earlier, we should let Nepolia have the bandits, but they will come to her with a slight alteration," he said calmly. Nepanities grin of pride grew and he knew she was beginning to see what he might mean. Princess Nepeslia started to ask what he meant, but he did not see her attempt and continued, cutting her off. "I think that a spell placed in the minds of those bandits, could turn them into the perfect of spies!" The eye brows of all but Nepanities, lifted. "Also, with the proper spell, their ability to perform to the level that Nepolia would desire, could be restricted." The Queens and Princesses looked to each other. Their smiles grew with their understanding. "Only your Majesties know how many spies are already in the castle of Nepolia," Carsanac drew their attention back to him; "but they could report what the bandit spies would learn." Crendoran and the Queens began to nod their heads. Nepanities smiled widely at her mate. None of the Neponian's saw Michele's worried look to Crendoran.

<hr>

Dasilan had led Belserlan to the safe web house. As the day passed and they waited on news from those sent to find the orb, they ate and talked of the new Natharia. Finally, Dasilan tried to learn the Overseer's plans. "Does the Overseer have idea what he is going to do for Natharia?" Dasilan asked quietly. Belserlan almost chuckled.

"Not completely, but I believe he has the beginnings of a plan. He has said that the orb must be found first, as well as those who have used it and what their message to Namsia was." Here Belserlan hesitated and Dasilan looked to him, waiting. "There are some other things you may not yet know, that the Overseer feels you should." Dasilan looked worried. "There have been some spies found and killed, in the Realm. The Overseer has no idea where they came from, or what they were after." Dasilan looked even more worried. "Also, six Gargoyles were captured when they invaded the Realm and supposedly, were going to capture someone and, the Overseer doers not know who, or why!"

"What is a Gargoyle?" Dasilan asked, trying to keep his voice calm. Belserlan seemed to ignore the question and continued.

"Also, there has been contact with a domain that is called Wereteran and it would seem that they are very worried that the domain called Gargoylia, which shares their world, is trying to make an alliance with the rebels of Namsia, to use them to help in the conquering of Weretoran." Dasilan, with coming of darkness, stared at Belserlan with wide outer eyes. Belserlan almost smiled again. "Yes, it is getting very complicated," he told the resistance leader. Dasilan's eyes returned to normal and a thoughtful expression came to him.

"It would seem that Namsia is in the center of all this," he said quietly and Belserlan nodded his agreement.

Gorsinbor, the largest of the wingless female slaves of the Ruler's castle, was the Controller of all female slaves in the castle. She smiled when the two spotters brought the struggling and yelling Gorastor into the induction room.

She pulled the knife from its sheath at her waist, as she approached the now standing and still struggling girl. She grabbed the neckline of Gorastor's shirt and the Gorastor saw the knife. Her eyes grew large and she stopped her squirming as Gorsinbor inserted the tip inside of the neckline of the shirt. With the left hand of the Controller guiding the direction, next to the blade, she pulled it down through the shirt and unknowingly, through the loosened bindings that no longer hid her maturity completely. The knife then went to her breeches and very quickly, Gorastor was completely naked. Both spotters growled, and leered at her, as Gorsinbor smiled widely.

"Master like you," she said as she looked over Gorastor. Gorastor now started to struggle and yell even harder than she had before. "Take pool," she heard the woman order the spotters and they dragged the fighting Gorastor through a door. In the next room, Gorastor saw a great pool and in that pool, were four; older wingless females and they too were naked. The spotters untied her and threw her into the pool. The four females grabbed her and bathed her. She did not, in the least little bit, enjoy the extra efforts the females made with her body. Gorastor screamed and fought even harder. Gorastor screamed and cussed as she heard the spotters laugh, as they watched, until Gorsinbor smacked the backs of their heads and ordered them out, back to work. They growled at the Controller as they left. When they had finished bathing Gorastor, the four brought her near the edge, close to the steps that led out of the pool. Gorsinbor knelt there and the females turned Gorastor around so her back was to the Controller. Gorsinbor fastened a thin metal collar around

Gorastor's neck and stood as the females turned her again. She now faced the large Controller.

"You trouble, get this," Gorsinbor said and pushed a button on a thin, rectangular box that she held in one hand. Gorastor couldn't even scream for the pain she felt. Her body was jerking violently from the affect of it. Gorsinbor released the button and Gorastor would have collapsed beneath the water except for the support of the other females. They then brought her out of the pool and two other females dried her and put clothes on her, though those clothes did very little to cover her body. They took her arms and led her out a different door and down a hall. They arrived at a cell, and the grinning male guard opened it. Gorastor was harshly thrown to a mattress on the floor. Gorastor could barely hear the guard chuckle as her landing was far from lady like and she knew that the guard could easily see all that she was. She heard the door shut and lock.

⸙

Gorastor lay in the position she had taken with her being thrown, still feeling the effects of the pain she had been given. Her breathing began to slow as she started to lose the effects of the pain. She slowly began to look around the cell. She saw a small table with a pitcher and a cup on it, a pot in the corner and then her eyes fell on the girl that shared her cell. The girl lay on her side, on her mattress, curled into a ball, her arms around her drawn up legs and her eyes wide with the terror she felt, as she looked back at Gorastor. Gorastor took a deep breath and crawled to the girl. She stopped, still on her knees and sat up. She looked to the frightened girl and tried to smile. "Me Gorastor," she said, pointing to herself; "you?" She pointed to the girl. It took several minutes, but the girl finally answered.

"Gorpeelia," the girl whispered, as her eyes went quickly to the cell door and then back to Gorastor. Gorastor nodded, still trying to smile and then copied Gorpeelia's action, looking to the door and back.

"When here?" Gorastor asked quietly. She could see the girl starting to relax, just a little.

"Before you," Gorpeelia said, starting to unwrap herself and sit up.

"How long?" Gorastor asked, as she sat and crossed her legs in front of her. Gorpeelia shrugged.

"Hour?" the girl guessed. Gorastor nodded and again looked to the door and then back. Anger came to her face, as she thought of why she and the girl were here.

"Garator pay this," she whispered, and nodded to the girl, who had again, found her terror. Gorastor looked to her and reached out, placing her hand on Gorpeelia's arm. "We survive, Garator pay!" she whispered to her, nodding with her words. In a few moments, Gorpeelia tried to smile and nod.

In Gartisia, after being led to another female's house, several understanding and sympathetic mother's set her broken arm and braced it with wrappings. Gorsentor immediately went to her house and using the small crystal, called to Weretilon, begging for the Werewolves do something to save her daughter. The witch had passed on her plea to Werelaran, when she arrived to greet the Realms envoy.

In the Council chambers of the palace of the Weretorians, Gordon looked to the witch. "Weretilon, what troubles you?" he asked quietly. The witch looked to him and then to her King. He nodded to her and she turned back to Gordon.

"Just before your arrival, I received a message from one of those who pass us information about what Garator is about," she spoke softly, but her eyes were telling of her concerns. "She said that those in their domain, whose job it is to take young females for Garator's pleasures, had taken her daughter and she begs us to help get her back." All those of the Realm looked to Gordon as all remembered the kidnapping of Isabella from Zentler. Gordon clenched and unclenched his jaws as he looked to the witch. He then looked to Werelaran, as Xanaleria passed on this new information. She nodded and turned to Gordon.

"Zachia says that it is your decision, but he needs information about Gargoylia and its Ruler," Xanaleria said softly. Gordon nodded and looked to Cartland. The younger man nodded.

"I will need to know what a regular male Gargoyle looks like," Cartland told Gordon and the Weretorians looked back and forth between them, not understanding what they were talking about. Gordon looked to the King.

"Cartland can shape shift to anything he knows the appearance of," he tried to explain. "Do you have a picture, or anything else, of what a male gargoyle looks like?"

"He can change form?" Weretilon whispered her eyes very wide and, frightened. Gordon nodded and looked to Cartland. Cartland smiled, and Weretilon sat where he had been. The witch screamed as she looked at herself and Cartland changed back to himself. Silence crashed down on them all.

"We have several Gargoyles here in Weretoran," Werelaran said quietly, trying to control his reaction to what he had seen. He was looking at Cartland, with surprise and concern. "There are no two that look the same, but there are certain similarities to them."

"All I would need is a male that I can copy, Your Majesty," Cartland said with a small smile.

"What level of magic do you possess?" Weretilon asked, rather loudly, quickly recovering from her shock. "Winged Gargoyles possess the highest level, except for their Wizards and they can be difficult to defeat." Cartland shrugged and looked to the others' of the Realm.

"Are they more powerful than you?" Xanaporia asked of the witch. She shook her head with a small smile of pride.

Xanaporia looked to the King. "Is there a place we can compare Weretilon's powers to Cartland's?" she asked. Werelaran looked to the witch and then around the room.

"Here would be alright, but how would you do this, comparing?" he asked. Xanaporia looked to her daughter. Xanaleria smiled and stood. She pulled her chair out a short ways from the table, dividing the length of the table and then came back to her place.

"Weretilon, you try to move the chair to that end of the table," Xanaleria pointed to the end that was closest to the witch; "and Cartland, the other direction, both using only your magic," she told them both. Weretilon looked to Werelaran and he nodded. She was smiling when she looked to Cartland. He shrugged as he looked to Gordon.

"Do what you can," was all he told Cartland, and Cartland nodded. He looked to the chair, as did Weretilon.

"Start," Xanaleria said, and both contestants lift their hands and the chair shot towards Weretilon's goal. But, it had only gone a couple of feet when it suddenly stopped and shot back the way it had come. It didn't stop again until it hit the wall, smashing. Every Weretorian in the room stared, wide eyed, at the ruined chair.

"How could you do this?" Weretilon asked in a frightened whisper, as she turned to Cartland. He shrugged, a grin coming to his face. Xanaleria took his hand and smiled with the pride of her husband. Weretilon looked to Xanaporia and then Xanaleria. "You two are even stronger in magic than he?" she asked in the same whispered voice. Both women nodded, as did all those from the Realm, including the wolves'. Werelaran looked to the single soldier in the room and almost laughed out loud at the wide eyes and hanging jaw of the guard.

"Please bring another chair," he instructed. The guard nodded. With the same open mouth and wide eyes, he left the room. He quickly returned with another chair, which he brought to and held as Xanaleria sat.

"Are all of the Realm, as powerful?" Wereselon asked as she looked to each of them. Gordon smiled and looked to his wife.

"No," Xanaporia said softly, as she slightly shook her head. "There are those who are even stronger than we are, especially the Overseer, who is the most powerful," she told the Queen. Wereselon's eyes opened wide again and looked to her husband. There was concern in her eyes.

"Your Majesty," Gordon said quietly to the King; "about these Gargoyles in your Domain, is there a male that Cartland could copy? Perhaps then, we could try to rescue this daughter that has been kidnapped." The King looked at him for a moment and then nodded. He turned to Weretilon.

"Can you open a portal to Werementran's farm, in the Haven of Weresola?" he asked and the witch nodded, still looking between the humans of the Realm. The King returned his look to Gordon. "There are six Gargoyles in Weretoran," he told them. "They were captured in the war that we fought to keep Garator from joining with Brandaro's forces. They have, since that time, proven their worth and their desire to stay in Weretoran. They all work on the farm of one of our council members, Werementran," Werelaran pointed to one of the council members who had raised his hand. Gordon nodded. The King and Werementran stood and the rest followed. Werelaran looked to the witch and Weretilon lifted her hands, starting her incantation. A portal appeared before them all. "Werementran, it is your farm, would you lead us please?" the King asked. Werementran bowed and walked into the portal. The King, Queen, witch, General, and then those of the realm followed. When the portal closed, there was a great roar as the voices of the remaining Council members, erupting with questions and, fear.

Zachia listened to Emma, as she told him the reports coming from Weretoran. He could see the worries she had about sending Cartland, her younger brother, into the Domain of Gargoylia, alone.

"He's very resourceful," Zachia tried to comfort his wife. "Look at what he did in the battle against Castope." His voice was gentle as he took her into his arms. She nodded against his cheek and pulled back from Zachia and almost smiled.

"I know what he can do, he is my brother," she said; "but Weretoran is not our only concern now." Zachia nodded and smiled his support for her. Carla walked into the room.

"I'm sorry," she said seeing the position they were in; "I didn't mean to intrude." Both Zachia and Emma chuckled.

"You're not interrupting anything Carla, what is it?" Zachia asked, as Pelkraen almost knocked Carla down as he rushed into the room.

"Namsia is responding to the messages from both Natharia and Nepolia!" he yelled. Zachia looked to the Meleret.

"Can you make out anything of the messages?" he asked and Pelkraen shook his head. Zachia looked to Carla. "What did you need Carla?"

"Only to tell you that there have been some strange actions, in all domains, concerning the behavior of some citizen who are seemingly, strangers," she told the Overseer, with worry in her eyes. Zachia nodded and thought for just a few moments.

"Pass on that these strangers are to be held, and questioned. We need to find out where they come from and, their intent," Zachia told her. She nodded and left the room. Zachia called to Michele, telling her to find the orb in Neponia, as quickly as possible! Emma sent the same message to Jennifer, in Namsia. Find the orb, and who controls it! Right after that, Emma went to the reading room, where the children of those sent, were playing. She sat next to Terressa and they talked of Benjamin's adapting to not having his father near. No one seemed to notice that Ava and Mike, Zachia and Emma's oldest, were talking quite earnestly to each other, as the other children pretended to play around them. Then all the children nodded at the same time and Ava walked to and began talking to Emma.

CHAPTER SIX

Brando rode into the town of Bentodon from the east side, not using the main road. He worked his way through the side streets, until he came to the back of the Mayors house. He tied the horse to the hitch, then went and knocked on the back door. The Mayor's eyes opened wide when he saw Brando standing on his porch.

"Are you crazy coming here in broad daylight?" he asked, almost whispering and looking around quickly. He pulled the much larger man into the house. "What if someone were to see you?"

"Somebody has found us out and has sent spies to the farm," he told the Mayor, as the door was being quickly closed. The Mayor looked to him in confusion and fear.

"What?" the Mayor asked in a whisper, his fear clear in his voice. "How could somebody find out about you? No one, but a few, knows of your identification." Brando nodded and he did not lose his angry expression.

"Somebody has learned about me and these spies could talk silently. They must have had considerable magical power, because they killed Barkoor when I sent him to question the two and now the spies have disappeared." Brando told him, his voice showing, very clearly, the rage that was trying to take control of him. The Mayors eyes were getting wider as Brando talked.

"What are we to do now?' the Mayor asked, still whispering. Brando looked into the frightened eyes of the Mayor.

"Find the ones who sent the spies and, their purpose!" he said and he wasn't whispering. "Contact our people on the council and have them find out what I need, now!" The Mayor nodded rapidly and grabbed his coat and started out of the door.

"Where do I contact you when I learn something?" he asked Brando. Brando smiled and there was nothing but anger in his smile.

"I will come back here in two days, after the sun has set," he told the Mayor. "I expect some answers when I get here." Brando pushed the Mayor out in front of him and went to his horse. "Do not disappoint me Mayor," he growled as he mounted. Brando then rode away, the way he had arrived. He didn't see the Mayor go around and reenter the house by the front door. Once safely inside, he called frantically to Somora.

In the Council Chambers of City Hall, Parsony was showing Melsikan and others' from the Realm, a map. He was explaining the layout of the area around the town of Bentodon. He knew the area well as that was where he had been born. He had moved to Namsia City as soon as Brandaro had been defeated, and joined the new police force there. He quickly volunteered for the head of the Mayors security force and Daridar had accepted his application.

"So, does everyone understand what they are to do?" Melsikan asked, after Parsony had finished his presentation and Melsikan had stated his intended plan. There were nodded heads by all. He nodded and a portal opened. He led all into it.

In Neponia, Neponities was still grinning as she asked her question of Carsanac. "What of these other facets you said were of your idea?" Neponities asked calmly, unable to keep the grin from her face. Carsanac bowed once, not taking his eyes from hers, joining in the grin. When he straightened, he glanced to his wife and then continued his telling.

"For the next part of my thoughts, I ask that you listen to Wenzorn," he said quietly and beckoned the leader of the Mearlies to come to his side. Wenzorn bowed to the Queens and their daughters. When he had straightened, he spoke calmly.

"It has been unknown to Your Majesties, but there has always been a line of communication between the leaders of Mearlies on Neponia," he told them and every eye in the room, with the exceptions of Carsanac and Phelton, opened quite wide.

"What say you?" Nepelia asked loudly. "Are you saying that you are in communication with the northern and southern Mearlie leaders? Why did you keep this from us?" The Queens voice told of her surprise and thusly, her anger. Neponities again placed her hand on the northern Queens arm, but Nepelia was not easily accepting her interruption. "Answer me Wenzorn!" Nepelia yelled at the Mearlie. Wenzorn glanced to Carsanac with an, *I told you so*, look and turned back to the Queen.

"Even as the faulty stones were being made by Weltizorn, the leader who made the power stones that were corrupted with his short cuts, both Wespozorn, the southern leader and I argued that he stop and what could come from his actions," Wenzorn told her calmly. Nepelia finally conceded to Neponities pull on her arm, to calm.

"Please continue Wenzorn," Neponities said quietly. The Mearlie nodded to her.

"As Your Majesties know, every five years, all Neponian's are issued new power stones, for the life expectancy of the stones is limited." Both queens and Nepanities nodded. Michele and Crendoran were looking around to all, trying figure out what everyone was talking about. "This exchange is done at the same time, in all three Sections. The old stones, that are taken in exchange, are stored away. All stones, past and present are stored!" Again the Queens nodded, but Neponities, Nepanities and Nepeslia, were again finding their grins. "I know not how Carsanac learned of our abilities to communicate, or the stored stones, but he had and he came to me with a question. I saw no reason not to agree with what that question led to." Nepelia's angry look was being replaced with one of curiosity.

"What question did Carsanac bring to you?" Neponities asked, joining the smiling glance to Carsanac, with her daughter. Wenzorn allowed a small grin as he continued.

"He asked how long it would take to remove all abilities of the old stones, to give any extra power," Wenzorn said calmly, his smile growing. All in the room looked to the Chosen Mate of Nepanities. "He also asked if those deactivated stones could be detected, by the appearance, from the new Power Stones."

"Can they be?" Nepelia suddenly asked, sliding to the front of her chair. Wenzorn slowly shook his head as his smile grew to fill his face. Neponities and Nepanities looked to Carsanac.

"Wenzorn has told me that within a few days, all of the old stones could be completely deactivated and then we only have to figure out how to get those useless stones, from the Northern and Central sections, to the Southern section and, the new fully powered ones, from the Southern section, spread out between the Central and Northern sections," Carsanac said quietly as his grin spread as far as it could.

"The exchange is due in a week, so we will have to have a plan quickly," Wenzorn added, with a chuckle and lifted brows. "We have already begun deactivating the old stones, in all three Sections." Even Michele and Crendoran joined the smiling faces and nods of those in the room. Then Michele decided that it was time for someone to answer the disturbing thought she had been stewing on.

"How do you plan to get the bandits to Nepolia, without raising suspicion?" she called to Carsanac, over the voices of the others'. Everybody immediately sobered. They looked to her and then to Carsanac. He looked to her and stood as straight as he could. He bowed his head to Michele and there was no smile to wear now.

"Lady Michele," he started; "all of Neponia knows that you have more magical power than even our Queens," Nepelia and Neponities exchanged looks as Michele, knowing she was not going to like what Carsanac was about to say, stared at him. "We would ask of you, to induce the spells into the bandit's minds and, those are to include a false memory of their escape from the jail. We then take them to the border and let them find Nepolia on their own. Also, there must be placed the idea that there was a border fight and all of Nepolia's forces were killed, but not before the bandits were able to escape, with instructions of where to go and who to talk to."

Michele felt her throat tighten. She knew that it was possible to affect the minds of others' with magic, but she had always thought it a most horrible and despicable acts that could be done, ever! They were now asking her to do that very thing. Michele stared, wide eyed at Carsanac, as Crendoran's hand settled softly on her shoulder.

———

Pastilan stepped from the front entrance of Bistalan's old and now, his new palace. The only thing he had changed in the palace, was to have a rear door added. He looked around and finally saw Daralan, carrying the orb, wrapped in leaves, coming towards him and, his aide was in a hurry. The web bounced with Daralan's landing and the aide hurried to him.

"Bandarson has answered Lord Pastilan," Daralan whispered. Pastilan nodded and led the way back into the web palace.

"What have they said?" Pastilan asked after they entered a room and were alone. Daralan set the orb on a table like webbing and looked to him. There was a mixture of fear and confusion in his eyes.

"They want to know if we have any of the stones that can block cast spells," Daralan said, almost whining. Pastilan stared at him and then looked to the ceiling.

"Where are we to get those?" he asked quietly. Daralan looked wide eyed at him, not realizing that Pastilan wasn't asking him.

"My Lord, only the Plain has those stones," Daralan said softly. "They guard them well and any that they share, they take back when the dangers are defeated." Pastilan lowered his eyes to the aide.

"Check the remains of those who attacked from the Realm and see if there are any on them," he ordered the aide, following the lead from Somora. Daralan almost smiled.

"It is too late to do that Lord Pastilan," Daralan said. "The remains have been spelled back to Realm." Pastilan continued to stare at Daralan and the aide was becoming very uncomfortable.

"Do we have any of the Realm, or any of the domains, that support us?" Pastilan finally asked. Turning his entire body, Daralan slowly shook his head. Neither had seen the one that hung upside down, looking in the top of window at them, and had heard all that had been said. Pastilan turned and looked out the window, but by then, Vastalan was speeding back to the web that held his leader and the ones from the Realm. "We have to find a way to get some of those stones," Pastilan told his aide and the trees outside of the window. The aide nodded, but the trees didn't.

Gorastor and Gorpeelia had been talking quietly and were beginning to relax with each other. Gorastor learned that Gorpeelia was a half year younger than she and Gorastor felt sorrow for what this young girl was to face, when a different male guard came to the cell door and unlocked it. Gorsinbor entered and beckoned them both. "Training start," she ordered them. The two girls stood and left the cell. There were two more guards waiting for them.

"Take kitchen," Gorsinbor told the guards. They nodded, each grabbing the arm of a girl and dragged them off, with Gorsinbor following. When they had arrived at the kitchen, the two guards shoved the girls into the center of the room. The cooks, all males, closed in around them and they were eyeing them thoroughly. Gorastor and Gorpeelia clung to each other in fear. "Get work!" Gorsinbor yelled, and the cooks grumbled as they went back to their duties. Gorsinbor went to the swinging door to the dining room and pushed it open. The two females, who served Garator, were beginning to set the room for Garator's lunch. "You," Gorsinbor called, beckoning one of the females to her. She pointed to Gorastor and Gorpeelia. "Train," she told the girl. The girl nodded and beckoned the two to come with her. Gorastor and Gorpeelia quickly followed the girl, but Gorsinbor stopped them before they passed through the door."Remember," she told them and held up two of the thin boxes. Both girls nodded and followed the other into the dining room.

<hr />

In Namsia City, while the Gaspilarians rested, Garplasar had found a window in a room on an upper floor, where he could watch the city through the destroyed gate. He was disgusted by the ugly appearance of the humans, but he knew he had to overcome that to get to the rebels. He watched and waited, quietly cursing the sun for its slow travels to the west.

<hr />

In the dining room, the two experienced servers had begun training the two newcomers on their duties. The first thing they had told Gorastor and Gorpeelia was to expect Garator's hands to go where he wanted. "You like, time," the one told them with a giggle, but Gorastor was quite sure she would never enjoy anything Garator did with her. As she looked around the dining room, she began to realize a plan of her own, a plan of rebellion. She started to work on the two servers, to turn them from Garator.

As those of the Realm exited the portal, all were astonished by the beauty of Werementran's farm. The trees were of different hues of greens and the grass was almost blue. The buildings were all painted different colors, but each seemed to glorify the other buildings around it. A gentle breeze ruffled the women's longer hair and the air smelled almost sweet.

"Your Majesties, Werementran, this is lovely!" Xanaporia said. "Is all of Weretoran like this?"

"Yes," Werelaran said with a smile. "This is what all of Weretoran is like, but Werementran does strive harder than many, in the keeping of his lands and buildings." Werementran bowed his thanks to the King.

"I will send someone to bring Garsendar," Werementran said and went looking for a messenger.

"Perhaps, you would like to look around?" Wereselon asked. The humans of the Realm nodded, as all the wolves' had their noses into the breeze.

"Would it be allowed that we look for ourselves?" Grrale asked of the King. Gordon exchanged looks with Xanaporia.

"I think it would be better that we all stay together for now," Gordon told the wolves' quietly and they exchanged disappointed looks.

"Perhaps there will be another time when we can show you our entire Domain," Werelaran said just as softly; "in our other form," he added with a smile. The wolves' grinned and nodded. Werelaran led them around the farm house area, trying to show all the means that were used to plant, harvest, and store, the produce of the farm. The humans were quite surprised that there was very little difference with what was done here, than what was done on the farms of their areas.

"Your Majesty," Werementran called. Everyone turned to the sound of his voice. Those of the Realm had to look twice at what walked beside Werementran. The creature was taller than the Councilor, even though it walked with its shoulders hunched. The simple short sleeved shirt and short breeches showed the thinness of the creature. Its eyes seemed to bulge out, on either side of the large, eagle beak like nose that stuck out quite far. When it got closer, they could just make out the very short and sparse hair that was on its head. Xanaleria could not stop the revulsion she felt for the thing. All four of the wolves' had to fight to keep their back fur from bristling.

"They are not pretty by any standards, but their own," Wereselon whispered to those of the Realm. All nodded, and they felt shame for their reactions to the creature. Werementran stopped short of the King and Queen and the gargoyle bowed deeply to them. The councilor looked to Gordon and the others'.

"May I present Garsendar," he said, his hand towards the gargoyle. Those of the Realm gave a slight bow and Garsendar responded with another deep bow. That's when those of the Realm noticed the smell that emanated from Garsendar. It was a heavy musk like smell, that when they first noticed it, repelled them, but it only took a few seconds and they could hardly notice it. Unfortunately, the wolves' continued to have difficulty with the scent and they moved so the breeze blew the scent away from them.

"Garsendar," the King spoke to him. "These people and wolves' are from the Realm and they have come to learn of Gargoylia, and Garator. They also come to try and save a young female taken to Garator's castle. Garsendar looked to the King with surprise and then to those of the Realm.

"Spotters take, no save," he said, slowly shaking his head, with a regretful look. The King barely paused. He placed his hand on Cartland's shoulder.

"This human can change his shape and plans to travel to Gargoylia, looking like a gargoyle," the King told him and

Garsendar's eyes opened very wide, which did nothing to improve his appearance.

"Can you copy the smell?" Gordon asked Cartland quietly. Cartland shrugged as he studied the gargoyle. Without warning, he shifted and another Garsendar stood where he had been. The original screamed and took off running. The creature was very quickly out of sight.

"Oh shit," Gordon and Xanaporia said at the same time, quietly. Cartland shifted back to his normal self, looking to the King, Queen, and Werementran. Weretilon and the General were chuckling.

"I'm sorry," Cartland told them. "I didn't mean to frighten him." The King, Queen and Werementran were struggling not to laugh.

"It will be alright," Werementran said. "We should have told you that the gargoyles that are here in Weretoran are rather easily frightened. Anything that is new to them, scares them." Werementran shrugged with his last words.

"Why don't we all go into the house and have something to drink, while Werementran finds someone that can chase Garsendar down and bring him back," Werelaran said and indicated the house with his extended hand.

"Yes, please," Werementran said; "the staff has been notified of your presence and I am sure they already have some refreshments ready." Everyone nodded and started for the house.

"How can they catch him?" Xanaporia asked Wereselon. "He was really moving when he took off." The Queen smiled and pointed to Werementran, who had stopped a young man and pointed in the direction the gargoyle had run, as he talked to him. The young man nodded and changed to wolf form, quickly followed the gargoyles path, his nose to the ground. Every eye of those from the Realm, stared at the departing, very large wolf. They then looked to each other and then all looked to the astonished wolves'. The Weretorians all started to laugh out loud, as they continued to the house.

Messages and representatives, from all of the Domains, were coming to Realm City. Zachia received them in order of arrival. Jarsalon, the Keeper of Magic for Dolaris, appeared in the entry hall of the palace. He was surprised that he was shown immediately into the Overseers office.

"Jarsalon," Zachia said from behind his desk. "It is good to see you," he said, standing and extending his hand. When Jarsalon shook Zachia's hand, the Overseer easily saw concern in Jarsalon's eyes. "Pease sit, what is it?" Zachia said and asked, as he sat. Jarsalon sat and took a breath, looking to Zachia.

"We had discovered four that we thought to be spies," Jarsalon started and Zachia nodded, waiting. "Two of them, disappeared right in front of me when I tried to question them and the other two died. We cannot find any explanation for their deaths," Jarsalon looked angry, sad, and confused, all at the same time. "What is going on

Zachia? Who are these people?" Zachia shook his head and tried to smile.

"We don't know Jarsalon," Zachia told him quietly; "but they're being found in every Domain and we have no idea what they're after."

"Perhaps they are after information and the planting of thoughts that would not be of benefit to Rightful Magic," Emma said as she entered the office holding the hand of Ava. Zachia and Jarsalon looked between Emma and the little girl, confused. "Go ahead Ava, tell Zachia what you just told me," Emma said softly. Ava didn't smile when she looked intently into the Overseer's eyes.

"Castope's Dark City still lives," Ava said, and there was the calmness of truth in her voice. The adults looked to each other in stunned silence.

"How could she know of Castope?" Jarsalon asked in a whisper, looking to Zachia. "She wasn't even born yet." Zachia looked to Ava's eyes and saw no lessening of her truth. He smiled and stood, going to Ava, leading her to the couch.

"Please, tell me all that you have sensed," he gently asked. Ava began her telling.

In a place that had once been called the Dark City, Somora was receiving news he did not want to hear. "Our spies are being discovered My King," Perilia, Somora's first mate, said as she and Dospora, his second mate, entered his office. "What are we to do?" Somora's face clouded with his anger and thoughts. Several others' followed his mates into the room.

"There have been many conversations speeding around, but they are being tight beamed and hard to read," Mestilia, the best talker of Somora's talkers, said as she came into the room.

"There is danger Somora," Bortenon, Somora's strongest sensitive, announced loudly, as he followed the talker into the office. All eyes turned to him. "A child of the town of Zentler has sensed our city and, you!"

CHAPTER SEVEN

Parsony had spent a considerable time explaining about the town of Bentodon and the farm of Cenlinas, who he told them was Brando and Brendo's mother. She had made it plain to anyone that would listen, that she had been a bed slave for a young Brandaro and had been impregnated by him and that her twins were the heirs to Brandaro's rule. Melsikan and the others' were very ready when they stepped through the portal, to the south of the town.

"The Mayor's house is across from the Court house, which is that tall building, there," Parsony said pointing.

"The farm is to the north?" Melsikan asked. Parsony nodded.

"About four miles, or so," Parsony said.

"All right, let's go meet the Mayor," Melsikan said, as he stepped off with Isabella on his arm and Parsony next to Daridar, behind them. Jennifer and Alan followed them and the twenty Realm soldiers, constantly looking everywhere at once, followed them.

At Corlaar's, which was a small farm in the shadow of a single bluff, Brando rode into the yard. Brendo and Corlaar came out to meet him. They walked with him to the corral without a word spoken by anyone. Brando took the saddle from the horse, throwing it on top railing of the fence, as Corlaar put the horse in the corral. Brando turned to his sister. "Have you heard anything?" he asked calmly. She shook her head. Brando turned to his second in command. "Have a couple of those from Bentodon check on the Mayor, I don't trust him anymore," he said and Corlaar nodded and trotted to the barn. Minutes later, several riders came from the opposite side of the barn and left for the town.

"What is it son?" Cenlinas asked as she came from the house. He looked to her and then his sister. His eyes turned hard when he answered.

"I feel that the Mayor of Bentodon has told others' of us and they are closing in on us. We must speed up our taking of Bandarson city!" His voice was soft, but all heard the intensity of his words and, the growl that came with them.

Nepolia paced the floor of the throne room. Calitoran had tried once to get her to eat and she had all but killed him on the spot. Now, everyone, male and female, stayed from her path. Her thoughts raced around the reply they had received from Bandarson.

"They demand power stones before they will even talk with us!" Depelia had told her in anger. "If we were to do that, what's to stop them from attacking us and destroying not just us, but all of Neponia?" she had added. Nepolia had stormed from the orb room and now paced the floor.

"There has to be a way to control these rebels, so I can do what I want!" she growled to herself.

In the meeting room of Neponities modest palace, Michele looked around the room, to all who looked to her. With her thoughts, she called to her brother.

"What is it Michele?" Zachia asked.

"They believe that the Queen of the Southern Section, Nepolia, has the orb and they want to use the bandits caught during the attack on Neponia, as spies against Nepolia. They want me to spell false memories into the bandit's minds and make them spy for them," she all but screamed at him. Moments of silence answered her. "Zachia?" Michele asked fearfully.

"Honey," Zachia's voice came to her softly. "I know how you feel about interfering with others' minds, so I cannot order you to do it and I wouldn't anyway, but we have to know what is happening between Nepolia, and the rebels of Namsia. I trust you to do what you know to be right and, what you know must be done," he told her.

"Thanks," Michele muttered sarcastically.

"I am truly sorry, but we must find the orb and stop any union of Nepolia and the rebels," Zachia told her. Michele nodded as she broke the connection with her brother. She looked to her husband, her confusion and fear of what to do, showing clearly in her eyes. He took her into his arms and looked to the Queens.

"You must understand that Michele has always strongly believed it the most horrible of wrongs to use magic to affect the minds of others'. The Neponian's looked to each other with worry. "What you ask of her now, goes against that belief."

"We are sorry Michele," Nepanities said to Michele, standing and coming to her. She looked around the room and then back to Michele."We will think of another plan." Michele pulled from Crendoran and turned to the Princess of the Center Section. As she looked to her, all in the room could see the turmoil Michele was experiencing.

"No, it is a good plan, and we will proceed with it," Michele said, drawing in a deep breath with the last of her words. "I will place the false memories, because of the nature of those I am to affect and, the fact that Nepolia cannot be allowed to make any kind of alliance with the rebels of Namsia, who have only their own greed in their hearts!" All those in the room began to breathe again, though quietly.

In Nepolia's throne room, the Queen came to sudden stop in her pacing. Her head came up and there was a smile on her face. The entire throne room became silent, no one dared move. "Somebody get me Wespozorn, immediately!" Several of the guards at the door collided, trying to make it out of the room at the same time, to fetch the Leader of the Mearlies of the Southern Section.

Vastalan raced the entire distance to the web that held Dasilan and Belserlan. He was panting heavily when he landed on the outer webbing and hurried into the web house. All looked to him when he entered.

"Have you found the orb?" Dasilan asked. Vastalan nodded and his eyes were wide from what he had seen and heard.

"The orb is in the palace that Bistalan had built and is now claimed by Pastilan," he told them; "but there is more Dasilan."

"Report," Dasilan ordered.

"I am not sure how to do that Dasilan," Vastalan told him, causing confusion in all eyes that looked to him. "What I have witnessed is difficult to describe, with sense," Vastalan added. Dasilan came closer to the still hard breathing Natharian.

"Tell us what you have seen and heard, we will decide its purpose," Dasilan told Vastalan calmly. Vastalan nodded and reported what he had seen and heard.

"I was at the window and I saw Daralan place the orb on a stand. He and Pastilan started to talk about the answer received from Bandarson," he told them. There were exchanged looks between Dasilan and Belserlan. "Daralan said that those of Bandarson want the stones that stop cast spells." Belserlan hissed. All looked to him.

"They must never get those amulets," he said and looked to the talker that had come with him.

"It was right after that, that Pastilan began to act very strangely," Vastalan said drawing the attention back to him.

"What do you mean?" Dasilan asked quietly. Vastalan's eyes told of his own confusion.

"He looked to the ceiling and seemed lost in thought, then suddenly, in a voice almost in a trance like state, asked where they could get those stones." Belserlan's eyes began to open wider. "Daralan told him that only those of the Plain had the stones and the stones had been taken back any that they had shared. Pastilan again seemed lost and then, in the same trance like voice, told Daralan to search the remains of those of the Realm, who had been slain in battle, and see if any had worn the stones. Daralan told him that all that had been slain had been spelled back to the Realm. I left then and did not hear any more, but it is the trance like speaking that is so odd," Vastalan said, almost to himself. "I have never seen a Natharian behave that way. It was as though someone else was speaking, through him." Belserlan again turned to the talker and nodded. The talker grinned and sent what she had heard from Vastalan, to those who were listening in the Realm. They were very interested in what they were told.

———

In Gartisia, the capital city of Gargoylia, Garteltor and the six of his gang, snuck into the recess of one of the larger waste outlets of Garator's castle. As much as it sickened him, Garteltor reached his arm into the waste water and found, as he had thought it to be, that the grill that blocked the entrance to the castle, only extended a short ways below the surface of what flowed through the opening. He withdrew his arm and nodded to his team. They all stripped off their clothes and placed them in bags that would repel any of the liquids of the small river. They exchanged regretful looks as Garteltor handed the thick and heavy staff he carried, to another and then stepped into the flowing water, took a deep breath and disappeared below the surface. He quickly appeared on the other side of the grating. The rest followed him, handing their staffs to the same one. When it was his turn, being the last, he thrust the staffs through the grate, and went under the grate. The staffs were handed back to their owners as they all gathered at the opening from the castle proper. They grasped the wrist of the one behind them, that held their staff and started into the dark tunnel, pushing their way through the over knee deep waters.

———

Across the city from their son, Gorsentor and Garpartor sat at the table, waiting for Weretilon to call on the crystal, to tell them that help was coming.

In Garator's dining room, Gorastor continued to work on the two servers who were training them. Gorpeelia had, much to Gorastor's surprise, immediately picked up on what Gorastor was trying to do and was helping all she could. They were both getting very scared as the meal time approached, because the other two had told them that as they were new, they would be receiving the majority of Garator's attention!

They all sat in the front room of Werementran's house and talked of the similarities between Weretoran, the Realm, and Zentler. Gordon and Xanaporia sat on the couch that was in front of the huge window. Gordon continually kept glancing over his shoulder, out that window. Werelaran started to chuckle and when all looked to him, he smiled at Gordon.

"Do not worry. The one sent after Garsendar is one of those who helped the gargoyles adjust to Weretoran. He will be bringing Garsendar back shortly," he told Gordon. Gordon smiled and blushed slightly. Xanaporia took his arm for support.

"I'm sorry Your Majesty," he said quietly; "but I worry of the passing time. Not just for the reason we are here, but also for the girl that was taken." Xanaporia's grip tightened with understanding. All of Weretoran nodded with their own worries.

"They come," Crrale announced suddenly. The other three wolves' nodded their agreement. All the rest from the Realm looked to them in curiosity, while those of Weretoran smiled at each other with understanding. "The scent," Grrale said softly, as an explanation. The humans nodded and looked out of the window. They could see the young man leading the gargoyle back.

"Shall we try this again?" the King asked as he stood. The rest grinned as they followed him out of the house, to meet with the nervous gargoyle, again.

———

Silence covered the room after Ava had finished telling of what she had sensed. Everyone looked from one to the other, with considerable concern about what they had heard.

"Somora is the one your father couldn't find, when he and the others returned to the Dark City," Ava had said to Zachia. He nodded as more a reaction to her speaking, than indication he had heard her.

"What are we to do now?" Emma asked, breaking the grip of silence. Everyone looked to Zachia. His eyes were looking at nothing, as he thought. He rose from the couch and Emma took his place next to Ava. He went and sat at his desk and spelled the Seeing Stone to him. The others' nodded as he put the amulet around his neck and took the stone in his hand. His eyes seemed to glaze and all waited. Minutes passed and the silence of the room seemed deafening. Finally, Zachia's eyes cleared and he looked around the room.

"We have to plan an invasion of what was the Dark City," he told them all and the Seeing Stone disappeared. "There are things happening there we need to investigate!"

"King Somora, I have felt an invasion of prying eyes!" Bortenon said. All eyes again, turned to him.

"What do you mean?" Somora asked in confusion. He and all in the room knew that Bortenon was a powerful sensitive. "What have you sensed Bortenon?"

"There was someone here, looking at us, My King, but they were not here in person, only their eyes, looking," Bortenon said, his voice telling of his fear. Somora stared at the nervous small man, feeling truth in what he had heard.

"What are we to do?" Perilia asked quietly, taking her comates hand.

"It has to be the Overseer," Gapilarian, a powerful seer, said in anger, as he too joined those in the office. "He is the only one with the power to cause this invasion!"

"They have found us out, we must run," Dospora said in fear and gripped Perilia's hand tightly. Somora held up his hand to them all.

"I have thought that something like this could happen, so do not panic!" he told them all as his eyes swept the room. He looked to Mestilia. "Have all the talkers contact the spies that have not been captured and tell them to be very careful and, do not be found!" She nodded and left the room. "Gapilarian, do you know who has sensed us?" The strongest of seers nodded.

"A girl named Ava, who is right now in the Overseer's palace," he said, with anger in his eyes, as well as his voice. Somora nodded and a very evil look came to his face.

"Have someone tell General Hantopan to come to me, I would talk with him." Gapilarian left the room. Somora looked to his comates. "Do not fear my pets," he told them quietly. "I am always one step ahead of those who would try to stop us!" Perilia and Dospora smiled back at him, with their confidence in him and went back to their duties. A few minutes later, Hantopan entered the room.

"You have called for me My King?" he said as he came to the front of the desk. Somora nodded.

"Learn from Gapilarian what the girl looks like and then send someone to the Realm, to kill this girl, Ava," he told his General in a snarl. The general saluted and went looking for Gapilarian.

Melsikan, with Parsony beside him, marched up to the front door of the Mayor's house, while the rest waited on the street in front of the house. They didn't slow down as they threw open the door and walked in. They looked all through the house and found nothing of the Mayor. When they returned to the others', Melsikan wore a very angry look. "We go to the farm," he told them all. A portal opened and they all marched into it. They walked out into the yard in front of the house and they could tell by the open door and emptiness of the coral that their quarry had already fled, but Melsikan signaled the twenty to search anyway.

"What now?" Daridar asked as she looked around. Melsikan looked to Jennifer.

"Call the Overseer and find out if they have learned anything that we can use," he told her gently. She nodded and concentrated. Her eyes were opening wider and wider as she got an answer. One of the soldiers came to Melsikan, from the barn and whispered to him. He looked to the soldier in surprise and looked to the rest. "All of you stay here, I'll be right back," he told them and followed the soldier back to the barn, as confused looks were exchanged. When he entered the barn, he saw the body. He walked to the body of Barkoor and knelt. He reached out and touched the neck of the man. "The bodies still warm," he said in a whisper. He stood and looked around as another soldier hurried into the barn.

"Melsikan, there are wagon tracks that lead to the northeast," he said, slightly out of breath. Melsikan looked at him for a moment and then turned to the officer who had brought him to the barn.

"Do you have a talker?" he asked. The officer nodded. "Good, take eight and follow those tracks. When you have found where they lead, call Jennifer and tell her where we can open a portal. Do not let anyone see you!" The officer saluted and left the barn. Melsikan returned to the main group. He looked to Jennifer expectantly.

"Emma says that they have found that the spies, in every domain, came from the Dark City," she told him; "but they still don't know what it's all about," she told him. Melsikan nodded as he looked around the yard again.

"Alright everybody, might as well get comfortable," he told them all. "The soldiers are following some wagon tracks and they will call as soon as they find out where they go. Until then, we wait." They all nodded and entered the house and sat on what they could find. Parsony went to the kitchen area and found that the cabinets were all full of food and other things.

"They must have left in a hurry," he said rather loudly. "They didn't pack any food to take with them." He pointed to the cabinets. "That also means that they didn't travel that far!"

"Might as well eat while we wait," Daridar said as she went to the kitchen. Isabella followed her, nodding.

Neponities and Nepelia led the way into the prison on the north side of Capital City. Michele and Crendoran were behind them and Nepanities and Nepeslia were behind them. All of the bandits yelled, whistled and hooted at the virtually naked women. The women ignored them and looked to Michele. They had thoroughly discussed what spells Michele was to impress into the minds of the bandit's. The Royals watched her as she lifted her hand and began her spelling. They all could see the tears that crawled down her cheeks as she implanted the false memories. The bandit's quieted as they were affected by those spells. Soon, they all just stood still, their faces blank. Michele lowered her hands and went into Crendoran's arms, crying freely. The others' waited, as they understood what she had sacrificed to do what she had. It took several minutes, but she finally turned to the Queens. "It is done," she told them softly. "They are ready now." Neponities nodded and turned to head guard.

"Bring them out and gather them in the yard. We will be ready to move them to the border soon," she told her. The woman bowed and signaled the other guards. The guards, carefully, began bringing the bandit's from their cells.

In Nepolia's castle, Wespozorn was brought before his Queen. "Why do you have me dragged here?" the Mearlies leader asked with an angry voice. Nepolia smiled at him and beckoned him closer. When the Mearlie stood at the foot of the two steps, Nepolia bent over, getting her face very close to the Mearlie ruler.

"How long," Nepolia asked, whispering; "would it take you to make power stones that would be faulty?" Wespozorn looked to her in confusion.

"Why would you want that?" he asked, thinking of the Power Stones that were already being prepared for her and the others' of the southern Section. Nepolia's face clouded up.

"Do not question me, how long?" she asked again, with irritation. The Mearlie shrugged.

"How faulty would you want them to be?" he asked, a sly grin coming to his lips. Nepolia smiled back.

"Very faulty," she said in a hiss. Wespozorn smiled.

"Not long after Exchange day," he said positively. Nepolia smiled with her nod.

"Make one hundred fifty, faulty stones, as quickly as you can and inform me as soon as they are ready," she commanded. Wespozorn bowed and left the castle. He chuckled as he returned to the mines and contacted Wenzorn.

"We need to get that orb and find out what this Pastilan can tell us of this other voice," Belserlan said. Dasilan nodded his understanding. He turned to several others' and held a quiet conference. There were tones of agreement. Dasilan turned back to Belserlan as some left the web.

"I have asked them to pass the word and all should try to find out all they can of the armies locations, and strengths," he told those of the Realm. "They are the ones who can stop any effort we make to capture Pastilan." There were nods by all. Again they were all required to wait, and the strain was beginning to show on Belserlan, for he had his own thoughts of what must be done. When the news came back that Mertilan now commanded all of the armies and that they were quite spread out, Belserlan pushed his idea forward.

"What if we simply use a small force to take Pastilan and the orb?" he asked. "Your spy got in and out without trouble, a small band should be able to do the same." He looked around the web. "If you concentrate on the armies, while I joined that small band, the armies can be directed as you need, if the current leaders are removed." There were exchanged looks by those in the web and smiles came to them. "But, the priority now is the retrieval of the orb and stopping any alliance with Namsia!" Belserlan stated. There were more nods made.

"You're right," Dasilan said, and pointed to Vastalan and four others' who were bigger than most present and were known to be the best fighters. "You are to lead Belserlan to Pastilan's web, to help capture Pastilan and the orb." The five nodded and beckoned to Belserlan to follow them. Belserlan looked to the four that had come with him from the Realm and they all followed the fives lead. Dasilan turned to a messenger with only one order. "Concentrate on the Commanders of the armies!" The messenger nodded and left the web.

Both Gorastor and Gorpeelia were close to panicking as Garator walked into the dining room. He eyed them thoroughly before he sat down. The one training her pushed Gorastor slightly. Nervously, she approached the Ruler with the pitcher of wine. As she poured the wine into the goblet, she felt his left hand on the inside of her right leg. She started to get angry when she felt it start moving up. She fought for control of herself as she finished the pouring and his hand came to a place that she had feared it would. She couldn't move for the grip he had on her. As he continued his manipulations, she found herself becoming angrier and she knew that she had to destroy this monster, somehow! Garator's chuckle, as he reached for the goblet with his right hand, only angered her more. She endured his hand, feeling disgust and loathing for what he did. He replaced the goblet as Gorpeelia came to his other side and placed the plate of food in front of him. He turned to her and chuckled again, as he reached under her short skirt, without taking his hand from Gorastor. Gorpeelia screamed when his hand reached its goal and tried to pull away from him. He roared and released Gorastor only to turn and slap Gorpeelia, knocking her across the room. Gorastor quickly went to the unmoving Gorpeelia. She held the girl, trying to use her own skirt to stem the blood that seeped from the split caused by Garator's slap. The two other servers quickly went to Garator and soothed him with their bodies. Gorastor looked to the Ruler as his hands mauled the other two. Her anger turned to rage. *You will die*, she swore to herself as she looked to the back of the Rulers head.

In the tunnel, the six counted ladders that came from different parts of the castle. They had done their homework completely and knew they needed the fourteenth ladder. That ladder would lead to the room, in which they would prepare for next part of Garteltor's plan.

⁓⁓⁓⁓⁓⁓⁓

They all could see that Garsendar was nervous and kept looking at Cartland, even though the young man that had brought him back kept a hold of his arm and was talking to him constantly. Cartland tried to smile, reassuredly, to the gargoyle, but Garsendar seemed unwilling to understand. They stopped six feet from the gargoyle and the King was about to speak, when Xanaleria spoke out.

"Who's that?" she asked and pointed. They all turned and looked where she pointed and saw another gargoyle peeking around the corner of the barn, which was only a short distance from them.

"Gorpendor!" Werementran called to the gargoyle, beckoning with his hand; "it is alright, come." He turned to the ones from the Realm. "She is Garsendar's mate," he told them with a smile. "I guess she was worried about him." A young woman went to the gargoyle and gently pulled her from her place of hiding, bringing her to the group. They could all see that the female was shorter than Garsendar, just coming to height of his shoulder and her features were less pronounced. She quickly grabbed Garsendar's arm as she looked wide eyed to the ones she didn't recognize. Again the King prepared to speak and again, Xanaleria interrupted him before he could start.

"You do not need to fear us," she said softly as she slowly took several steps towards the female, both of her hands held out waist high, palms up. "We have come to help Weretoran and all those of Gargoylia, who seek peace and freedom from Garator." She stopped just short of Gorpendor and smiled. Gorpendor looked at her for several seconds and then glanced at her mate and then to Xanaleria's hands and then to her face. She removed one of her hands from Garsendar's arm and slowly reached out and placed her hand on one of Xanaleria's. The gargoyle stood for several seconds, just barely touching Xanaleria's hand. Then she started to smile and nod, slowly.

"Talk truth," she said quietly and slowly took Xanaleria's hand into her grip as her other hand came from Garsendar's arm, and took Xanaleria's other hand. No other sound was heard as those of Weretoran stared wide eyed, at the surprising connection between Gorpendor and the much shorter, Xanaleria.

Zachia talked with Tarson about the security of the Realm, for quite a while. With Tarson's nod, Zachia called to Pentilian and Pelinoria, as they inherited his name sakes ability of invisibility that could not be sensed. The two women did not come alone. Each had brought their husbands and Pentilian had also brought her daughter Paolaria, as well.

"We have a strange situation on our hands right now," Zachia told them after they had all found a seat. They all looked to him waiting, but Zachia could see in their eyes, that they already had some information on the situation, especially Paolaria. "Someone has taken over the Dark City, and they are sending spies into all of the Domains and we have no idea of their purpose." He looked to them all, but it was Paolaria's eyes that kept drawing his attention. "We need to investigate what is happening there and, why," Zachia continued. "I want to send you two," he pointed to Pentilian and Pelinoria; "invisibly, and see if you can find out what we need to know." The two women looked to each other and smiled, as they looked back to Zachia.

"We have already anticipated your request Overseer," Pentilian said quietly, and Pelinoria nodded her agreement. "We believe we have a better idea." Zachia and Emma, both tried and failed, to hide their surprise.

"What do you have in mind?" Zachia asked, as a small smile found his lips. The two women smiled wider as they glanced to each other and then Pentilian pointed to her daughter.

"Her," Pentilian said as her grin widened. Zachia looked to Pelinoria and saw the same grin on her face. He looked to Paolaria and his smile vanished when he saw the look in the woman's eyes. "She is younger, has the same ability of invisibility and is a greater magical power than either, or both of us," Pentilian said softly. Zachia looked into Paolaria's eyes and saw strength, as well as anger. "The only difficulty is that she cannot talk as we can," Pentilian said in a hushed voice.

"I will go," Paolaria said and Zachia could hear the badly hidden anger. "I can travel quicker and I know to get out if confronted," she said as a false smile came to her face. Zachia and Emma exchanged glances. Zachia returned his look to her.

"We need to learn what this group is about and who their leader is," he told her. Paolaria nodded only once, slowly.

"I will learn these things," she said, still holding the false smile. "Pelinoria and mama have told me all about the layout of the city, so I know where to go." Zachia watched her for a moment and there was no slacking of her intensity. He nodded and glanced again to Emma, seeing the worry in her eyes.

"Alright, are you prepared to go now?" he asked and Paolaria nodded. He spelled a communication crystal to himself and handed it to Paolaria. "I'm going to put you on the north side of the city." Again Paolaria nodded, as she put the small chain around her neck and tucked the amulet into the top of her shirt. She quickly touched her mother's hand and then turned back to Zachia.

"Be careful," Zachia said softly. Paolaria nodded, with an angry smile, just before she disappeared.

———

"Remember, those that are sent here, must not see that anyone is here. They must think that we have left, in a hurry," Somora told the vast crowd around him. There were grins and nods throughout the gathered. "Alright," Somora yelled; "everyone to their places!" Those gathered, began to disperse. Somora and his comates, plus a few others, went to the hidden tunnel in the southern mountains. Others' went to places that were hidden deeply. Food, water, games and pots had already been stored there, so there was no reason that any should need to leave until Somora called for them.

"Why don't we just destroy them?" Gapilarian growled as they settled to their mats, inside the tunnel. Somora looked to him, trying to control his anger.

"We have made the city appear as though we left," Somora told him; "leaving things that would too bulky or heavy to carry. Those who come will think that we have gone elsewhere and leave. We can then return to the city and resume our ways. They will not think that we would return to the city and will not look there again. If we destroy them, they will bring their armies against us and we would lose that battle. That's why!"

"What if they don't believe our ruse?" Dospora asked quietly. Somora smiled as he looked to her.

"Oh, they will," he said, chuckling. "I have left further evidence for them to find." His comates looked to each other and then to his grinning face, in wonder.

Paolaria appeared on the north side of the city and went immediately to invisibility. She listened for awhile, but couldn't hear anything but the breeze as it stirred the trees around her. Looking carefully around her, she slowly made her way into the city proper. She went slowly, checking everything as she moved about. She was beginning to doubt that any were left here, for it appeared as though the inhabitants had indeed fled, in a great hurry. She moved to check the fortress her mother had so meticulously described and had found the door open and again found the evidence of hasty packing and leaving. She stepped back into the sunlight and grabbed the communication stone around her neck. She called to the Overseer.

"Yes Paolaria, what have you found?" he asked.

"Overseer, it looks as though the ones that had been here, have fled, for there is no one here now and it looks as though they packed quickly, leaving many things behind," she told him.

"What kind of things?" he asked with a tone that worried Paolaria.

"Large things that would be harder to move and some clothing that would not be needed for daily living. Many foods were left as well," she told him.

"That's not right," Zachia said softly. "These people have magical powers; they would have not panicked like that. Be careful, something is…."

"Mommy!" a small voice echoed through the city.

"Overseer, I hear a child calling for its mother. I'm going to find out about this."

"Be careful Paolaria, I think there is something very...."
Paolaria released the stone, cutting off the Overseers words.

"Mommy?" the tiny voice called again, louder. Paolaria became visible and followed the sound of the child. She came upon the child, several blocks from the fortress and the girl, she thought to be around eight years old, was standing in the middle of the narrow street, looking around. "Mommy!" the girl screamed and Paolaria felt a mother's sympathy for the girl. *How could parents just run off and leave a child like this?* She wondered. As she neared the child, the girl turned to her and Paolaria saw the tears that flowed down her cheeks. Paolaria got closer.

"Do not fear little one, I will save you from being alone," she told the girl.

"Who are you?' the girl asked, taking a step backwards.

"No, don't be afraid," Paolaria said softly. "I am going to save you. I am going to take you with me to safety."

"Who are you?" the girl asked again as Paolaria neared her.

"My name is Paolaria, and I am going to take you to the Realm," she told the girl as she pulled her into her arms. The girl came reluctantly.

"Where is my mommy?" the girl cried onto Paolaria's shoulder.

"I don't know sweetheart, but you will be safe in the Realm. What is your name honey?"

"Mesetere," the girl said meekly.

"Well Mesetere, I am taking you with me," Paolaria told her and grabbed the communication stone again. "Overseer, I am bringing the child with me. There is no one here and I cannot leave her here alone."

"Paolaria, wait, you don't know why…." Paolaria released the stone, cutting off Zachia's words again. Holding the child, she disappeared. While Paolaria was speaking to the Overseer, Mesetere told Somora, through her mother, that his plan was working.

CHAPTER EIGHT

Garplasar watched the sun as it finally went below the horizon. He smiled as he went to the Gaspilarians and woke them. He led them from the building, to the broken gate. He was totally shocked to see that there were lights being lit on the streets and there were as many humans walking around, as there was before. "Don't humans ever sleep?" he whispered angrily. The Gaspilarians shrugged.

Isabella had dozed on the couch, but then suddenly woke, jerking with the beginnings of a nightmare that she had already lived. She sat up and looked around. She saw Melsikan through the door opening, standing on the porch. She rose from the couch, and went to him. She slid under his left arm and he smiled as he put it around her shoulder, drawing her to him. She shivered with the cool night air. He started to rub her arm with his other hand and it helped. "Are you alright?' he asked quietly. She nodded against his shoulder.

"Just started to have a bad dream I didn't want to relive," she told him softly. He hugged her a little tighter as he looked in the direction the soldiers following the tracks had gone. "You haven't heard from them yet?" Isabella asked. As if cued, Jennifer walked out on the porch.

"I just received word that the soldiers have found the ranch the tracks lead to," she said.

"Did they send a picture?" Melsikan asked and Jennifer nodded. "Give it to me and get the others' ready." She nodded, sent him the picture of where to open the portal and then went back inside. In just minutes, they were all assembled and entering the portal.

On Neponia, in the field outside of Capital City, the sun was close to its setting, when they started the bandit's for the border. They marched along, their faces blank. Nepeslia kept looking from the bandit's, to Michele. Finally, Nepanities asked what was wrong.

"How are they to be valuable when they act like they do?" she asked in a whisper. "Nepolia will not believe this." Nepanities chuckled.

"Michele will activate them when we release them. Do not worry, they will be back to their repulsive manners when they cross the border," she told Nepeslia. The princess again looked to the silent bandit's, then Michele, with doubt and fear.

Wenzorn went among the boxes of amulets being stacked in the building. Even he was surprised at the speed the Mearlies were deactivating the old Power Stones and were still able to continue preparing the new stones for Exchange Day. Carsanac arrived and took the Mearlie leader aside. "I have thought of how we can get these deactivated stones into the southern section," he told Wenzorn. The Mearlie looked to him, waiting. "There are fruit shipments crossing the border at every crossing, all over the sections, every day. Some of them are designated for the Mearlies mines and driven by Mearlies. There is no reason for anyone to suspect anything. We just put the boxes of amulets among those shipments. They are never checked all that thoroughly and it will be the quickest and easiest way." Wenzorn looked to him for several seconds and then began to nod slowly as a grin grew on his face. Then he frowned.

"How are we to get the active stones out of the Southern Section?" Carsanac smiled and pulled a map of the border lines around the planet. He pointed to the many passes and ravines that crossed the border, that were closest to the southern mines. Wenzorn nodded and looked to the human. "Does Her Majesty approve?" he asked. Again Carsanac grinned.

"She will when she sees this," he said as he waved the parchments in his hand. He was still grinning as he started towards Capital City.

"Carsanac, wait, please," Wenzorn called, stopping Carsanac. He walked back to the Mearlie.

"What is it?" he asked the concerned looking Wenzorn.

"Nepolia has instructed Wespozorn to make one hundred and fifty faulty Power Stones," he told Carsanac in a whisper. Carsanac looked surprise for a moment and then nodded.

"I will talk with Lady Michele about this," he told Wenzorn. "Perhaps Nepolia plans to give those stones to those she is dealing with in Namsia. If so, that will work to our advantage! Keep me informed on your progress and I will talk with Her Highness." Wenzorn nodded and Carsanac returned to Capital City.

Belserlan was in the middle of the line, as Vastalan led them to the web of Pastilan. They were making their way carefully through the gigantic trees, single file. Even with their amazing night vision, the clouded sky blocked whatever moonlight there might have been and it was necessary for them to travel slowly. At one of the stops, so Vastalan could scout ahead for troops, Belserlan turned to the young female talker, who was directly behind him. "Tell the Realm that we are going after Pastilan and the orb. We hope to capture both and get some answers from this Pastilan," he whispered. She nodded and concentrated. Vastalan returned and signaled all clear. They started forward again. Belserlan was one of the largest of the group, but he still felt a nervousness for what they were about to do. Suddenly, Vastalan signal a halt. He turned and signaled Belserlan to him. When Belserlan had moved to Vastalan's side, the leader pointed with one of his legs.

"Look outs," he whispered. Belserlan nodded his seeing of them. "Wait here, we will take care of them. We are near the web." Belserlan nodded as Vastalan pointed to two of his squad and they snuck forward. Even Belserlan had difficulty hearing the taking of the look outs and the three quickly returned. "Come, we are almost there," Vastalan whispered and they all moved forward slowly. They stopped again in a short time and signals were given for all to spread out. Belserlan and Vastalan moved closer to the web. When they stopped again, they could plainly see the web and the many widely spaced guards that stood watch around it.

"Oh shit," Belserlan whispered to himself. Vastalan chuckled.

Instead of being returned to the cell they had been taken from, Gorastor and Gorpeelia went with the two servers, to the server's quarters, but not before a warning from Gorsinbor to Gorpeelia. The Controller had told Gorpeelia that she was lucky that Garator had only slapped her. She warned them both that if either failed to comply with Garator's desires again, here she had pulled the flat boxes from her pocket and waved them in front of the girl's faces, they both would be severely punished. When the two were led into the server's room, they were shocked to see ten other young females, most of them lounging naked. The girls rose and laughing started to grab and probe at Gorastor and Gorpeelia. Gorpeelia cried, but Gorastor got mad, again. "Who you?" she yelled at them. The others' stopped for a second and looked at her. "Is all want?" she screamed at them as her hands waved at the dirty room, shoddy beds, one shower, and several pots along one wall. "Forget life?" she asked them, only slightly softer in her tone. "Forget family?" she added. The other girls looked to each other and then to her. Many of their faces showing the memories that they had forgotten, or had had beaten out of them, for many showed scars of beatings. "Remember life," she told them. "Remember family!" One of the other girls stepped up and she looked angry.

"Who you ask?" she growled. "All is," she added waving her hand at the room. Gorastor shook her head.

"No," she told the girl; "life more, family more, not Garator!" Silence followed as they all looked to each other.

"How out?" another asked quietly.

"We no agree Garator," she told them. "We resist, we plan."

"How?" the first girl asked, her eyes narrowing. "Garator, army." Gorastor looked to her and moved closer.

"No like Garator," she said in a normal tone. "No react Garator touch. No wiggles, giggle, Garator touch." She looked to each as she spoke, nodding. "No give pleasure Garator!"

"How plan?" the first asked again. Gorastor grinned an evil grin."

"Females, no like Garator. Find weakness, then kill, together!" All of the girls opened their eyes wide and looked to each other.

———————

Garteltor and the six with him had climbed the fourteenth ladder and crawled into the dark room. The only light was what could sneak in under the door. They had managed to get most of the slim of the water from them and had dressed. The muted sounds of shouting came through the wall and Garteltor could have sworn that the loudest of the voices, sounded just like his younger sister!

———————

The Weretorians stared as Gorpendor and Xanaleria pulled Garsendar away from the others' and the three talked for several minutes before Xanaleria beckoned her husband to the group. There were exchanged looks between the King and Gordon. All Gordon could do was shrug, with a small grin. Weretilon moved closer to Xanaporia and whispered something to her. Xanaporia looked to her, smiled, and those two walked a short distance away and were talking. Shortly, they beckoned the Queen, Terryle and Serryle, to join them. Again, the King looked to Gordon and this time the General of the Armies joined him. Gordon could see that the General wasn't all that happy.

"I do believe that there is a chance this might work," Werelaran said softly as he moved closer to Gordon and the General followed. The three, plus Grrale and Crrale, were watching the gargoyles, Cartland, and Xanaleria, but the King and Gordon were taking turns glancing to where their wives', witch, and the female wolves', talked. Cartland shifted and again, there were two Garsendar's. Both gargoyles had jumped, but didn't run. After a few moments, Gorpendor leaned closed to the Gargoyle Cartland, and made an obvious smell test. She drew back and shook her head. They all could hear her as she loudly stated; "stronger." Cartland nodded and in a second, Garsendar leaned closer and nodded his approval and so did Gorpendor. Then the gargoyles indicated they should sit, right there in the road. Both Garsendar and Gorpendor started talking earnestly to Cartland.

"Maybe, Your Majesty," Weretustran said softly, looking from the talking group sitting in the road, to the females that talked, sometimes giggling; "we should try to find out what at least one of the conversations are about?" Werelaran and Gordon both chuckled.

"I believe General," Werelaran said just as softly; "that this is one of those times when the best leadership, is to be the one that does not interfere," the King said, looking from one of the groups to the other. Gordon and the two male wolves' nodded slowly, in their agreement. Weretustran looked to the four with confusion. He then looked to the two groups talking a distance from them. He sighed, loudly.

Kris stepped from the indoor outhouse, which was directly under the stairs that led to the second floor of the palace.

They had all come with Melsikan and Isabella, when they had returned to the palace, for their trip to Namsia. The rest were in the reading room. She suddenly felt a shiver go up her spin and the old feelings of close danger came back to her. She froze in place, listening. The sound of a gentle step came from the balcony above her, and that was followed by the sounds of someone slowly coming down the stairs. She flattened against the door and then carefully peeked around the corner, looking towards the entry hall. She saw the barrel of the dart gun first, and then the man carrying it. The man was looking everywhere as he turned towards her and came forward. She was looking around frantically as she again flattened to the door. She saw the solid chair as the gun barrel and then the man, came passed the corner. She looked to him and saw that his eyes were fixed on the partially open door of the Overseers office.

Paolaria, holding the child, appeared in the office. All the adults crowded around her and the girl. That was why Ava, still sitting on the couch, didn't see her immediately. The girl seemed frightened by the sudden mass of people around her and buried her face into Paolaria's shoulder, that's why she didn't see Ava immediately. Zachia pulled a chair from in front of the desk and Paolaria sat down, the child still in her arms. Ava slowly started to look where Paolaria sat and then someone moved as the girl lifted her head from Paolaria's shoulder and turned. The two looked to each other. The girl hissed at Ava, as Ava jumped from the couch, lifted her hand and placed a shielding and holding spell on the girl and Paolaria. The back of the couch exploded, right where Ava had been and the crash of a breaking wood and then a grown were heard, at the door. No one but Ava had moved until it was all over. They all looked to the door that had been pushed open by the falling body of a man. Kris stood, looking to them with wide and frightened eyes and, the remnants of the chair still in her hands.

"She's a spy!" Ava announced, drawing all their attention back to her. She pointed to the one in Paolaria's arms. When they all looked to the girl, and they could see that now, the girl appeared much older than she had before. She was still the same size, but definitely older. She hissed at Ava again, loudly. Zachia lifted his hands and separated the girl from Paolaria. Freeing Paolaria, but keeping the girl in a shielding and holding spell. Pentilian went to her daughter as the rest kept looking from Ava, to the girl, to the couch and then to the open door and Kris and the fallen man. Emma went to Ava, going to one knee and putting an arm around her.

"Are you alright?" she asked quietly. Ava nodded, never taking her eyes from the girl.

"She was to fool us into believing that all had fled the city and to learn what she could while here," she told Zachia, still looking to the sneering girl. Zachia allowed his eyes to survey all of the room before he looked to Ava, a small grin coming to his lips. He moved his eyes and looked to Emma.

"Do you think they know how powerful their daughter is?" he asked her quietly. Emma grinned and nodded.

"Probably," she told him calmly. Zachia nodded as well and looked to the girl, who still glared at Ava.

"What is your name?" he asked her. The girl glared at him and then went back to sneering at Ava.

"She told me her name was Mesetere," Paolaria said, blushing with her embarrassment that she had been so easily fooled. Pentilian tightened her arm around her shoulder. Zachia looked to Kris, who had dropped the remainder of the chair. Guardians were tying the man's hands behind his back, as Pelidora was checking, and then sealing the gash, on the back of his head the chair had caused. He looked to her.

"Will he be alright?" he asked the elfin healer. She smiled as she looked up, nodding.

"He's going to have a very powerful headache when he wakes, but he will live," she told him. Zachia nodded and looked back to Mesetere, his face and eyes, turning hard.

"Alright young lady, start talking," he told her. She kept her sneer as she looked to him.

"Somora will defeat you and he will rule all the domains!" she yelled, and then clamped her mouth shut.

"Who's Somora," Zachia asked.

"Our King and savior," Mesetere yelled at him; "and he will defeat you all. You cannot win against him!" Zachia looked to Emma and saw her confusion, and the beginnings of her anger.

"What are you going to do?" Glornina asked as she came into the room. She had been in the reading room tending to the other children and had come to Kris after the sound of the breaking chair had come to her. She then saw the couch and her eyes opened slightly, as she turned to the dart gun held by one of the Guardians, and then to the man still on the floor. "Who was he after?" she asked very quietly, turning back to her son. Zachia pointed to Ava.

"Oh shit," Glornina whispered, very softly.

———

With the message received from Mesetere, through Mestilia that she was being taken to the Realm Somora told everybody they could move back to the city, but there was a worrying thought, nagging at the back of his mind. As soon as most had returned, he called Hantopan to him. The General arrived and he came with Mestilia, Mesetere's mother.

"The assassin has been sent Somora," Hantopan said as he entered the room. "Kaltersan is the best there is. He will not fail!" Somora nodded and looked to their most powerful talker.

"Is there anything from Mesetere?" he asked her. She shook her head, but Somora could see the worry in her eyes. "What is wrong?' he asked the mother. She looked to him and shrugged with only one shoulder.

"I'm not sure," she said quietly. "She could just be too busy to talk, or something else that is innocent, but she has gone completely silent to me." Somora looked to her for a moment, his nagging thought grew stronger.

In Namsia, Melsikan lead them all from the portal, into a gully. A soldier waited for them and immediately held a finger to his lips. He then beckoned that they should stay low and follow. The soldier turned and started up one side of the gulley. They came up behind a row of bushes, about two hundred feet from the farmhouse. As they knelt and looked to house, the Commander came to Melsikan's left and Parsony to his right.

"There are four or five inside," the Commander whispered. "Their movements have been normal, as if it were any other day." Melsikan nodded and looked around the grounds.

"What about the back?" he whispered to the Commander.

"There are two of the best there, watching," he answered as the front door of the house opened and a very large man stepped to the porch. A woman, almost as tall as the man followed him. They all watched as the two seemed to be talking.

"Brando and Brendo," Parsony whispered to Melsikan. Again Melsikan nodded as he tried to study the two. Isabella gasped quietly and Melsikan looked to her.

"He looks just like Brandaro," she whispered, not taking her eyes from the one on the porch. The two on the porch turned and reentered the house and everything got very quiet. Minutes passed as Melsikan looked around again. He didn't like the feeling he was getting.

"They've spotted us," he said in a normal tone and rose, charging the house. The rest followed quickly. As they neared, Melsikan sent a blast spell, blowing the door to pieces. He ran into the house and immediately saw that the house was empty. He ran for the back door and found it wide open. "Where are your watches?" he yelled at the Commander. The commander pointed and Melsikan ran to the spot and found the two bodies, twisted with their deaths.

"By the Divine One," Isabella said softly as Melsikan went to the bodies and checked them.

"Blast spell?" Parsony asked, coming to his side. Melsikan shook his head as he stood. He looked to Parsony and all could see, even in the dim light coming from the back door, the anger that had taken over Melsikan's face.

"This was done by someone with great strength, with their bare hands," he said, almost in a growl. He turned to the rest of the soldiers. "Spread out, in groups of three and see if you can find any tracks, leading away." The soldiers nodded. Teaming up, they began to search for foot prints. It didn't take long and a group called out that they had found tracks. Melsikan, with the others' in close pursuit, ran to them. They followed the tracks and they led straight to the corral. All could see that a section of the fence railings had been removed, and they could see the hoof prints leading to the east.

"Damn," Melsikan said, loudly.

"What are we to do now?" Daridar asked with worry in her voice.

"Jennifer, call to the Realm and tell them we need a sensitive, immediately!" Melsikan's voice told all of his anger. "Everyone, back to the house, they left in too big of a hurry to take too much with them, which means we may be able to find something personal of this Brando and Brendo!" They all returned to the house to begin their search, as Braxton appeared in the center of the main room.

On Neponia, a full squad of soldiers had preceded the parade of bandit's to the designated spot on the border. Once arrived at the crossing point, that squad spread out. They stayed to hiding, as they surveyed the area. One soldier was waiting for the Queen's, and bandit's, as they neared. "All is clear and the soldiers are in position and ready, Your Majesties. There are at least four full squadrons of Nepolia's forces nearing. Two each, from opposite directions" a soldier told them. Neponities nodded and looked around.

"Take them to the spot, I will signal when to start," she told the soldier and received an answering salute, as the others' moved forward and took control of the bandit's, pushing them closer to the ridge. On the other side of that ridge, was the border and the closing Nepolia's patrols. Neponities saw them stop, just short of the top of the ridge. She raised her hand and the soldiers scattered and hid, watching to the south. She turned to Michele. "When you see the signal, Michele," she said softly and backed away. Michele stepped forward, watching the soldier who would signal when the patrols were close. Suddenly, the soldier turned and pointed at Michele. She nodded numbly, and lifted her hand.

The bandits came alive and without looking around, ran up and over the ridge. They were quickly captured by Nepolia's forces. Once the ones on the ridge had made sure of the capture, they snuck back to the Queens. Then all returned to Capital City. Michele walked as in a trance, her head down. She was held by Crendoran's arm, for comfort.

It was after sunrise before Neponities and the others' arrived back at Capital City. Carsanac was waiting for them. The first thing he saw was the tiredness that showed on all of their faces, and the numb look to Michele's eyes. Neponities and her daughter saw him at the same time. Nepanities went into his arms and he held her as they entered the palace. The soldiers went quite happily to their beds. Servants brought coffee, spiced with brandy, as they all went to the meeting room. After they had all settled in their chairs and had several sips of their coffee, Neponities looked to Carsanac.

"I assume that all is on schedule?" she asked quietly. He nodded.

"We are actually a little ahead of schedule, Your Highness," he told her with a small grin. She looked slightly surprised.

"You have figured out how to get the deactivated stones into the southern Section and the active ones out?" she asked.

"Yes, Your Majesty," he said with a nod. "I have the plans all laid out for you," he added, sliding a small stack of parchments towards her. She reached for them and started to go through them. "Weslizorn has already begun to ship his deactivated stones, from the north and Wenzorn has stock piled the ones here, all ready to transfer to the southern section. Wespozorn has all the active stones ready to ship north." There was something in Carsanac's voice that caused Neponities to look to him. "Nepolia has ordered Wespozorn to make one hundred fifty faulty stones," he told her softly. Neponities looked at him for several seconds. "If she intends to give these stones to the rebels, it could work in our favor, as well as the defenders of Namsia," he added, explaining. Neponities nodded and glanced to her daughter, then to Michele. She worried at the look of Michele's face, but went back to reviewing the parchments Carsanac had given her. Nepelia was leaning over Neponities shoulder and looking at the papers Neponities was reviewing. Both began to nod. They glanced at each other, grinning and then turned to Carsanac.

"Do it," they both said, at the same time. Carsanac nodded, and took Nepanities to their quarters for needed sleep. Traredonar, Neponities Chosen Mate, led her to their quarters. Nepelia and Nepeslia were led to their rooms and Crendoran led Michele to theirs. Once Carsanac had Nepanities in bed and asleep, he went to the Mearlies and started the transfer of all stones. The active stones north, and deactivated stones, south.

———

Nepolia was woken, very early in the morning and told that the bandits were on their way to the castle. That gave her reason to wake completely. Then she was told that the bandits had told their newest captors that the Center Section troops had caught the rescuers near the border and a battle had been fought. The squad leader had sent the bandits on, but the bandits doubted that any of her troops had survived. Nepolia shook that off as though of no importance and quickly was dressed and went to the court yard of the castle, to greet her new troops.

———

Pastilan lay on his sleeping pedestal, but could not sleep. He had heard the warning from Somora, and he was worried. *How many of the spies had been caught?* He wondered. *Are they coming to find me?* His thoughts continued. His panic was growing with each thought. He lifted from the pedestal, went to the window and looked out. *I have got to get to a place of hiding*, he thought as his panic continued to grow, completely ignoring the number of protecting troops that stood on the web, around the building. He scurried down the ramp to the main room and then into the small room that held the orb. He quickly wrapped the orb in his extruded webbing. Taking the orb with his left front leg, he headed for the rear entrance of the web palace. His paranoiac panic was in complete control now!

In the trees around the Rulers web palace, plans were made to attack, just before sunrise. They all thought that, that would be when the guards would be the most tired and more easily surprised. Belserlan had not been able to rest, as the others were, waiting for the time to pass and had snuck in closer to the web palace that held the orb, and Pastilan. Peserlan, nearly as large as Belserlan and the one Balsarlan had sent with Belserlan, to act as his personal guard, came with him. They stopped where they had a good view of the rear door of the palace and the guards that were on watch, on the deck around the palace. They didn't speak as they both looked to all that could be seen. Peserlan was the one to spot Pastilan at the window. He nudged Belserlan and pointed. Belserlan nodded and he too watched the newest leader of the rebels. The Natharian disappeared from the window and Peserlan leaned closer to Belserlan. "You should try to get some rest," he whispered. Belserlan seemed to not hear him and Peserlan was about to repeat his advice, when Belserlan moved a little, staring intently at the rear door of the palace. Peserlan looked to where Belserlan was looking and he saw the two guards to either side of the door, swivel and go to the door and enter.

"What do you suppose that is all about?" Belserlan asked in a whisper. Peserlan was about to answer, when Pastilan stuck his head out of the door and swiveled, to look around.

"What is he doing?" Peserlan asked. Belserlan didn't have a chance to answer as Pastilan suddenly scurried from the door and into the trees, straight at Belserlan and Peserlan!

"He carries the orb," Belserlan whispered louder than he had intended.

———

Gorsentor and Garpartor nearly jump out of their skins when the crystal that had been hidden beneath a towel on the table where they sat, spoke in Weretilon's voice. "Yes!" Gorsentor said, louder than she had meant to, lifting the crystal to eye level. They listened as Weretilon told them of what was to happen. They in turn, told Weretilon what they and their son were about. They would occasionally look to each other, quite wide eyed at what they heard. When Weretilon had finished, Gorsentor said that they would be ready. They looked to each other, and then hurried to alert those working with Garteltor, that he needed to wait at least four hours, before beginning his assault.

———

In a small room, next to the server's quarters, Garteltor sat with the six, as they prepared to begin their efforts to stop Garator. They were very surprised when the lid that covered the ladder from the sewer, opened, and the youngest of Garteltor's group, crawled into the room.

"Why here?" Garteltor whispered harshly, grabbing the lad. The boy smiled and then looked very serious.

"Gorsentor say wait four hour," the boy told him. "Help come, Realm!" Garteltor looked to the boy and then around to the others'. There was confusion in every pair of eyes he looked to.

It was at least a half hour after the groups had formed, that the women of the Realm, the Queen and Weretilon returned to the King, General, and male wolves. The witch nodded to the Queen and opened a portal and the witch walked into it. Shortly, Gorpendor led the two Garsendar's, the female wolves', and Xanaleria, back to the King, General, and Gordon. The female wolves' went and stood beside their mates and Xanaleria stopped next to her mother. The two Garsendar's stopped, but Gorpendor came closer by a few steps. She looked to the King and lifted her hand towards the other two. "Real Garsendar?" she asked them. Werementran, who had used this extra time, to attend to some of the business of the farm, walked up at that time. He stopped next to the General, looking back and forth between the two Garsendar's, rather wide eyed.

"They're exactly the same," he whispered. The King, and General, nodded their agreement. Gorpendor smiled and went to the Garsendar to the Kings left. She took his arm.

"Garsendar," she told them. She then went to the other and placed her hand on the gargoyles shoulder. "Garperdar," she told them all. Those of the Realm, and of Weretoran, grinned in unison. Xanalaria turned to the King and Gordon, who stood together.

"Garsendar and Gorpendor have given Cartland a very good description of the capital city, Gartisia and, the two he will be meeting," Xanaleria told them all. Everyone nodded. "They are now going to work with Cartland on how to walk and move and how to talk, so as not to draw attention to himself. We should be ready to send Cartland in a few hours," she told them. Xanaleria then sent her message to the Realm.

"Weretilon has gone to tell Gorsentor what is planned," Xanaporia told all. Again, nods were given as looks were exchanged.

Mesetere had been taken to a separate room, and Zachia had put a shield around it, so the child couldn't send any messages. The would-be assassin had been taken to a shielded cell, not far from the captured Gaspilarians. Zachia was in his office reading all the reports that were coming in from all those in the troubled domains, though he was having difficulties trying to keep his thoughts on them. He was pleased as it seemed that all were closing on their goals. Glornina and Emma entered the office as he finished the last report. He looked to them as they sat in the two chairs in front of the desk. He immediately saw the look of concern that was in each of their eyes.

"We are not going to hurt the girl, but we do need to get as much information as we can from her," Zachia told them gently. They both nodded and Emma almost made a smile.

"Glornina and I have been talking and we think it would be best if she and I, with Ava, question her," she told him, and his mother nodded her head in agreement. Zachia looked to them both for a few moments and then nodded his concession.

"I will talk with the would-be assassin and find out what his role is in this Somora's plans," Zachia said more to himself then either of them. They nodded and the three stood. They each went to their assigned prisoner. Each held their own level of regret for what they must do.

Perilia and Dospora walked into Somora's office, talking quietly with each other. They were surprised to only see one of the lesser sorceresses cleaning the room. Before either could ask anything of her, the sorceress looked to them and told them that Somora had told her that he had something he had to do and didn't know for sure when he would be back. He had then disappeared.

"When did he do that?' Perilia asked. The sorceress looked to her and Somora's two mates saw the concern in the woman's eyes.

"Right after Mestilia and Hantopan had left," she told them. They both saw that there was an intensifying of concern in the sorceress's eyes.

"What is your concern?" Dospora asked, feeling some worry of her own. The sorceress looked to her and her concern had turned to fear.

"He was talking to himself when I came to clean, and I heard him say that moving day was coming," she told them both, looking from one to the other. Perilia and Dospora exchanged looks and left for their quarters.

CHAPTER NINE

"Brando?" Cenlinas asked as they walked the horses, allowing them to rest from their hasty departure from the farm; "where are we going?" He didn't answer right away and Cenlinas prepared to ask again. Brando, who had been leading, stopped his horse at a small stream, so the horses could drink. He looked to each of those with him, a small grin coming to the corner of one side of his mouth.

"Where is the one place they won't look for us," he asked. "The one place we can carry on with our reclaiming of Bandarson?" Corlaar and Cenlinas exchanged looks, but Brendo began to chuckle. They all looked to her, but Brando was the only one smiling. She looked to him as her grin grew to match his.

"Bandarson City," she said calmly; "that is the last place they would look." Corlaar started to join in the grin, but Cenlinas just frowned.

"We can't go there," she said. "There will be guards all over the place." Brando turned to her, his grin not lessening, and nodded.

"In the city, yes, but not in fathers castle," he said and Brendo's chuckle turned to laughter. "The castle is vacant and none want to enter. We can stay there; entering the city at night, to plan our revolt against the fools who had called for the Realm forces, and who had caused the reelection of the dwarf, Daridar and the ruining of Bandarson!" Cenlinas started to grin as Corlaar and Brendo checked the horses. In a short time, they all remounted and started for Bandarson City. Towards what they thought was to be their prosperous future.

Nepolia watched the over seventy bandits as they were marched to the holding cells, in the lower caverns of her castle. She was later told by one of the squad leaders, that almost twenty of the bandits, had tried to molest the female soldiers and had either been killed outright, or had had their hands cut off and left to bleed to death. She brushed that news off and reviewed her plans on how to use these bandits.

Carsanac and Wenzorn were progressing well with beginnings of the transference of the deactivated stones to the south. Squads of soldiers, all over the section, were starting to receive active stones from the south, through the many ravines and gullies that lead from the mines. The Queens and Princesses slept in peace, but Michele was having nightmares and Crendoran was having a difficult time trying to keep her calm.

Pastilan had sprinted a hundred feet into the trees before he stopped. He turned around to see if anyone chased after him and saw that it seemed that none had. He waited for several minutes, until he was sure his escape had not been noticed. He turned again and started to move carefully ahead, trying to think of a place he could hide safely. He had to move slowly for a Natharian had very limited peripheral vision and had to turn its entire body to look around. Belserlan and Peserlan moved to stay ahead of him and plotted how they were going to take him. They knew they had to wait until he was far enough from the web, so that any sounds made in the taking, would not be heard by the guards there.

Gorsentor and Garpartor waited at the spot they had been told that the newcomer was to appear. They looked around nervously, even though they were in a very isolated part of Gartisia. They had managed to send a messenger to their son, telling him to wait until the newcomer came to him. Suddenly, they were looking at the one from Weretoran, wide eyed.

"Who you?" they asked quietly. Cartland, in gargoyle form, smiled.

"Me Garperdar," he said in perfect accent and tone.

"Go," Gorsentor whispered harshly and the two took Cartland's arms. They pulled him into an alley. As they traveled to the meeting place with their son's cohorts, Gorsentor and Garpartor told Garperdar what was happening in the Rulers castle. He listened intently as he looked around to the squalid conditions of the city. It sickened him that these creatures were required to live this way!

Immediately after Garperdar/Cartland had disappeared, with Xanaporia's spelling, Gordon turned to the King; "There's nothing to do now, but wait for Cartland's report." The King nodded and looked to Werementran.

"You do have some burtanlias, don't you?" The Kings voice told of the strain he was feeling for the events of the day. Werementran nodded and led the way to the house and the brandy like drink that they all thought a good idea.

"Would it be possible for one or more of your staff to now show us the area around your farm?" Grrale asked of Werementran, as the wolves' were not really interested in the brandy idea. Werementran looked to the King, who looked to Gordon.

"I don't see why not," he told the King with a shrug. "There's no telling how long it will be before Cartland can report." The King nodded and looked to Werementran and nodded. Werementran nodded and beckoned the same young man that had chased down Garsendar.

"This is Weresanran," he told all, when the young man had come to them. The ones from the Realm said hello, with a slight bow, at the same time. "Would you and your wife take our wolf visitors on a tour of the area around the farm, so they can see what Weretoran is like?" Werementran asked him. Weresanran looked to the wolves and smiled as he nodded.

"It would be my honor," he said with a slight bow. "I will fetch my wife and rejoin you in seconds," he told them and turned and walked to a building next to the barn. Shortly, he returned with a very attractive woman, who was only slightly shorter than he. The two stopped short of the wolves' and those of the Realm. "This is my wife Weremislon," he told them and the woman bowed. Her bow was answered with bows.

"Try to stay within fifty miles or so," Werementran said, as the rest turned back to the house and the burtanlias. Weresanran nodded to their backs, and then looked to the wolves'.

"Are you ready?' he asked. The wolves' nodded their readiness. The man and woman shifted to their wolf form. "Alright, follow us. If you have any question, do not hesitate to ask. Me, or Weremislon, will be very happy to tell you what you seek." He and his wife led them eastward from the farm, towards the fields and the lands past them. They quickly settled into the traveling trot, that all wolves' seemed to know. They talked as they traveled. The first thing that the wolves of the Realm learned, was that the Werewolves usually only shifted to wolf form when they slept, played, traveled, or battled. Xanaleria had looked over her shoulder just in time to see the werewolves shift to wolf and she was able to compare them, side by side,

to the wolves' of the Realm. She was surprised to see that
they weren't any bigger than those who had come with her.

———

Zachia entered the cell that held the assassin. The man
glared at him from the bunk he lay on. The gargoyles
had started to holler and scream at Zachia, as soon he
had come to the cell block. He looked to them. Abruptly,
though they still jumped to the bars of their cell and,
around in it, there was no sound heard. The man had seen
this happen. His eyes had opened with realization of the
power the Overseer possessed, but when Zachia turned
back to him, a glare had returned to his face.

"What is your name?" Zachia asked, his voice hard. The
man continued his glare. Zachia began to find anger. "I
asked you your name and I would recommend that you tell
me, or this is going to get very unpleasant for you!" The
man blinked, but his glare stayed. He was trying to figure
out why Somora was not spelling him out of here, or killing
him. "Alright, have it your way," Zachia said tiredly. The
assassin was suddenly hanging upside down, his feet near
the high ceiling of the cell. Zachia sat down on the bunk.
"How many times to you think you can be bounced off of
the floor, before you die?" Zachia asked quietly, looking up
to the man. The man looked to him, then the floor, and
then back to Zachia.

"Kaltersan," the assassin said, his voice a little higher
pitched and panicked, than he would have liked.

"Who sent you here, and why?" Zachia asked without changing the tone of his voice.

"Put me down first," Kaltersan demanded. Zachia had a small grin as he shook his head slowly. Kaltersan's glare returned. Zachia let him drop within a foot of the floor and then put him back to the ceiling, rather harshly.

"Who sent you, and why?" Zachia asked again, his voice was much less patient. The now wider eyes of the assassin looked to him with fear.

"Somora," he said; "and I was to kill the girl, for she sensed Somora City and, him."

"What is Somora's purpose?" Zachia asked. Kaltersan looked to him, hesitating. Then, without warning, Kaltersan went limp. "Kaltersan?" Zachia called to him. There was no reply. Zachia looked to the man for several moments and then lowered him to the floor. He went to the body and felt the neck. He felt no pulse and pulled his hand back. Still kneeling on one knee, he stared at the remains of the assassin. "Did Somora take your life to stop you from talking?' he asked the obvious.

Mesetere had been trying to send a message to her mother since she had first seen Ava. She continued her efforts as she sat in the room, alone. She heard the lock working and got ready. She knew that the room must be shielded and she also knew that when that door opened, it would be the only chance she had to get a message to her King.

She watched the door and when it began to swing open, she began to send with all of her might. Ava pushed the two in front of her, into the room and quickly slammed the door. Glornina and Emma looked to her. "She was trying to send a message," Ava told them, not taking her eyes from Mesetere. The two women looked to the girl, their eyes harder than Mesetere liked.

"Alright Mesetere," Glornina said, coming closer; "we've got some questions, and you are going to answer them!" She was shocked when the girl looked at her and smiled, as she shook her head. Mesetere started to mutter as her hand suddenly shot up, aimed at Glornina. Ava was faster. Mesetere could not send her blast spell, as she was now locked in an immobilization spell. Glornina and Emma jerked their sights to Ava and worried for the small grin they saw on the girls face. They looked back to Mesetere in time to see the girl's eye lids flutter and then close. Her body, locked in the spell, couldn't move much, but it sagged slightly. Glornina and Emma exchanged looks and went to either side of the girl.

"Release her," Emma said to Ava. The girl lifted her hand again and Mesetere's body started to fall off the stool she had been sitting on. The women grabbed her and Glornina's hand felt the neck of the girl. She looked to Emma, her eyes wide, and sad.

"She's dead," Glornina whispered.

"Somora killed her," Ava said softly, her young eyes beginning to fill with tears.

Mestilia, Gapilarian and Hantopan entered Somora's office and found it empty. They looked around and then talked of what they were to do. A good hour passed before Somora appeared. He looked to them and he wore a half grin. "I have received a message from Kaltersan," Mestilia told him immediately. "He has been captured before he could kill the girl and asked to be taken out of there." Somora looked to her and shook his head slightly. He lifted his hand and then looked to the three.

"He should not have failed me," he said coarsely. "Prepare to move our people. The Overseer has found us. We will have to move to another location. I have found a domain that is safe, remote, and should serve our purposes well. We will go there. Now hurry, time is our enemy now!" The three looked to him and then turned to leave, when Mestilia cried out. "What is it?" Somora asked with considerable concern. Mestilia turned to him.

"Mesetere has screamed a message. She says to get out, the Overseer is coming!" Mestilia looked to Somora pleading. "Please bring her back to me," she begged. Somora looked to her and lifted his hand, muttering. When his hand lowered, he looked to Mestilia and slowly shook his head.

"The shielding was too strong to teleport her," he told her. She stared at him as the meaning of his words penetrated her mind. Tears came to her eyes, as the truth settled into her heart. "She did not suffer," Somora told her, trying to soften his words, but failing. Mestilia's heart became empty at that moment, but it refilled quickly, with hate, for the endangerment done without care, by the murderer of her daughter.

It was early morning, not long before the sun was to rise, before Garplasar could get into the city. He was thoroughly enraged by that time and even the Gaspilarians didn't want to be near him. The people had finally stopped walking the streets, though he could still hear the loud voices of some, coming from somewhere. He eased onto the street from the deserted castle and started to where the boys mind had told him, the mayor's house would be. He was sure that the mayor would know where to find the rebels and he intended to get that information! He had finally found the building he had sought. He started to cast a door opening spell, but was startled by a roaring of a voice behind him.

"Hold it right there you!" someone yelled. An enraged Garplasar turned to see who would dare challenge a Wizard. He saw at least two dozen men around him and the Gaspilarians, and they were armed! This was the last straw as far as Garplasar was concern!

"Grab!" he yelled to the Gaspilarians. With very little hand movement, he spelled himself and Gaspilarians, back to his castle. He was shaking with his rage when he appeared in his magic room. The Gaspilarians knew it and scattered just as soon as they were sure they were home. "Those rebels," he started to roar, causing any in hearing range to flee, or hide, which was just about everyone; "are not worth the trouble! If Garator wants to deal with them, he can. I will have nothing more to do with them!"

In the cabin, those of the Realm had found many personal items the rebels had left behind and it only took a few minutes for Braxton to separate them to the ones who had last handled them. Once he had knowledge of them, Braxton began searching for them with his senses. The rest waited, watching him, as the sounds of the night came through the doors and windows.

"There are four of them and they travel south west," Braxton told them. "Brando, Brendo, Cenlinas and a man called Corlaar."

"Can you read their destination?" Melsikan asked quietly. Braxton nodded.

"A place called Bandarson City," he told him.

"The castle," Isabella whispered and all turned to her; "that is the last place anyone would expect." Melsikan nodded and turned to Parsony.

"Gather the soldiers," he told him. Parsony nodded and left the room. Melsikan looked to Braxton again. "Can you see if they carry the orb?" he asked. Braxton nodded.

"They do," was all he told Melsikan.

"We are ready," Parsony said, entering the front door.

"What do you plan now?" Daridar asked. Melsikan didn't answer her immediately. He turned to Jennifer.

DEFIANCE OF THE REALM

"Can you talk with any in Namsia City?" he asked her. She shrugged. "Start looking and find out please." She nodded and started sending to the city. Melsikan turned to the Mayor and Parsony. "It will take them several days to get to the castle and I intend to be waiting for them when they get there!" Melsikan looked to Jennifer and she shook her head. "Alright, everyone outside," he ordered. They all left the house and gathered in front of the soldiers. Melsikan sent Braxton back to the Canyon and then opened a portal. The sun was just lighting the eastern sky, when they came out on the street, directly in front of the castle gate. Melsikan turned to Isabella and Daridar. "How much do you remember of the layout of the castle?" he asked them both. Isabella shook her head and Daridar smiled. Melsikan looked to her strangely. She turned to Parsony.

"Find Besaline," was all she said to him. Isabella nodded her agreement, as her grin grew, remembering the female slave master for Brandaro.

———

Neponities was the first of the royals to wake, shortly after mid day. She quickly bathed, dressed and went to her rather small dining room for coffee. She was very shocked, and worried, to find Michele being comforted by Crendoran, sitting at the table and it was very obvious that they had slept little, if any at all. "Michele?" she asked coming to the woman, her concern showing in her voice. "What is the matter?" Michele just shook her head slowly. It was Crendoran who answered her.

"She didn't sleep well," he told the Queen. "She kept having nightmares."

"Oh no," Neponities said as she gently touched Michele's shoulder. "Is what we asked you to do with the minds of the bandits, the cause of these nightmares?" Neponities saw Michele's small nod as her tears fell.

"If I had thought for one second, that you would suffer so, I would not have allowed you to do it," Neponities said softly, kneeling beside Michele. Neponities saw Michele's efforts to try and smile. Neponities could plainly see the pain in Michele's eyes, when the woman answered. "It was what was needed to be done," Michele told the Queen, her tears trying to interfere with her voice. "Don't worry, I'll be alright soon." Neponities tried to believe her, trying to give a smile of support, but she fell short of her goal. They were suddenly interrupted by Nepanities voice.

"Has anyone heard from Carsanac?" Nepanities asked as she, Nepelia and Nepeslia, came into the room. Two of the three at the table shook their heads. "What is the trouble?" Nepanities asked noticing the look on her mother's face.

"Michele couldn't sleep for nightmares, because of what she has done to the minds of the bandits," Neponities said softly. There was immediately looks of concerns on the three new arrivals faces.

"Are you alright Michele?" Nepanities asked softly, as she too knelt by Michele, next to her mother. Neponities easily saw Michele fight for another smile.

"I will be. I just have to get used to it, that's all," she told them all. Crendoran squeezed her shoulders gently. "Don't worry, I'll be alright soon." They all heard her say. Neponities was not the only one to then hear Nepelia's voice.

"Can we get some coffee?" Nepelia asked one of the servants, loudly; "and add brandy to hers!" Neponities saw that she pointed to Michele. Even Michele managed to laugh, but only a little.

Although the clothing worn by the women of the Southern Section covered more of their bodies than either the Central or Northern sections, there was still a lot of exposed skin. When Nepolia walked into the holding cell area, the bandits showed their desires for her and the other female's, loudly! She smiled at the lewd and vulgar things the bandits said they wanted to do to her and the rest. She turned to Calitoran. "Find some of the local women that are mostly willing and bring them for our guests," she told him. Calitoran nodded and left to pass on his mistress's order. *Yes*, she thought as she looked over the brutish males; *I will train them and they will serve me in the defeat of Neponities. Then I will let them have her and, that daughter of hers!*

Belserlan and Peserlan had stayed ahead of, but still near the panicked Pastilan for almost an hour. Finally, Pastilan stopped to rest, high in the trees. Belserlan and Peserlan moved closer, carefully.

"I will try to wrap Pastilan, to capture," Belserlan whispered. "You get the orb." Peserlan nodded and they closed in on the fleeing Ruler. Belserlan could easily see that Pastilan was tired and that he was obviously trying to find a place to get some sleep before he moved on. The two watched as the would-be Ruler, found a place that satisfied his needs and went to a resting position. They moved even closer as Pastilan started to sleep. They moved behind and above him and prepared to attack. "Now," Belserlan whispered and the two landed on the unprepared Pastilan. Pastilan screamed out in fear, as the larger Belserlan began to wrap him with his webbing, as Peserlan tore the orb from Pastilan's surrounding leg. In less than a minute, Pastilan was completely helpless and Belserlan was holding the orb that Peserlan had given him. "Go for the others', I will stand guard over this coward," Belserlan told Peserlan. Peserlan nodded, and scurried away into the darkness of the night. Belserlan moved around so he could look into Pastilan's terrorized eyes. "Now tell me, who has been guiding you?" he asked. Pastilan started to open his mouth, but then suddenly stiffened. His eyes closed, his body becoming quite still. Belserlan looked to him for several minutes, but Pastilan never moved, or opened his eyes again. Belserlan moved closer to check Pastilan. It did not take long for him to realize that Pastilan was dead. "Now what has caused this?" he asked himself in a whisper. It was many minutes later when the reinforcements arrive. Belserlan told them all what had happened and the talker of the group passed the word to the Realm. There were many relieved people in the Realm, that at least one of the orbs had been recovered.

———

With Garperdar/Cartland in tow, Gorsentor and Garpartor arrived at their home. They found the six that were to be the second stage of their sons plan, waiting for them. They told them that a messenger had been sent, but were not sure that Garteltor had received the word in time. That he may have already begun the first part of the plan to destroy Garator. Gorsentor introduced Garperdar/Cartland to them, explaining that he was from the Realm and was here to help with the rescue of Gorastor and the overthrow of Garator. They all bowed to him, but there was more than one that looked to him with less than trust in their eyes.

"Hurry, go," Garcordor, Garteltor's second in command and leader of this group said, pointing to the door. "Garteltor wait." They all nodded and started out the door. Garperdar/Cartland reassured Gorsentor and then quickly followed the others'.

———

They were all sitting the large dining room, eating breakfast and talking, while the wolves' shared their breakfast with Weresanran and Weremislon, in their wolf form, out on the lawn. Jennifer suddenly grinned widely, looking to Gordon.

"What is it?" Gordon asked, drawing the attention of all present.

"The orb on Natharia has been recovered and the rebels there, have been beaten," she told them. "Blautdarn, fourth son of Bleudarn is now the Ruler and very willing to continue the agreements with the Realm!" The ones from the Realm cheered quietly as those from Weretoran looked at them with doubt of their sanity.

"Has there been any word from Namsia?" Xanaporia asked Jennifer quietly. Jennifer concentrated for a moment. She then looked to her and then the rest from the Realm, her eyes told of concerns.

"They say that the unknown ones have eluded their first attempt of capture, but feel that they will have them soon," she told them softly. There were exchanged looks among the visitors.

"What does this mean?' Werelaran asked. The rest of the Weretorians nodded their interest. Gordon looked to him and then the others' around the table.

"As you all know, there have been messages from the Domains of Natharia and Neponia, sent to the rebels in Namsia," he said gently. The Weretorians nodded. "Well, it seems that these rebels seem to be at the center of all the activity and Zachia has sent a team to try and reclaim the orb they have stolen and, to stop them from creating the rebellion. The capture of the orb in Natharia, takes away one leg of those threats." The King nodded. The rest of the Weretorians looked to him, and joined in his nodding.

"So, if they can stop the rebels, there will be no chance of Garator joining them in his plans to conquer Weretoran?" Werelaran said more than asked. Gordon nodded to him.

"That leaves only to stop those of Neponia from joining the rebels on Namsia and the stopping of Garator, and recovery of the girl taken," Gordon told him. The Weretorians looked to each other, and then to those of the Realm.

"Let us hope that those endeavors end soon and, simply," Wereselon whispered. They all nodded their same hopes.

Emma, Glornina, and Ava, met Zachia in his office. The two women went immediately to the brandy cart and poured their glasses quite full. They each took a rather large drink before turning to Zachia. Ava had gone to the couch and had sat, her head down, her hands gripping each other.

"The girl is dead," Emma said, her voice breaking slightly as she went and sat on the couch with Ava, putting her arm around the girl.

"Ava said that Somora had killed her," Glornina said as she sat in the chair in front of Zachia's desk. "Whoever this Somora is, I would like some personal time with him, to explain that it is wrong to kill children!" Her voice told of her rage. Zachia nodded his understanding.

"The assassin was killed also," he said softly. The three looked to him. "I would like some one-on-one time with this Somora, myself!" His voice was soft, but his words showed the rage that had come to him as well. After a few minutes, he turned to Ava. "You said that these people are in the Dark City?" he asked her and she looked to him, nodding. "Can you sense if they have returned to the city yet?" Ava stared at him for a moment and then closed her eyes. Minutes passed as they watched her. She was nodding even before she opened her eyes.

"They are still there, but I sense a fear and a panic. I think they prepare to leave," she told Zachia. He nodded and looked to Emma.

"Spread the word, I want Tarson to prepare a small army, for we are going to try and catch this Somora!" he told her. She nodded, as she began to send messages.

Somora had not given Mestilia time to mourn her daughter and had had her sending messages to the yet unfound spies, that they were to stay put and they would be contacted as soon as Somora had moved all to the safe domain. Mestilia was now in her house, packing what she had been told to, but she kept finding the clothes and toys of her daughter and her tears couldn't stop. Her rage against Somora grew with each item of Mesetere's she found. She finally decided that she had to do something to stop Somora. She wrote a long note to the Overseer, knowing that any he would send must find it, so she left it on the table. As she carried her bag to the area where Somora was to open the portal, she

DEFIANCE OF THE REALM

plotted what she could do to spoil Somora's plans, while she was with him in the new domain. She almost smiled as thoughts came to her. She started her efforts by sending some messages to some of the spies who had places of power if the Domains of Rightful Magic.

Somora opened the portal and all of his people, demons, goblins, dragons, and all of the Gargoyles, followed him through it, except for six. These six began going through each of the houses, looking for things that might lead any invaders to where they might be. One of them found Mestilia's letter, and told his superior, who told Somora. Somora did not waste any amount of time before he killed Mestilia.

CHAPTER TEN

Nepolia and Depelia walked in the court yard of castle, talking. "Wespozorn will have a hundred and fifty faulty stones ready, shortly after Exchange Day," Nepolia said softly. Depelia looked to her wide eyed.

"Why would you have him make faulty stones?" she asked in a harsh whisper. Nepolia smiled as she stopped and looked to her.

"We will have fresh and fully powered stones, when we bring the rebels here, including their leader, Brando. We will give the faulty stones to them and then send them back to Namsia." Depelia looked more confused than before. Nepolia's smile widened. "We will follow them and when they try to use the stones to beat their enemies, we will be there to take over when they fail!" Depelia's eyes were widening with each of her Queens words.

"But You Majesty," Depelia said; "why would we want to do that?" Nepolia's eyes turned harder than normal.

"Because," she said in a quiet, enrage voice; "we will be able to not only have the remaining rebels as a force to use against Neponities, we will have the entire population of the Bandit's Domain to use!" Depelia began to see that her Queen was quite insane. "We must send a message to Brando that we will bring him here in four days, to give him what he demands," Nepolia said, taking Depelia's arm and leading her roughly, to the orb room.

———

Beling listened to the report from the Squad Leader of the Mayors guards, of the strange creatures they had tried to capture at the mayors house. "It just disappeared?' he asked quietly. The Commander nodded.

"It, and the little ones that had grabbed its cloak," the Squad Leader said; "and believe me, those things were really, really, ugly!" Beling knew that he had to tell Melsikan of this and left for the castle, with the Squad Leader in tow.

———

As they traveled, Brando and Corlaar led, Brendo and Cenlinas followed. Their pace was faster than would normally be done, but Brando wanted to be in the castle as quickly as he could, so he pushed the horses and those with him, as hard as he dared.

"Brando, we must rest the horses," Corlaar said. "They cannot keep this pace constantly." Brando glared at him.

"He's right brother, we must rest them," Brendo added. Cenlinas agreed. Finally, even Brando nodded to the need. They slowed and then stopped and dismounted. They started walking.

"There is a stream about a mile from here," Corlaar said. "We can get a drink there." Again Brando nodded. All could see that his thoughts were at the castle and what must be done there.

"What about something to eat?" Cenlinas asked. "I'm starving!"

"The Benderlese farm is near there as well," Corlaar said, looking back to her. "We should be able to get something there." Cenlinas nodded and walked on, as Brendo watched her brother. Brando suddenly stopped and looked to her.

"When we were at Corlaar's, did you receive anything on the orb?" he asked her. She didn't turn from his eyes as she slowly shook her head. He stared at her for several seconds and turned started walking again.

"What are your thoughts Brando?" Brendo asked. He glanced over his shoulder at her, and then looked forward again.

"We are on our own now," he said softly. That was when Brendo heard a muffled voice coming from the large bundle behind the saddle on her horse.

When the reinforcements had arrived, Belserlan told them what had happened to Pastilan. His explanation was immediately accepted. The wrappings were cut from Pastilan's body and it was shoved from its perch, to fall to the forests floor. The dead were mourned on Natharia, but the bodies were sent to the forests floor, where scavengers would quickly make it disappear. Vastalan lead them back to the web house where Dasilan awaited them. When they entered, Belserlan saw that that there was another Natharian there. The new one was almost as big as Belserlan and standing with a power that gave Belserlan a confidence in this obviously young Natharian.

"Belserlan, this is Blautdarn, fourth son of Bleudarn," the resistance leader told him. "He will be the new Ruler." Belserlan bowed to the new ruler.

"May I ask," Belserlan said softly; "what your intensions are concerning the association with the Realm?" Blautdarn smiled.

"I see no reason to change the agreement that had been before," the new Ruler stated, in a young voice. Belserlan grinned and bowed again.

"The Overseer will be glad to hear that," he said and glanced to the talker. She nodded and started to pass on the news to the panel in the Realm.

"You can also tell them that the Commanders of the armies have been defeated and the armies are turning to Blautdarn, as he is well known to most of them," Dasilan told her. She looked to Belserlan and he nodded. She smiled as she sent her message.

When Gorastor and Gorpeelia were led back to the dining room by the two trainers, to prepare for Garator's evening meal, they had a simple plan. The three would try to keep Gorpeelia as far from Garator as they could. Thankfully, when Garator came to the dining room, he was not in the mood to molest them, as he had other thoughts on his mind, though those he had brought with him to the meal looked them over, completely. He had brought several of the council members, as well as his Armies General with him and they were all too busy to grab any of the females. Gorastor listened to all that was said between the Ruler and the ones who had come with him, unconcerned of the eyes of these strangers. She was surprised that Garplasar had not found a talker yet. In fact, the Ruler had not heard from the wizard in days and Garator seemed furious about that! When they returned to the server's quarters, after the meal, Gorastor had the beginnings of a final plan. She gathered all the servers and began asking many questions. She was very pleased to learn that most of the servers knew many of the females in the harem, as the harem was only a short distance from their quarters. She smiled at them as she told them what she plotted. It did not take long, and all the servers were smiling with her!

Garperdar/Cartland was led through many dark alleys. He was trying to ask question of those closest to him, when Garcordor, the leader, stopped them all and put his hand to Garperdar/Cartland's chest, pushing. "Garteltor tell," he whispered harshly, with anger in his eyes; "quiet!" Garperdar nodded, and followed quietly, as he was led on. They arrived at the grated recess and Garperdar/Cartland looked to the sewer river. Even with the limited sense of smell his Gargoylian body had, the smell of that water was sickening. He looked wide eyed as the others' took their clothes off and were putting them into bags. The one closest to him, held out his bag to Garperdar/Cartland and pointed to his clothes, then to the bag. He stripped and shoved his meager clothes into the bag. The staffs that had been carried were handed to one as the leader waded into the water, took a breath and disappeared below the surface. He reappeared on the other side of the grate. The next in line followed his actions. The last one, before Garperdar/Cartland, handed the staffs through the grate and followed the others'. When all were on the other side of the grate, Garperdar/Cartland took his breath, fighting the want to vomit; he too went under the water. He surfaced next the others'. Without waiting, they all took the next ones wrist and started into the tunnel.

By the end of breakfast, they had decided that it would be a good idea that the humans get to see some of Weretoran, as the wolves' had. The problem was that they didn't have any animals that could be ridden, on the farm. They only had the humongous draft animals that pulled the huge cargo wagons that carried the produce from the farm. Werementran had an answer.

"You can open a portal?" he asked Xanaporia. She nodded, as did Xanaleria. The council member smiled. "There is a mountain top that is flat and large, that overlooks this entire area," he told them.

"If you could describe where it is, I can open a portal to it," she told him. He nodded and pointing in the direction of the mountain top, he told her all about it. She finally nodded and they all readied as she opened the portal. Werelaran and Wereselon led the way and they all traveled to the mountain.

They walked around the huge plateau, looking out over the beauty of Weretoran. Each of the Weretorians pointed out different places of interest and the wolves' added the things they had seen the day before. All of the Realm raved about the splendor of Weretoran. It came lunch time and Xanaporia opened a portal back to the farm. The staff of the farm had arranged a large picnic on the vast lawn. They all enjoyed a very pleasant meal and the lazy afternoon after. Completely relaxed and swapping jokes, they all shared the moment. Suddenly, Cartland's voice screamed into Xanaleria's mind.

"I need help, now!" he screamed to her. She opened her mind to all that she could. "The girl has started a revolt and it's a battlefield here! I need help!" They not only heard Cartland's call for help, they could also hear the background noises he could hear. There were screams of pain and anger, both male and female. There were the sounds of things exploding and crashing. Even the Weretorians could hear what was happening. They looked to each other and then to Xanaleria, in fear.

Zachia looked out over the small army Tarson had gathered. He felt a gentle tap on his arm and looked to his son, standing beside him.

"I'm going with you," Mike told him. There was no mistaking the seriousness of his words. Zachia looked to Emma. She showed a very worried grin, with a small shrug of her shoulder. He nodded and started to open the portal when Ava stopped him.

"They're no longer there," she told him. He looked to her for several moments.

"Do you know where they went?' he asked as calmly as he could. He could see her concentrating. She looked to him and her eyes told him before her voice did.

"No, I can't find them anywhere," she said quietly and Zachia heard the regret in her voice. He gave her a one armed hug and opened the portal.

Almost every one of Somora's people gasped as they exited the portal, except the goblins and the fire dragons. They grinned as they looked over the land before them. The goblins had all heard the stories of the land that Palakrine had taken their ancestors from and although this was not that planet, to them, it was. The dragons simply enjoyed the heat. The temperature was hot, but not unbearable. The air seemed heavy with the humidity. There were some trees that looked almost familiar, but most of the foliage was of an unfamiliar nature. The stone ruins of a city, that Somora was leading them to, lent an eerie aspect that most found uncomfortable. When Somora had reached the outskirts of that city, he climbed up on a fallen statue, that seemed not quite human in configuration and he looked over those gathering in front of him.

"We are where we can rebuild our purposes," he told them after they had settled. "We cannot assume, as we did before, that we are invincible. We need to move slower and, more carefully." His voice turned harsh. "We will also, move with more determination to cause havoc and panic, for those who feel superior! Those who would have us follow, as pets, to obey without question, or need!" There were many nodding heads answering him, but a few looked to him with worry and fear. Somora lifted his hand and pointed to the ruined city behind him. "This city will become our home. From here, we will teach those who would rule, that we are not to be denied!" A great roar from those before him, told of their continued devotion. Somora smiled.

Two large creatures stood, hidden in the brush and trees, not too far from where Somora spoke to his people. They were tall, even though the legs they stood with were slightly bent. They were powerfully built and the claws at the end of fingers and toes, told of their capabilities. Their muzzles were wide and there were fangs showing, even with their mouths shut. A mane of dark orange-red fur circled their necks, blending into the red hair that covered their heads. Their noses, were very wide, but did not extend very far out from their faces. Their yellow, slit eyes, watched and their lifted, short, pointed ears, listened to Somora and the response of those gathered around him. "We will again have to feed on those who know nothing," Liaganost growled softly, looking at the distant gathering. The one standing slightly ahead of and to Liaganost's left slowly shook his head. Liaganost looked to him strangely. "What are your thoughts Lianost?" he asked the larger Listaman.

"These are different than what was before," Lianost, Pride leader of the Listamans, said softly. "These are smarter and, I sense a power in them," he told his second in command. "We will watch them and learn of this power. Then I will decide what we shall do." The two eased back into the bushes and trees, returning to the bramble covered main den that was their home.

—·—

Zachia led the army of thirty, which included six sensitive's, from the portal on the east end of what used to be the Dark City. Ava, holding Emma's hand was to his right side. Mike, his eyes going everywhere, was to his left. The portal closed and they stood looking over the city. The absolute silence that stared back at them, tried to unnerve them.

"There are no birds singing," Ava whispered. They all nodded, but Mike had a strange look on his face, that his father did not miss. Zachia turned to the army.

"Spread out in groups of five and start searching. You are looking for anything that might give us an idea of what they were about while they were here, or where they might have gone," he commanded. There were nods of understanding. The army split into six groups, fanning out into the city. Zachia, Emma, Mike, and Ava, started for the central fortress. Zachia could not stop the old stories of those who had attacked that building, searching for Castope, from haunting him.

Nepolia and Depelia entered the orb room and the Queen pointed to the orb. "Tell the ones in Bandarson that we will bring them to us in four days," she told Depelia quietly. Depelia nodded, not looking to her Queen and went to the orb.

Salirous, the talker who had come with Belserlan, whispered to him. The others' looked to him. Belserlan nodded and looked to Blautdarn. "The Overseer has said that until the other orbs have been found and, those who took them are caught and punished, I am to bring this orb back to the Realm," he told the newly announced Ruler. "Have no fear," he added, seeing the look that came to Blautdarn's eyes. "As soon as the others' has been found and returned, this one will be returned to you." Blautdarn nodded his understanding of the need for this. "In the name of the Overseer, and all those of all the Domains of rightful magic, I say thank you. We are happy that Natharia has been returned to those whose heart lies with the Rightful Magic," he told all. He and the ones from the Realm disappeared.

———

Gorastor, Gorpeelia, and one of the lead servers, snuck into the harem. They had heard that Garator had not visited there that night and Gorastor had said that they needed to talk with the girls there immediately. The other servers spread out through the castle, talking with other females and males, who were the slaves that worked the many other jobs that were needed to, keep the castle running. No one saw, or even thought about, the one in the harem that stayed separate from the group huddled around Gorastor. She listened to what was said and then slipped out another door, heading for Garator's office. She met up with a few others' who carried the same message for their Ruler.

———

The General of Garator's Armies and several of the council members, from the more powerful provinces, were in Garator's throne room, trying to calm the irate Ruler and not doing a very good job of it. Finally, Garator stood and looked to them, one by one. His eyes settled on his general.

"Find Garplasar," the Ruler growled deeply and quietly, at the general. The general nodded several times, turned to his aide and waved his hand, shooing the aide from the room. The aide nodded several hundred times, very rapidly and left to find Garplasar. The aide was very happy to be out of the presence of the enraged Ruler, even if that meant going to the Wizard's castle! The girl from the harem and those with her arrived just seconds after the aide's departure. They burst in the door, screaming of Gorastor's plot of revolution!

Those of the harem had readily agreed to Gorastor's plots. They all spread out through the castle, passing on the talks of revolution. Very quickly, hundreds of slaves began to gather in the main hall of the castle and, they were ready to fight!

In the dark room, near the server's quarters, Garperdar/ Cartland told Garteltor what was to be their plan, as, unknown to them, the slaves were gathering in the main hall. They became alerted when the sounds of a squad of castle guards passed the room, yelling of the revolution. One of them even yelled the name, *Gorastor*. Garteltor looked around to the twelve in the room and then to Cartland. "Sister," he whispered and started for the door. They surged from the room and followed the guards. They had not traveled far when they were challenged by four guards, with drawn swords. There were two in front of them and two who had come up behind them, from a crossing passageway. The fourteen were unarmed, except for staffs, and Cartland saw a disaster in the making. He made his decision quickly. Dismissing the plans that had been made for him to infiltrate the castle personnel, Cartland changed back to his human form and sent four wide spread blast spells, in less than a second. The ones with him were so stunned by what he had done, that he had to tell them three times to get the guards weapons. As this was happening, most of the guards, of the castle, were attacking those gathered in the main hall. The problem the guards had, was that most of those slaves had taken swords, lances and anything else they could from those they served, or from the armory! The guards were quickly driven back by the weapons and numbers of the slaves. Cartland and Garteltor, and the other ten, ran into the back of one of the main groups of retreating guards, and they could hear the sounds of guards coming from behind them. That's when Cartland called for help.

Gordon immediately started to organize their forces. He told Serryle to stay with the King and Queen, as Xanaleria could talk with her. He told Xanaporia to be ready to teleport them all to where Cartland was.

"We will fight with you," the King said, standing tall. Wereselon looked at him, stunned. Gordon looked to him and shook his head.

"You must stay here, Your Majesty, to make the preparations, in case we fail," Gordon told him. Wereselon took her husband's arm.

"He is correct Werelaran. You must plan our defenses," she told him, with pleading in her eyes.

"Have you got a lock on him?" Gordon asked Xanaleria and she nodded. Gordon could see the worry in her eyes. He looked to Xanaporia and she nodded her readiness. "Alright, let's go!" Gordon said. Xanaporia waved her hand and said her spell. Gordon, Xanaporia, Xanaleria and the three wolves', now stood in the middle of the battle.

Zachia entered the fortress with Mike beside him. Emma was behind him and she held Ava's hand. They carefully searched the fortress, room by room, floor by floor. They found nothing that would give them any idea, or sense, of where those who had been here had been up to, or, where they had gone. Then they found the room that had to be Somora's office. Zachia went directly to the large desk and began going through the drawers. Emma went to the different tables and even looked behind the couch that was against one wall. Mike stopped next to Ava and placed his hand on her shoulder. Ava stood in the center of the room, her eyes closed. Emma spotted the two first and told Zachia with her mind. He looked first to his son, who stood tall for his age and saw the boy's eyes were slightly glazed. He looked to the girl and then to Emma, confusion in his eyes. She shrugged back at him. Ava slowly opened her eyes and looked to Zachia. He saw the fear that had come to her eyes.

"They have gone to some that will help them and they will be a danger for all domains. Especially those to be found in the future," she said softly, but clearly. A single tear rolled down her cheek as Emma came from one direction and Zachia, the opposite. They both knelt and put a hand on the girl's shoulders. "I want my daddy," Ava said in a whisper. Emma and Zachia looked to each other, after a glance at Mike. They both saw that their son now looked to the floor, but slowly lifted his eyes until he looked at his father. Zachia worried for the hard look in his son's eyes. He and Emma again looked to Ava and they were both unsure of how they could help the girl.

———————

The Fire dragons, now eight in number, took off immediately after Somora's speech, looking for a place they could call home. The rest walked into the stone ruins, and began the process of figuring out how to make a home of what was there. It did not take them long, with their magical powers, and the ruins began to become livable buildings, though all of the Gargoyles stayed to one area of the city. Somora, with Perilia and Dospora, went to the largest of the ruins and Somora began planning his castle. By the end of that day, most all had a home and were spelling the items for their needs. Firewood was brought to all and they began to settle into their new domain. All during these transformations, Somora thought about what he was going to do about his desires. He had done the initial transformations to the ruin that was to be his castle, but then his two comates took over to finish. He went to the roof of the building. He watched as those who had come with him, changed the ruins into a living city. His thoughts raced as he plotted. He talked with the two spies that only he knew were still in the Realm, of what was happening around the domains. At first, the news of what Mestilia had done with her messages, enraged him, but as they talked further, with a few ideas the spies had imagined, slowly a smile was soon fighting for control of his lips. He went to his comates, telling them that he would be back shortly. They watched as he walked off in the direction of the second strongest talker. They looked to each other and shrugged.

CHAPTER ELEVEN

"You should have Kris here too," Isabella said to Melsikan, after Parsony had left to find Besaline. "She knew the castle very well." Daridar nodded her agreement. Melsikan looked to them with a smile and nodded. "Jennifer," Melsikan called to her. When she came near, he told her to ask someone from the Realm to send Kris to them. Jennifer smiled, with a glance at Isabella and Daridar, and then concentrated. Kris suddenly appeared in the court yard and she did not look particularly happy about being there. Isabella went to her with a hug.

"I thought I had seen the last of this place," Kris said as the two parted. Isabella almost smiled.

"You aren't the only one, I assure you!" she said with feeling. Kris nodded with lifted brows and hugged her again.

"Alright," Kris asked as she pulled from the embrace, straightening her shoulders and looking around. "What's going on?" Isabella quickly filled her in on all that happened since her arrival. Kris waited until Isabella had finished and Melsikan had joined them. She then told them of what had been happening at the palace, including the attempted assassination of Ava. Isabella gasped when she heard what had almost happened to her daughter. She went into Melsikan's arms. When she pulled back slightly and looked to his eyes, she feared the enraged look that had come to his face.

"Is she alright?" Melsikan asked in a very quiet voice. Kris smiled and nodded to them both.

"Yes, she is," she told them; "but she is looking forward to your return to her." Isabella tightened her grip on his arm. He looked to her and tried to smile.

"We are almost done here," he told her. "We will be with her soon, I promise." Isabella tried to smile. She nodded slowly as Besaline was led into the court yard, followed closely by the heavily panting Beling and the guardsman, for they had tried to run most of the way.

Brendo pulled the bundle from the horse and carefully unwrapped it. She set it on the ground and the rest gathered around her. "This is Brendo, what is your message?" she asked the orb. Two faces appeared and there was no smile on the face that spoke.

"Queen Nepolia says that Brando and you will be brought to the Southern Section in four days. Then we will supply the Power Stones you ask for and inform you of what is to be," Depelia told her. Brendo looked to her brother and could see the thinking he was doing. He finally nodded to her. She turned back to the orb.

"We will contact you in four days and give you our location," Brendo said, seeing that one of the faces had left. The other face looked somewhere else and moved closer to the orb she talked to.

"Be careful, the Queen plots treachery," Depelia whispered, and broke the connection. Brendo again looked to her brother and was surprised to see a small smile as he nodded slowly.

"Alright, let's get moving," he said loudly, turning back to his horse and mounting. The rest mounted their horses as Brendo retied the orb behind her saddle and then mounted her horse. She stared at her brothers back as he led them off at a fast pace, towards the Benderlese farm. She wondered what his thoughts were, because she was beginning to not have a good feeling about their future.

———

Nepolia walked from the room after she had heard Depelia tell the bandits that they would be brought in four days. She was smiling as she climbed the few steps to her throne. *Three days until Exchange Day,* she thought to herself. *Then I will have the power I will need to rid myself of those who had tried to drive me down,* she thought. Calitoran watched her. He was very sure he did not like the intense and wild look in her eyes.

———

Xanaporia and Xanaleria turned and faced the forces coming from the rear. They very quickly began convincing them that there were other places they could be, that were much safer, by hurling blast spells at a rate that was hard to follow. The guards learned the lesson with surprising skill and ran for their lives as Gordon and the wolves' joined Cartland and the Gargoyles with him. The soldiers they battled were so panicked when the huge wolves attacked; they tried to run the other way, convinced that Weretoran was attacking. They very quickly ran back into the attacking slaves. In a surprisingly short time, silence fell over all, as the two forces trying to free themselves from Garator's rule, met over the bodies of the castle guards, who hadn't escaped.

"Garator!" Garteltor yelled as he lifted the sword he had captured. He charged off, leading the slave army back down the hall they had just fought their way through, towards the quarters of the Ruler. Their calls for freedom from their slavery and, for the death of Garator, echoed through all of the halls. Those of the Realm watched as they charged away. They then looked to each other.

"What the hell do we do now?" Cartland asked, a half grin coming to his lips as he looked to the others'. Gordon looked down the hall the slaves had gone, and then down the hall the fleeing guards had gone. He then saw the young boy who stood, looking at them wide eyed.

"Do you know where the girl Gorastor is?' Gordon asked. The boy blinked several times before he slowly shook his head.

"What about the two who met you?" Xanaporia asked, turning to Cartland. "Would they know enough about this castle to help us find the girl?" He shrugged. She frowned at him. "Give me a picture of what you saw and where they led you," Xanaporia said rather harshly. He closed his eyes and sent her all he could remember. Xanaleria watched her mother and saw her smile. "Alright," Xanaporia said; "I'll see if I can bring them here." She closed her eyes and suddenly, two very wide eyed gargoyles stood before them. "Do you know the castle?" Xanaporia asked them. The two stared at them, slowly shaking their heads.

"Great," Cartland muttered again; "now what?" Xanaleria turned to the wolves.

"Is there a scent difference between the gargoyles?" She asked them. Grrale looked to her and chuckled.

"The only difference we can tell is that the males have a stronger scent then the females, but they all smell the same otherwise," he told her. The other wolves' nodded their agreement. All of the Realm sighed.

"Gorsentor?" a hushed voice asked. The two gargoyles spun around and those of the Realm looked at the six, rather scantily clothed females entering the hallway, from a crossing hallway.

"Gorastor!" Gorsentor screamed and charged, with Garpartor right behind her. The humans and wolves' exchanged wide eyed looks, as one of the six females ran forward and was grabbed almost as hard as she grabbed the two. The other five females had stopped and were staring, with a very wide eyed intensity, at the humans and wolves.

———————

Garator, his General, several Councilors, and the eight slaves who had come to warn them, most of which were females, snuck through a hidden tunnel. They slowly made their way passed the battles and finally came out almost a hundred yards outside of the castle walls, in the middle of a small grove of trees. They stopped and listened, as the sounds of the battles came from the castle. Those sounds were being joined by the sounds of other battles being fought outside the castle walls. "What do?" one of the frightened councilors asked quietly. Garator smiled.

"Go Garplasar's, survive!" he growled and led them off towards the Wizard's castle.

———————

Werelaran stared at the vacant area those of the Realm had just occupied and his thoughts raced. "Majesty?' Weretustran asked quietly. The King looked to his General, and then to his wife. He turned back to the vacant area and a portal opened in the center of that area. Weretilon hurried from the portal.

"Your Majesty, I have lost contact with Gargoylia," she said, her worries clear in her voice. Werelaran looked to her for just a moment, when Serryle spoke out.

"Gordon says that the slaves of Garator's castle have revolted and most all of the castle guards have either been killed, or have fled. The girl, Gorastor, has been recovered and seems to be well. In fact, if Gordon can believe what is being said, she is the one that started the revolt!" Serryle was smiling as she said the last. "Gordon also says that they are going to stay in Gargoylia and see what they can do to help the gargoyles find their freedom and, a healthier life style. He also asks that your Majesty begin to form a force of those who can help the Gargoylian's to find the same freedoms that are known to be in Weretoran." The King nodded to her.

"Tell them we will begin forming that force immediately," he told Serryle. The wolf nodded, sending her words to Xanaleria. He took his wife's arm, glanced at the General, then looked to Weretilon. "We need a portal to the palace," he told her. She nodded and a portal opened. They entered it. Back at the palace, they began the preparations for a force to travel to Gargoylia.

<hr/>

In the Dark City; it took several hours before the search parties were gathered around the fortress. They all told Zachia the same thing. There was nothing they could find that gave purpose, or direction of travel, for those who had been there. Zachia nodded to each report and then opened a portal. They all returned to the Realm. Ava immediately went to the reading room, to be with the other children. Zachia, Emma, Glornina, Tarson, and several others, met in Zachia's office. Mike hesitated at the door. Zachia looked to him.

"What is it son?" he asked. Mike turned to him and there had been no lessening of the hard look in his eyes.

"Papa, when the time comes, I will have to face Somora," he said softly; "I will not be beaten." He turned towards the reading room. There was silence in the room for several moments. Zachia glanced at Emma and saw the worry in her eyes. He touched her shoulder with his hand, for support, going to his desk.

"What do you think?" Glornina asked her son quietly after they had all found their seats. She had seen the look in his eyes, for both what they all faced and, for what his son had said. Emma fought through her own worries, trying to give her husband the support he needed, but she had also seen something else in his eyes, the look of worry. She stayed near him, giving what peace to his thoughts, she could. Zachia looked to each and was about to speak, when Marcus entered.

"Overseer," Marcus said softly; "I think it would be best if we returned to Zentler. Ava is pretty upset, and I think being where things are more familiar to her will help." Emma nodded and looked to her husband. Zachia nodded as well and led Marcus from the room. They entered the reading room and Zachia opened a portal to Zentler, which led to the yard behind Penelope's and Marcus's house. They all entered, and Zachia returned to the office. When he sat down, he took the time to look to each there.

"There is nothing to do right now except to wait for the outcomes in Namsia, Neponia, and Gargoylia," he told them. There were nods around the room. They all left to try and resume what duties they thought they should be about. Emma stayed near Zachia, because it was obvious to her that there was more in his mind then what was happening in the places he had named. In the reading room, Mike, his sisters, Mergania and Minsitoria, Heather, Glorian's oldest, and her twin brothers, Telkor and Belkor, and Michele's three, Mearlanor, Dafnorian, and Ramnarson, who was spoiled more by his older sisters, than his parents, met by the pile of toys and talked among themselves, very quietly and, very intensely.

———

Melsikan was sure that Brando would try to enter the castle through the rear gate, which had also been destroyed in the attack on the castle. With the guidance of Kris and Besaline, Melsikan positioned his troops around the small court yard, as well as setting up different rooms for different purposes. They all settled down to wait for Brando. Beling was finally able to get Melsikan's attention and had the Squad Leader describe the ones who they had found trying to enter the Mayors house. Melsikan had Jennifer contact Xanaleria and she passed on the description she had heard. Xanaleria confirmed that it was a gargoyle that had seen and told Jennifer that she should tell Zachia about the little ones that were seen with the larger one. Jennifer called directly to Zachia and did as Xanaleria had told her to. Zachia was very interested in the news!

———

Nepolia had begun the instructions of the bandits. They seemed quite willing to cooperate, with the promise of the wealth they would receive. Much to the relief of Nepolia and those instructing them, they had found enough willing females to calm the bandits. Nepolia was very happy about the progress of her plans.

In the Southern Section, Wespozorn couldn't stop the grin that had claimed a large portion of his face, as he walked among the Mearlies carefully stacking the boxes of deactivated Power Stones. All of the Mearlies he walked among wore the same grin.

Wenzorn and the Mearlie leader from the Northern Section were wearing similar grins as they stacked the boxes of active stones from the south. They had quickly found that there were far too many of the active stones from the south and they didn't have the capacity in the mines, to store them. The two queens of the Northern and Central Sections came up with a plan and asked Michele to call to her brother, the Overseer. Once they had a connection, they explained their thoughts and Zachia agreed.

Another day passed and there had been good news for many, but bad news for those in Namsia. Brando had not been spotted by any of the lookouts sent out by Melsikan.

After leaving the Benderlese farm, with fresh horses and a few supplies, they traveled many miles. It was getting late in the day, when they came to the small river. They got off the road and to a small clearing where they and the horse, could reach the water and, there was plenty of grass for the horses to gaze on. Brando paced, not liking having to stop for any period of time, but he knew the horses needed the rest and the feed. Brendo sat, leaning against a small boulder, holding the orb, as she watched her brother. Cenlinas had gone to the nearby forested area, hoping to find some berries to nibble on. Corlaar moved to a position where he could watch the bridge that crossed the river. He heard the sounds of galloping hooves long before he saw the rider. When he was sure of the identity, he raced for the bridge, causing both Brendo and Brando to find places of concealment. Corlaar flagged down the rider and the twins watched as they talked. They were rather surprised when the rider dismounted and followed Corlaar to the clearing.

"Lord Brando," Corlaar said, as the twins came from their hiding place; "this is Marcan, from Bandarson City." The rider bowed to Brando and eyed Brendo. She didn't sneer at him, but came very close to it. "He brings news you should hear," Corlaar said, with a tone in his voice that caused Brendo concern. Brando looked to the rider, waiting.

"My Lord Brando," Marcan said; "there are many from the Realm, in the city. When I had left, they were questioning the council members and there was talk that you were identified. There was also a lot of talk, of their search for you. Do not go to Bandarson City My Lord, they await you." Brando looked to the man for a moment or two and then turned slightly, to Brendo.

"I told you that they were from the Realm," he told her, speaking of the ones he had spotted at Corlaar's farm. She nodded and looked to the rider.

"How long have you been gone from the city?' she asked the rider.

"This is the third day, My Lady," he said. Brendo looked to her brother.

"Do you think they may have returned to the city and wait for us at the castle?" she asked him quietly. He nodded.

"It is a possibility we must accept, but I have an idea that may just ruin their plans," he told her in a growl and looked to the rider. "There is a farm, two hours to the north east." The rider nodded his knowledge of the place. "Tell them that you ride for me and get a fresh horse from them. Return to the city and find out all you can." Again the rider nodded. "We will arrive in just over a day and we will seek you at the large hay barn on the west side of the city, just after dark." The rider nodded as he vaulted into the saddle.

"Yes Lord Brando, I will be there!" the man said and pulled the horses head around and rode off to the east.

It was long after darkness had come to Gargoylia, when Garator and those with him, got to Garplasar's castle. They had walked the entire distance, much to the dislike of most of the councilors, for the slaves who were with them couldn't fly and Garator knew that they could be spotted much easier if they were in the air. The Wizard met them in the main hall and he was scowling. "Why here?" he asked Garator, growling.

"Slaves revolt, need safety," Garator told him in a loud growl of his own. "Need sleep, then plan." Garplasar didn't let Garator see the smile that wanted to be seen. He turned to a servant and indicated that the Ruler and those with him should be taken to rooms. Garator grabbed the arms of several of the female slaves that had come with him, and the others' did the same, as to their preferences. When they were led off to their rooms, Garplasar hurried to his magic room. With this unexpected good news, he began his plotting to take over as Ruler of Gargoylia!

Renstimar, the next most powerful talker, had told Somora that she had been able to hear some of Xanaleria's tightly beamed reports from Gargoylia. He told her to give him her thoughts. He quickly located on Xanaleria's talking and spelled himself there. When Somora appeared in Gargoylia, he was hidden from the sight of everyone. It did not take him long to find out that Garator would seek out this Garplasar, that there seemed, was a considerable amount of discussion about. He captured a gargoyle and stole the location of the Wizards castle from his mind. He then appeared in the entrance hall of that castle, scaring the servants that happened to be there. It was the Wizard he wanted first. Garator would just be a bonus. Garplasar appeared in the hall and immediately sent a blast spell, which Somora was able to easily block. The Wizard looked first shocked and then worried. Somora held up both hands and smiled. "Are you Garplasar?" he asked calmly. The Wizard nodded as a wary look came to his eyes. "Is Garator here?" Somora asked with the same calmness as before. Again the Wizard nodded. "Bring him to me and I will tell you both my proposition," Somora said. Garplasar began to sense the possibilities that this ugly stranger had brought with him.

Zachia and Emma appeared in the street, outside of Neponities palace. There was an immediate flurry of activity. After a few minutes, Neponities and Nepelia led the rest from the building. There were greetings, and then they all returned to the palace. When all were settled, they talked of the Overseers agreement and responsibility, for the Power Stones he was going to store in the secret chamber that held the other things that Mike, the Overseer who had trained his father, had hidden.

"How many crates are we talking about?" Zachia asked with a small grin. Neponities looked to Carsanac.

"One hundred, seventy-six, Lord Overseer," Carsanac told him. Zachia and Emma's eyes opened wide to that news.

"Send me back and I'll gather some ogres," Emma said with a quiet chuckle. Zachia nodded and Emma disappeared.

Zachia had not missed the dark circles under Michele's eyes, as she was held in Crendoran's arm. He went to her and placed his hand under her chin and lifted her face.

"What is it?' he asked her quietly. She didn't answer at first, so Crendoran did.

"She has been having nightmares about the spells she placed in the bandit's minds," he told Zachia. Zachia saw the doubt in his sister's eyes as she spoke.

"I'll be alright in a while," Michele whispered. Zachia shook his head as he looked to her.

"Come on, let's you and I have a talk," he said and took her arm. She came with him easily and they went into the other room. It was at least a half hour later that they returned and Michele seemed to be doing much better. Emma called to him that she was bringing at least twenty ogres and a portal opened. Ogres started to arrive in Neponia.

Zachia never told his baby sister of the calming spell he had placed in her mind, so she could better deal with what she had done.

———————

Melsikan had begun to worry. It had been days, and still no word had come as to the whereabouts of Brando. He called for a meeting with Parsony, Beling and Daridar, in the large throne room of the castle. Isabella, Kris, Jennifer, and Alan, were with him when the three arrived. Melsikan looked to Parsony and then Beling. "Has there been any large numbers of peoples coming to the city recently?" he asked them both. Beling answered first, with a nod.

"I am receiving reports coming from all parts of the city," he said; "of people from all of the provinces, from every direction, coming into the city. Many are being housed in the homes of those who already live here." He was frowning at Melsikan, in worry. Melsikan nodded.

"He's getting reinforcements before he even arrives," Isabella said, more to herself. Alan began to shake his head slowly, as he looked to Melsikan.

"He has to be in the city already," Alan said. "He has had enough time to get here, even though the lookouts haven't seen him. He must have snuck in somehow and he is planning his attack!" Melsikan again nodded and looked to both Parsony and Beling.

"Alert your forces to watch for any large gatherings," he told them and they nodded.

"Or the travel of many in any similar direction, or to any particular area," Alan added quickly. Melsikan nodded his agreement, as did Parsony and Beling. They stood and started to leave. Melsikan turned and looked to Daridar.

"I think it best that you stay here, in the castle with us, for your protection," he told her. She glared at him.

"I know you do not want to hear it Mayor, but he's right," Parsony said to her. "The guard can then help the protective Force, knowing you are safe here." She glared at him, and then looked around at the rest. There were nodding heads all around her. She sighed and nodded her acceptance.

———————

It had taken Brando and the rest, just over a day to reach Bandarson City. They came in on the west side of the city after dark, to the huge hay barn there. Marcan and a small army of supporters met him there. They ate and drank as Marcan, with the input of several of those who had come with him, told him of the happenings at the castle and the rest of the city.

"How many of the city, are with us?" Brando asked. Marcan and those with him, grinned.

"Hundreds, Lord Brando," Marcan said rather loudly. "There are many from the city and those who have come from the provinces, from every direction and, there are more arriving everyday!" Brando allowed a small grin with his nod. He then looked to his sister.

"Call to Neponia," he told her. "We cannot wait two more days for the promised Power Stones. We need those stones now!" She nodded and went to where she had hidden the orb. She returned in a short time. She did not look happy when she looked to her brother.

"I was told that we have to wait," she said. "They have not finished the making and we cannot have the stones until they are completed." Brando stared at her, without really looking to her. All could see the rage that had come to his eyes. He turned to Corlaar.

"Begin the building of four armies from all those who are with us," he ordered. "Have them begin to gather on four sides of the city. I will tell of the rest of my plans soon." Corlaar nodded to Brando's orders. He took Marcan and all but six of those with him and left the barn. Those six were to be guards for Brando, Brendo, and Cenlinas.

Garator raged at the interruption of his rest and pleasures. He glared at the hideous thing that was sitting and, didn't stand, when the Ruler was led into the room. "What?' he raged at Garplasar. The Wizard smiled at the Ruler.

"This human has come with a plan that I think will be a benefit to us," he told Garator, who stared back at him, his eyes wide and mouth hanging open. Garplasar's smile grew with Garator's shocked look.

"How talk that?" Garator asked quietly, still in shock of hearing a full sentence from the Wizard.

"Garsalar, my tutor and master, taught me to speak in complete sentences, like all those of the other domains," Garplasar said. "So I do not sound as an idiot!" Garator became enraged with the Wizard's words and grin. Garator started towards him. Garplasar lifted one hand and started to mutter, the smile never leaving his face. Neither accomplished their goals, for Somora put an immobilization spell on them both. He slowly rose from the chair and walked to the two who could not do anything, but glare at each other. He extended both hands, the index finger of both, pointing downward. He muttered and swiveled his fingers, in opposite directions. The two would-be combatants, without moving any part of their bodies, slowly turned so that they both now faced him, still unable to do anything, but glare at him. He smiled at them both.

"Now listen, both of you," he told them calmly. "I know that you both wanted to make use of the rebels of Namsia, to take control of this planet," he said looking to Garator. "And, the Realm," he said to Garplasar. "Well, I'm offering you both a chance to do exactly what you want and, more!" The two frozen in place, stared at him and blinked.

As the night deepened in the Realm, Zachia sat at his desk. He was making a list of events that had occurred in the domains of the Realm, Natharia, Namsia, Nepolia, and Weretoran, and Gargoylia. He was looking for more than the obvious connections of the domains. He was trying to find the purpose of the one called Somora and how it connected with the domains. Emma entered his office and came to his side.

"It is time for bed my love," she whispered with a kiss to his cheek. He looked to her and almost made a smile.

"I know, but I feel that there is something I am not seeing," he answered her, looking back to the list he had made. She leaned closer and she looked at the list. She sighed and he looked to her, questioning.

"What I don't understand is where this Somora came from and, how is it he came to be in the Dark City?" she said softly, still reading the list. Zachia looked at her, stunned. He looked back to the list. He suddenly pulled another paper from the drawer. Emma looked at him with concern.

"What?" she asked.

"I think you have just given me a direction to follow, to find what is missing," he said and began making another list, different than the one before. She watched as he wrote and began to nod. She was seeing where his ideas were leading, for the first thing that was written on the paper was; *interrogate the captured from the battle of the Dark City*!

CHAPTER TWELVE

It had been the day before the regularly scheduled exchange day, that those of the Central and Northern Sections had received their new Power Stones. Neponities, Nepelia, Nepanities, Nepeslia, Carsanac, Michele, and Crendoran, met in Neponities palace. They plotted their assault on the Southern Section. Making their plotting easier was the knowledge that the Southern Section would be receiving the deactivated Power Stones. The next day would be the day of their attack.

"Even though they won't have the power of the stones," Neponities started the talks. "There are many who have a strong magical talent and have great fighting skills." There were nods of agreement from Nepanities, Nepelia and her daughter. Nepanities looked to her mate.

"Do you have thoughts of this?" she asked him. The others' looked to him and he wore a small grin as he looked to Michele.

"Lady Michele, would it be possible to get some of the larger warriors from the Realm?" he asked to her. "Their size alone will deter most of the southern soldiers from fighting without thought."Michele nodded, joining his smile and called to her brother for some ogres, Natharian's and dragons, as reinforcements.

Two days had passed and the activity in the domains had intensified. Nepolia stood in front of her mirror, in the throne room and smiled at the bright new medallion around her neck. The reflection in the mirror showed the crate of faulty Power Stones that sat on the floor behind her. Her smile turned deadly as she stared at it. She turned to Depelia. "Tell those in Bandarson that we will bring them in the morning," she said with a sneer, as she looked back at her reflection and the new Power Stone she wore. Depelia bowed and went to the orb room. One of the serving males slipped from the room and told Pelinon, the Seamstress. She then had her daughter Benilon; pass on what Nepolia had planned, to Seastaria, who told her grandmother, who told Neponities and the others'. Plans were revised.

Somora had sent a message to Renstimar and had told her to inform all that he would be a few days finishing his business. It took two days for him to convinced Garator and Garplasar of his plots, but he had been required to concede to Garator's demand that a punishment must be enforced on the gargoyles who had rebelled. A very drastic and severe punishment was finally agreed on by the three.

The rebellion of the wingless gargoyles had spread quickly to all of the provinces. All winged gargoyles were brought to the castle and given the choice of joining in the new free Gargoylia, or death. There were a few who refused to accept an equal's role with the wingless gargoyles. They were quickly slain. The rest, seeing the results of noncooperation, joined in the common Gargoylia. Within a day, a wingless elder was elected as Governor and all celebrated the new Gargoylia!

Werelaran wanted to lead the force of teachers, doctors and builders, to Gargoylia, but Wereselon and Gordon, through Weretilon, were able to convince him that it was still much too risky for him to appear in Gargoylia yet. So, with almost a pout, he sent Werepetran, the second General of the Armies, as leader of the force. That force was very surprised at the cheering welcome they received when they walked from the portal, into Gartisia.

Melsikan read and listened to, the many reports of the actions of those coming to Namsia City. He held a conference with Daridar, Parsony, Isabella, Kris, Jennifer and Alan. "I see that there is going to be a larger than expected force that will try to take control of this city," he told them. They looked to him waiting, after shared glances of worry. He looked to Jennifer. "I think we should get some help from the Realm, just to be sure. Make sure that they wear Milky Crystal amulets and make sure they bring enough for us!" he added. She nodded and sent a message to the Realm, calling for reinforcements.

———————

"They will not give us the true Power Stones," Brando told the small gathering with him.

"What do you mean?" Corlaar asked, his anger evident in his voice. Brando smile was angry and Brendo shivered with the sight.

"They will give us stones that do not hold the power of the stones they have," Brando growled and those around him exchanged looks. "I think that this Nepolia has desires to conquer us and use us for her own goals!"

"What do you plan son?" Cenlinas asked the same kind of smile on her face as Brando's. Brendo shivered with her mother's smile, as she had for her brothers. Brando turned his eyes to Corlaar.

"I want six of the strongest fighters we have, for they will travel with us to Neponia," he told him. Corlaar bowed and left the meeting. Brando looked to those still around him. When he spoke, his voice was quiet, but deadly. "I will have a true Power Stone and I will control all!" Brendo now smiled with her understanding of her bothers intents and there were more than a few, who feared the cruelty of her smile.

———————

The celebrations of freedom were profound in all parts of Gargoylia, but none were equal to those of the capital city, Gartisia. Those who had lived closest to the rule of Garator, partied the greatest, in number and, volume. Somora, Garator and Garplasar appeared in a dark alley, just out of sight of one of the largest parties that seemed to never end. Somora lifted his hand and cast his spell at the revelers, as Garator and Garplasar chuckled deeply. Once his spell had been cast, the three disappeared, reappearing at Garplasar's castle. Those loyal to Garator, which were the council members, the General, the slaves, mostly females, and the gathered army of Gaspilarians, awaited them. Somora opened a portal and led the gargoyles to his new domain.

It was the following morning that the arriving force from Weretoran was met by a cheering crowd of gargoyles, but there were none from the gathering that Somora, Garator and Garplasar had visited. They, each and every one of them, woke with effects of Somora's spell. They would infect any that tended them. A call for aid was sent to the Weretorians that had come, as one entire section of the capital city, became sickened.

Lianost and his mate Liornora, Liaganost, and his mate Liorpanora, and ten of the strongest Listaman fighters, approached the main gate of the newly formed wall around the rebuilt city. A cry went out from the guards at the gate. General Hantopan, with a squad of soldiers, came running to the gate. The two parties stopped just back from their sides of the gate and a silence came to them.

"Who are you and what is your purpose here?" Hantopan asked, breaking the silence. His voice was neither harsh nor soft. He had some concern that he had to look up to the visitors face.

"I am Lianost, leader of the Prides of Listaman," Lianost said, his voice a growl sound. "I have come to talk with the one called Somora."

"How do you know our leaders name?" Hantopan asked, after a moment of thought. Lianost smiled, which showed the teeth that could easily tear flesh from bone.

"We have been watching and listening to your kind since your appearance," Lianost said calmly. "I now come to speak with your leader, to learn his purpose here." Hantopan's brows lifted for a moment and then lowered, as a cunning smile came to his lips.

———

Even the rehabilitated sorceresses, sorcerers and Dremlor, who had been captured in the Dark City, were questioned of all they might know of Somora. All of the interrogators reported their findings to Zachia. The more Zachia learned from these reports, the less he liked this Somora. Zachia could now clearly see that the goals Somora seemed to be seeking and that those goals were to be yet another threat to all of the Domains of Rightful Magic. Because of Zachia's intense study of Somora's plots, the call for reinforcements for Nepolia and Namsia was turned over to Tarson. Zachia knew that Tarson could quickly and easily, selected the soldiers and races and, the numbers of each, to go to both domains.

In Zentler, Ava seemed to be doing better with the familiar settings. She began to spend a lot of her time with the younger GeeBee. Kris and Carl, who had been very shocked to realize that GeeBee had magical sensing, were worried of what else she might possess and what she was learning from Ava. All of the children seemed to separate themselves, slightly, from their parents, as the number of quiet conversations between them grew. Penelopy and Marcus tried to keep the other parents from worry, as these separations occurred. They tried talking with their children about what was happening among the others'. Terressa began to worry more than the other parents, because her son, Benjamin, the unknowing son of a Dremlor, was staying more and more to himself. Four year old Nathan, Giorgio and two year old Bella, struggled to keep Benjamin from pulling from others' and still stay in touch with Ava and GeeBee. What only the children knew was that Ava was also doing a lot of talking with Mike, the Overseer's son.

Isabella had already gone to bed when Melsikan called to Michele, in Neponia. "I have a feeling this all is about to come together," he told her. She gave a very tired chuckle.

"You have no idea," she said. "Nepolia is going to bring Brando to her tomorrow morning and she is going to give him a crate full of faulty Power Stones."

"What?" he said louder than he meant to. "Do you remember what happened with Brandaro?" She sighed.

"Yes, that's why we're going to attack before she can give those stones to him," she told him; "hopefully, catching him there at the same time." Melsikan nodded to himself.

"That's not going to be easy," he told her. "This Brando is big and has no hesitation to killing."

"Yeah, I remember his father," Michele said. "Don't worry, we've got some ogres, Natharian's, and dragons from the Realm. We will be ready for him."

"Alright, have someone keep me informed," he said. "We will have to face his forces here, whether he is caught there or not."

"Alright," Michele said; "I'll tell you myself, what the outcome here is."

"Good, thank you, and goodnight," he said softly, and broke the connection. He stared at the table he was sitting at. After some time, he slowly rose, and went to join Isabella, but he knew sleep would not come to him tonight.

Hantopan sent a messenger to the palace and then led the Listamans towards it. Lianost stopped about twenty feet from the building, looking at it with dislike. Hantopan looked to him with surprise, as the returning messenger told him that Somora awaited their guests. "My King awaits you, inside," he told the leader. Lianost looked to him; a snarl came to his face.

"We do not enter these strange dens," he growled. "If this Somora cannot come to me, there is no need of talk!" Hantopan stared at the Listaman for a few moments and then told his aide to watch their guest, and entered the palace. It was several minutes later that Somora came out, with Garator and Garplasar and, a small collection of Gaspilarians behind him. He stopped about ten feet from Lianost. He looked all of the Listamans over, one by one. He returned his eyes to Lianost.

"Do you speak for your kind?" he asked. Lianost nodded slowly. "What is your reason for coming here?" Somora asked, with a small arrogant smile on his face.

"As you have led these people to invade our world, it is my demand that you tell of your purposes here!" Lianost told Somora, eyeing the gargoyles carefully. Somora's look became angry, as a squad of his soldiers began to spread out, behind the Listamans.

"Be very careful," Somora said quietly. "I have invaded nothing and you are in my compound and therefore, will obey me!" Lianost snarled and a growl came from deep within him. The warriors who had come with him, turned around, forming an arc around the rear of Lianost and each crouched with their claws showing. Each growled as Lianost had.

"This was our world before you came and it is ours now!" he said, taking a step forward. "You have invaded our world. You will now obey me and explain what you are doing here!" Somora saw that he would have to convince this stranger who was boss, but he didn't want to kill them, for he saw a potential in them. He snapped his hand without lifting it, casting a blast spell that was meant to stun, not kill. Lianost did not change his expression as he easily deflected the spell from him and then sent a spell of his own, which sent Somora, Garator, Garplasar and, the Gaspilarians, tumbling. Lianost's wife, second in command Liaganost and his mate, stood to Lianost's side, prepared to meet any that would attack from the front. Behind the front four, the squad of soldiers started forward and the Listaman warriors prepared to meet them, with growls that were very close to roars. Bunched muscles and extended claws, showed their readiness to battle. Somora yelled for them to halt. Somora stood, brushing the dust from him. Garator and Garplasar stood as well and their rage was clear in their eyes. The Gaspilarians formed a line behind those two, their rage obvious. Somora slowly walked back to within ten feet of Lianost.

"It would seem that this did not go as well as it could have," he told Lianost gently. Lianost took another step towards Somora, his eyes blazing with the rage that would control him.

"You have invaded our world and now you try to start a war you cannot win. Now what is your purpose here?"

Lianost roared his words, as the soldiers backed from the Listaman warriors. Somora's mind raced as he slowly lifted his hands, palms forward.

"There is no need of battle and I am sorry that I misunderstood you," he said, trying to soothe the obviously enraged Lianost. Lianost waited, his expression never changing. "I was not aware that there was any living on this world. I am trying to save my people from those who would hunt and kill us. I am sorry that I did not see that there was a peace to you and I would ask that we start over. That we try to work out any differences we might have." Lianost did not change his outward expression, but his mind was warning him of the manner of speaking this intruder had.

"Why would any hunt you?" Lianost asked his growled words quieter, but not yielding any power. Somora allowed a small grin to form.

"Because we knew of their danger to us and we tried to spy on them to learn their true plans, to attack and kill us!" Somora told the leader. Both Garator and Garplasar looked at him, in surprise, something Lianost did not miss. "The ones that hunt us have great powers and they try to kill us because of their greed for more to control," Somora continued. "We were forced to flee, to save ourselves, until we could properly defend ourselves. We have not come here to conquer, we came here seeking refuge." Somora had slowly lowered his hands until they now hung at his sides.

Lianost did not trust all that Somora had said, but he felt that there was a power to this one before him. He thought that he might be able to finally, using this stranger, spread his prides among the world's that those who had been here before, had spoke of. The prey on this world was running low in numbers and his prides hungered for new meat!

Nepolia was smiling as the preparations for the arrival of those from Bandarson were being made. Even the panicked report of the combined forces of the Central and Northern Sections, fighting their way towards her castle, couldn't completely steal her grin. At least until she was told of the ones from the Realm, who were leading the way.

"What did you say?" she screamed at the messenger.

"Dragons fly the skies, flaming our troops to panic. The large hairy ones are capable of taking on many of our soldiers at one time and the huge ones with the many legs are impervious to our spells and weapons," the messenger told her. "Neponities, and her daughter, as well as Nepelia and her daughter, lead their troops and are destroying any resistance with ease. They will be attacking your castle within an hour, at the latest!" Nepolia stared at the messenger for a moment.

"Tell the guards of our bandit troops, to prepare them to fight the invaders," she ordered. The messenger bowed and left the throne room. "Tell Brando to be ready, we will open the portal in minutes!" Nepolia ordered. Depelia bowed and went to the orb. She returned quickly and told Nepolia that Brando, and those coming with him are ready. She then told Nepolia where she had been told where to open the portal. Nepolia nodded and lifted her hand and began her incantation. She was surprised that the portal didn't form as quickly or as solidly as she had expected. She didn't have time to consider the point, for Brando, Brendo, and the six huge warriors, quickly entered the throne room.

"Where are the stones you promised?" Brando demanded, loudly. Nepolia glared, as two of the male servants brought the crate forward. Brando easily took the crate from them, in one hand, and tore it open with his other hand. He quickly put on one of the amulets and handed out one to all who had come with him. He then set the crate down. He then turned to face Nepolia, starting towards her. "I know that you intend to cheat us and I am here to stop you from that end!" he lunged at her as she started to lift her hand, to cast the spell that was forming with her words. His right hand closed on her power Stone, as his left hand slapped her, hard. She was driven back by the force of the slap and the chain that held the amulet around her neck was broken by her movement and Brando's pulling. All of those with him had also targeted others' in the room and very quickly, they each held a Power Stone taken from Nepolia's people.

"You will die for this insolence!" Nepolia screamed and again tried to cast a blast spell, but without a Power Stone to support her, it had no strength and Brando was barely rocked by its affect. He laughed at her and again advanced. The soldiers of Nepolia tried to defend against Brando's forces, but they were no match for the shear brutality of Brendo and the six. Very quickly, all were unconscious, or dead. Brando picked Nepolia up by her hair and held her easily at arm's length. The echoing sounds of Neponities forces attacking the castle, was heard in the halls and those sounds were coming closer. Nepolia screamed with her pain and surprise. Her hands grabbed his arm. She was feeling true fear as she looked into the enraged eyes of the one she had thought she could easily conquer and control.

"You are not so much, but I am," Brando growled at her. Her eyes opened wider with her terror. He laughed loudly. Using her hair, he gave a severe twist to her head. Nepolia's neck snapped with the sudden movement of her head, that her body could not match. Brando dropped her body and turned to his sister and the warriors, smiling wide. He lifted his hand as he picked the crate from the floor. A portal opened, and Brando led them into it, easily carrying the crate under one arm.

Emma, with Glornina, Carla, Edward, Tarson, and Prelilian, entered Zachia's office as he gave the last of his instructions to the sensitive's he wanted to look for Somora's hiding place. They waited until he looked to them. When he did, he wore a surprised and questioning look.

"We have just received a message from Michele and she says that Brando has the Power Stones Nepolia was to give him and he also has the deactivated stones that Nepolia and those in the throne room with her, had wore. She also said that Brando killed Nepolia and has fled back to Namsia, with the stones," Emma said, almost smiling. Zachia looked from one to the next and each nodded their knowing of these facts and each developed a grin, of sorts, of their own.

"He has gotten the faulty stones Nepolia was going to use to control him?" Zachia asked quietly. Again, all nodded. Zachia thought for a moment and then looked to Carla. "Warn Melsikan of this situation. Advise him of the danger those stones could be and that he should take all precautions with his forces." Carla nodded and concentrated, as Zachia looked to Tarson. "Who and how many have you sent to Namsia?"

"A full battalion of soldiers, as well as ogres, dragons, eagles, and Natharian's," Tarson told him, getting a serious look. "I also sent wolves for scouts and guards, fairy folk for communication and scouting, plus bats for night recognizance." Zachia nodded and continued to think, his head down slightly. They all waited.

"There will be considerable danger if they combine and try to use more than one with stones at the same time," Glornina said quietly. "It took years for all to recover from the affects of Brandaro and the two with him." Zachia nodded without looking to her. He lifted his head and looked around to those there.

"Prepare, we will go to Namsia and see for ourselves what is happening," he told them. They all smiled and turned to leave the room, with nods of agreement. They stopped short as they all looked to the determined eyes of seven year old Mike, who stood in the doorway.

"I will go too," he said with a determination that frightened Emma and caused worry in Zachia. Emma glanced at Zachia and then looked to her son.

"You are going nowhere near Namsia, not now. This trouble will be settled without you being in danger," she told him, coming closer. Mike looked to his father.

"I must prepare for the future battles that are to come, from Somora," he said. Zachia stood and came around his desk.

"I'm sorry son, but your mother is right, you are not going," he told Mike, kneeling and placing his hand on the boys shoulder. "As to what is to come from Somora in the future, is something that you and I will face, together." Mike stared into his father's eyes for several seconds. He finally took a deep breath and nodded, but Zachia, and the others' of the room, could plainly see the determination in Mike's eyes. Emma put a hand on Zachia shoulder and he could feel the slight tremble of a mother's fears. Mike turned and left the room, but they all saw him join with his younger sisters and the three went into the reading room.

"By the Divine One Zachia," Emma whispered; "what could he be doing, so young?"

"The same thing that both of you, your father and I, and those before us, have done, what he feels he must," Glornina's voice was a whisper, but it echoed in each of their minds.

Through talkers, Blautdarn, ruler of Natharia, had been kept informed of events that had been occurring. He talked with his councilors and it was decided that they would send any requested by the Overseer. He ordered his talkers to inform the Realm of their decision. Zachia and Tarson were very happy to hear the news, as most of the Realm tribe had been sent to Neponia and there were only a dozen in Namsia. Just prior to their departure to Namsia, Zachia opened a portal and fifty Natharian's marched into the Realm.

———

The doctors, who had been sent to Gargoylia, almost immediately discovered that the disease that was spreading quickly through the population of gargoyles had no affect on those from the Realm, or the werewolves. Because of that, many more doctors and nurses were sent to Gargoylia, from Weretoran. They fought as hard as they could against a plague they could not identify. It was Serryle who noticed that there were a few gargoyles that seemed immune to the disease. She had been working with Gorastor and Gorpeelia. Both of the young females had already lost their families to the plague. She quickly saw that neither of the girls got sick, even working with those who were. Serryle told Xanaleria, who told Gordon, who told the doctors in charge of those fighting to find a cure. Gorastor and Gorpeelia were quickly called to the command center of doctors and blood samples were taken. The doctors found that the girl's immune system attacked the plague virus, destroying it. Word quickly was spread to locate any others that were immune, as more blood was drawn from Gorastor and Gorpeelia. A serum was formulated from the collected blood samplings and was quickly distributed throughout Gargoylia. Within a week of its outbreak, the plague was stopped, but not before over half of the population of Gargoylia had died!

⁓⁓⁓⁓⁓⁓⁓⁓⁓

Werelaran had learned of the status of events on Neponia and Namsia, because he had had Weretilon in constant communication with the Realm, as was Xanaleria. He now stood next to the crystal, with Wereselon at his side. He looked to Weretilon. "I wish to speak to Zachia directly. Please tell them of this," he told her. She nodded and turned to the crystal. She passed on her Kings request. She was surprised how quickly the Overseer replied.

"Your Majesty, I am listening," Weretilon announced to her King, repeating Zachia's words. Werelaran looked to the crystal, but talked to Zachia, as Wereselon took his hand.

"Lord Overseer," he began; "I know that we are new to the Domains of Rightful Magic, but I now offer our troops as aid, to any effort to defeat this Brando and the rebels of Namsia." He worried slightly as the time passed without a response, but finally Weretilon spoke. She wore a smile when she did.

"King Werelaran, I, and those of the Domains of Rightful Magic, would welcome you and your troops, in the effort to defeat Brando. If you can gather your forces together, I will open a portal to the Realm, in your court yard, in three hours. We would welcome any that you send." Werelaran nodded to Weretilon. She almost giggled, as she told Zachia that they would be ready.

"Please send a Weriron to General Weretustran, that he is to have a battalion ready and in the court yard of my palace, in two hours and tell him why," Werelaran instructed Weretilon. She nodded, pointing to Peritor, who had been listening. The Weriron bowed and flew from the room, faster than Weretilon had ever seen her fly. Werelaran and Wereselon exchanged confident, yet worried looks. Werelaran told her that he would lead the troops that they send. Wereselon worried at first and wanted to go with him, but Werelaran explained to her that she needed to stay and work with the remaining Gargoyles, to help them in their recovery. She tried to smile as she nodded, for she already had many ideas of what must be done, but she knew she would not rest until her husband returned to her. Werelaran was very surprised and proud, when four battalions of troops, with the General leading them, arrived at the palace.

It was decided that Gordon, Xanaporia, Grrale and Terryle would return to the Realm. The King and the Weretorian battalions entered portals to the Realm. Cartland, Xanaleria, Crrale and Serryle, would stay and help Wereselon, with the aid to Gargoylia.

When they arrived in the Realm, Zachia immediately sent Gordon and Xanaporia back to Zentler. Zachia opened ten portals and he and Emma went to Namsia, with the leader of the wolves' of the Realm and his mate and, those from Weretoran. There was also a great many others', from all domains, which entered the portals to Namsia.

Neponities and Nepelia, with their daughters beside them, led the soldiers of the Central and Northern Sections. Ahead of them were the ogres, Natharian's, and dragons, driving the Southern Section soldiers back towards Nepolia's castle. They could have laughed, if it had not been so tragic, because what blast spells the soldiers tried to cast, had no power, for the soldiers wore deactivated Power Stones. They stopped and watched as the soldiers tried to make one last stand at the gate of the castle. Neponities gave the signal and her soldiers charged. The fighting was not as fierce as she would have thought, because the Southern Section soldiers started to realize that they could not win. Many lay down their weapons as the charge was begun, while others retreated into the castle, hoping their Queen could protect them. Neponities forces quickly cleared a path to the throne room. Neponities, Nepanities, Nepelia and Nepeslia charged into the throne room, just as Brando stepped into the portal.

"Halt," Neponities yelled. Brando turned to look at her as the portal closed. He wore a very terrifying grin. Nepanities chuckled and everyone looked to her in shock.

"Did you see what they carried in their hands?" she asked and all shook their heads. "They carried the Power Stones taken from Nepolia and others here, the deactivated ones!"

After the portal had closed, Brando turned back to his sister and the six. "Make sure that the commanders get those first, then hand them out by rank," he ordered, pointing to the crate. All six bowed and left with the crate.

He beckoned to Brendo to follow and he led her behind some bushes where they couldn't be seen. "Now I will show you the difference between what they gave us and the stones they wore," he told her as he slipped off the one taken from the crate and put on the one he had tore from the Queen. He smiled at her and lifted his hand and muttered a blast spell at a tree near them. Nothing more than some broken bark, happened. He stared wide eyed at the tree. He looked to Brendo, his confusion showing. He tried his blast spell again and again, nothing happened.

"What is happening?" Brendo asked in a whisper. Still wearing the one taken from the crate, she lifted her hand, muttered a blast spell and the tree blasted apart. She looked to Brando and saw the rage that was taking him.

"They planned for us to try and take their stones! So they wore stones that had no power!" he roared. He jerked the useless amulet from his neck and threw it to the ground. He turned to her. "Tell those who also took stones from those in the room that they are useless and to throw them away!" She nodded and hurried off. Brando slowly placed the amulet taken from the crate, back around his neck. He muttered as he walked to the barn; "at least that dead parsha will not be able to try anything!" He was all the way back to the barn, before the possibilities of the inoperative stones, became understood. He sent one of his guards for the stone he had cast down and to gather the other inactive ones.

Zachia, Emma, Grrale, and Terryle, the remaining wolves'
of the Realm, dragons, and ogres of the Realm, exited the
portal, into the rear courtyard of Brandaro's castle. They
were followed by fifty Natharian's. Melsikan, Isabella,
Jennifer, Alan and Daridar met them. The Weretorian
troops, who had arrived through a different portal, were
shown where they would sleep. The Natharian's were led
off by the commander of those already there. The wolves'
went with the leader that was already there, to the wolf
grounds that had been established. Werelaran joined
the rest as they were led to the command room, which
happened to be Brandaro's old throne room. There, they
poured over the reports, maps and everything else that
concerned Brando's efforts. At first, Werelaran was having
difficulties trying to concentrate, for all the new sights
around him, but the new quickly wore off and he was able
to stay with all that was said. He even began to present
ideas that the rest agreed with. They then gathered on
the large couch, except for Isabella and Daridar. They
couldn't sit there, for their memories of what had sat there
before. Refreshments were brought and the conversations
and plotting, continued for several hours. Without any
warning, a dwarf, who had been spying on Brando, came
charging into the room.

"Lord Melsikan, Brando and his troops are wearing the
amulets you told us to look for!" he managed between
gasps. Melsikan rose and went to the dwarf, trying to
get more information from him. He and Zachia, and the
others' were surprised at the volume of information the
dwarf possessed, especially the location of the barn Brando
was using as a command center!

During the conversation with the Listamans, Somora learned that they not only possessed a powerful magical talent, they needed and wanted new hunting grounds. He planned on using both of those traits. It had taken him over an hour to convince Lianost of the value of following his plots, but finally the leader seemed to understand that there was an advantage to both races, if they worked together. Unknown to Somora, Lianost, as well as all of the other Listamans, saw through his lies. After leaving Somora, the Listamans returned to their den.

"I do not like the idea of following that Somora's orders," Liaganost stated loudly. "He has purpose for only himself!" The others' nodded, as did Lianost.

"Yes, but through him and his ideas, we can spread among the domains and then we can hunt. Our prey will be plenty and easy," Lianost said quietly, but with force. "We can establish our own dens, unknowing to Somora. We can cut him from our victory, when we are ready!" His head was down as he swept the den with his sight, filtered through his thick brows. "We can take what we want, when this puny human has run as far as he can and is trapped by our hunt!" The tribe roared their support of their Leader. Runners were sent to other tribes, which there was at least two dozen, telling of Somora's plans and the secretive plans of their leader. It did not take long and all the tribes were ready to follow their leader and, pretend to follow Somora.

Brando called for a meeting of the commanders of the four armies that were being formed. They met at the barn, completely unaware of the fairy folk, most of who could talk silently to someone back at the castle, which now hid in any recess or crack they could find. They listened to and reported every word that was said! "You all know of my basic plan to attack Bandarson City from four sides," Brando started his address. "Well, that will be what most of our attack will be, but I have added a twist and the ones from the Realm are going to be very surprised," he told the commanders and they exchanged confused glances.

"What are you talking about Brando?" Brendo asked, as her brows furrowed. He smiled at her and turned back to the commanders.

"We have all heard the story of the female that my father had sought and how she had been helped by a girl that had been hiding in the castle. She knew of many hidden passages that allowed her to go anywhere in the castle and never be seen, or heard." Heads were nodding by all of the commanders. Brando leaned down, placing both hands on the edge of the table. "Well, that very same girl is now back in the castle, with the one my father was looking for and, they both know these tunnels!" Again the commanders exchanged confused glances, but Brendo and Cenlinas began to grin. Brando pulled a dwarf female to him. "This dwarf was in service of my father and knows the castle layout well. In fact, she was the one to tell me of the two's presence in the castle," he told them all and looked to his sister. "You will pick four. Tonight, with this dwarf leading, you are to capture these two females and bring them to me," he told her and she nodded slowly. "From them, we will learn the tunnels we can use to send some of our forces into the castle and surprise these fools from the Realm, with a defeat!" The commanders and Cenlinas cheered as Brendo selected the four she would take with her that night.

CHAPTER THIRTEEN

In the throne room, a large group had gathered to discuss what they had heard from the fairy folk spies. "Don't worry my love," Melsikan whispered to Isabella as she was held in his embrace. "I will not allow that bastard to come anywhere near you, or Kris." She wanted to believe him, but the terrifying memories of her time as a captive of Brandaro could not be erased with his assurances. She pulled her head from his chest and looked to Kris, who sat on a small couch nearby. She saw the worry in her eyes. Isabella pulled from Melsikan's embrace and went and sat next to her, putting her arm around her friend.

"I won't tell them anything of the tunnels," Kris told her with bravado, but Isabella heard the slight tremble in her voice. Isabelle almost smiled with her nod and took Kris into an embrace.

"Maybe you should show our troops these tunnels and then we can better defend against Brando's infiltration," Daridar said softly.

"That's an excellent idea Daridar," Zachia said. Kris managed a real smile as she slowly shook her head. They all looked to her in confusion.

"Most of the tunnels are either too narrow or too low of a ceiling for a soldier to pass through them easily and, forget being able to battle with a weapon," she told them. Isabella nodded, remembering the tunnel Kris had led her through, from the cell she had been put in. Melsikan looked to the others' in the room and Werelaran took a step closer to the two on the small couch.

"What about wolves'?" he asked calmly. "Could a wolf pass through them?" Kris looked at him and then looked to Grrale and Terryle. Werelaran changed to his wolf form and stood next to the Realm's wolf leader and they were the same size. Kris began to smile and she nodded.

"There are some that even wolves' would have to crawl through, but yes, wolves' would do better in the tunnels than any others'," she said, looking to Zachia and then Melsikan, her eyes shining. Grrale and Werelaran looked to each other and grinned as well.

"Alright, Werelaran, Grrale, Terryle, figure out which ones are going to keep the patrols outside the castle and whose to be the patrols in the tunnels," Melsikan ordered. The three nodded and started to turn to leave. "As soon as you have the answers, let Kris know and she can start teaching you the tunnels." Again they nodded and looked to Kris.

"How many tunnels are there?" Werelaran asked.

"Around fifty," Kris told him; "but there are only about fifteen that are the main ones." The wolves' nodded and trotted out of the room.

—————

Brendo and the four she had picked listened to the female dwarf as she explained the layout of the castle, by drawing maps on the floor of the barn. They then rested in the afternoon, for it was to be long night for them. Brando came and talked privately with Brendo for a few minutes. He then met with his commanders and the spies who had been watching the goings on in and around the castle.

"My lord Brando," a rather small man started his report; "The patrols around the castle are staggered and over lapping. The large creatures, with the many legs, patrol the outer limits. The dragons and huge eagles are constantly in the air, yet they do not follow any set pattern. The huge bats fly the night patrols and it is hard to see them in the dark skies. The large, hairy ogres, and the other large ones, who wear clothing, travel with a mixture of police of the city and soldiers of the Realm. Wolves travel in packs of no less than five and they are constantly sneaking around everywhere." He lowered his eyes a moment and then looked to his leader. "I do not see how you can launch any force against them that will not be found out quickly and they will meet the threat with a great force of their own!" Brando smiled at him and looked to a male dwarf, who had access to the castle regularly.

"What of the inner guards?" he asked quietly. The dwarf looked to him, his face showing fear.

"The patrols are the same inside of the castle," he whined. "I have not been able to detect any pattern to their patrols. They travel quietly, in forces that are never far from each other." Brando nodded and his smile faded slowly.

"My lord," Corlaar said; "what do you plan?" All eyes looked to the ruler and waited. They exchanged concerned looks as silence answered Corlaar's question. Finally Brando straightened and looked to those gathered around him.

"When we attack, we will come as three fronts," he told them and the confusion in their eyes deepened. Brando allowed his smile to return, but only to the right side of his lips. "I will tell of these three fronts to those who will be of them, but not now and not here," he said in a growl. "Rest now, while we wait for Brendo's return with the two who will give us the information we will need for one part of that attack." With that, Brando stood and strode to his quarters, beckoning two of the many women of his troops, to join him. They happily followed him. Fairy folk spies sent silent messages to those at the castle who could receive them.

Neponities, Nepelia, Nepanities, and Nepeslia, met in the dining room of the castle that had been held by the deceased Nepolia. Their purpose was to try and figure out who was to now rule the Southern Section. About an hour later, Nepalisia was called to the room. She was the commander of the most efficient battalion from the Northern Section. She was also Nepelia's niece, as well as Neponities, by way of her Chosen Mate. She was therefore, Nepanities and Nepeslia's older cousin. Her father, Praredonar, was the older brother of Traredonar, and was the Chosen Mate of Nepelia's sister, Nepetilia. Nepalisia had other talents that all respected. She was almost as good at combat as Nepanities. She was loved by her troops and one of the best strategists of the Northern Section commanders. Nepalisia entered the room and stopped short of the Queens and Princesses. She bowed.

"Your Majesties," she said, as she straightened. Both Queens smiled at her.

"Relax Nepalisia," Queen Neponities said softly. The newcomer looked to her strangely. The four laughed. Nepelia stood and came to her. She placed her hands on the arms of her niece, and smiled wider.

"It has been decided that you are to be the new Queen of the Southern Section," she said loudly and the others' clapped their hands, laughing again at the woman's wide eyes.

"I do not understand aunt Nepelia," Nepalisia said in a whisper. Nepelia chuckled and glanced at the three still at the table.

"We feel that you are the best qualified to lead this Section of Neponia," Nepelia said, as the rest stood and came to her. They were nodding their heads as they formed a half circle behind Nepelia. Nepalisia looked to each, still not understanding everything. Neponities reached out and placed her hand on Nepalisia's shoulder.

"You are an excellent leader and we need you here, as an ally, uniting all of Neponia, as one," she told Nepalisia.

"But, what of my troops," Nepalisia muttered as the news finally began to sink in. Nepelia smiled.

"You will keep your Battalion with you, to help in your acceptance as Queen," she told her niece. Nepanities and Nepeslia laughed at her again.

"You have been promoted cousin," Nepeslia and Nepanities said together, laughing even harder, as they both hugged her. The two Queens stepped back and let the young women share the moment, as the muted sounds of those who celebrated the death of Nepolia, gave them an encouraging serenade.

The night was closing in as Melsikan went and personally checked all watches. He was taking no chances that the rebels could sneak in and take his wife, or Kris. Returning to his and Isabella's quarters, he saw that she was lying on the bed, but her eyes were open and she was watching him.

"Is everything alright?" she asked in a whisper. He smiled and nodded.

"Yes my love," he told her as took his outer clothes off and climbed into the bed with her. "Everyone is on high alert." Isabella sighed as she snuggled into his arms.

"I'm worried," she whispered. "What if they do get in?" He chuckled softly.

"They will find many surprises waiting for them," he said, pulling her even tighter to him. "Try to get some sleep, you're completely safe," he assured her. She closed her eyes, but knew she wouldn't sleep until Brando and his troops were defeated.

Brendo lead the dwarf female and the four soldiers she had picked, from the barn, not long after the sun had set. The dwarf took the lead, as they made their way towards the castle. Brendo's eyes and ears were constantly searching for the patrols. Several times they had to find hiding places as they neared the castle, but managed to avoid being discovered. It took hours for the dwarf to lead them to the entrance that no one else seemed to be aware of. The same entrance that Porkligor and Rentaring had used to infiltrate the castle. They looked for several minutes before the dwarf moved forward, to what seemed as any other part of the wall. She opened the stone door that the others' hadn't been able to see. Once inside and the door closed again, they donned the face coverings they had brought. As they prepared to move further into the castle, Brendo pulled a bottle from an inside pocket of the dark coat she wore, that held the sleep inducing liquid, that she intended to use on the two they were to capture.

The dwarf had explained that the one called Kris, shared a room with Daridar and Besaline, the old slave master. The one called Isabella shared her room with her husband.

The dwarf led them, carefully, avoiding the patrolling soldiers. They stopped outside the door that the dwarf said was the room that held Kris. She again whispered the location of Kris's bed. Brendo nodded as she eased the door open. They snuck into the room silently. Two of the soldiers stayed at the door, as a lookout and Brendo and two soldiers approached Kris's bed. They did not see that the dwarf female slipped away, trying to escape, or that Daridar had her eyes open and was watching them as they neared the sleeping Kris. They also couldn't hear the silent message that Daridar sent to Jennifer, who sent a message to the defense teams. She also sent the alert to Melsikan and Zachia, waking them to action.

Brando had followed Brendo's group. He was convinced that there was a possibility of Brendo not succeeding and he wanted to see how his sister was captured. He had followed Brendo into the castle and now watched the door they had entered, from a dark alcove not far from the door. He was not surprised when there was a sudden appearance of a lot soldiers, staying out of sight of the doorway.

Brendo pulled the cloth from the bottle, making sure to keep it far from her face and started to reach for Kris's face. That was when a great many things began to happen, all at once. Daridar screeched as she sprang from her bed. Six wolves came from an opening in the wall that a second ago, had not been there and the soldiers of the castle charged into the room, throwing the two at the door, who had turned at Daridar's screech and weren't looking out the door, to the floor. Brendo tried to send blast spells, but a wolf closed its jaws on her arm and pulled her to the floor, the other five wolves' taking an attack positions over and around her. The two other soldiers immediately knew they were going to lose and threw their hands up in surrender. The entire capture was accomplished in less than a minute and with the exception of Daridar's screech, silently. Brando smiled as he snuck back out of the castle and returned to the barn.

Zachia told a messenger to gather all of the army's commanders and leaders of the races, in the throne room, as he and Melsikan went to Kris's room. When they walked into the room, Brendo had been bound with magical restraints and the Power Stone amulet had been taken from her neck. The wolves' stood watch around her. She glared at the smiling muzzles of her guards. The four soldiers were bound and stood in one corner, the amulets they had worn, had also taken from them and their heads were down. He looked at Kris. She smiled and nodded. He nodded his answer and turned to the leader of the troops. "Place them all in cells, far apart from each other," he said pointing to the four soldiers, as the screaming rage of the female dwarf was heard, getting closer. He looked to the scowling Brendo and smiled. "Make sure she is kept very far from the others'. I will interrogate her later." The soldiers nodded and led the invaders away. Melsikan stepped from the room and the dwarf, still raging at being held, was brought before him.

DEFIANCE OF THE REALM

"We caught her sneaking down the next corridor," one of the soldiers holding her said, with a half smile. "She claims she couldn't sleep and was just walking." Melsikan nodded and looked to dwarf as Daridar stepped up beside him.

"How did you get them inside the castle?" he asked and the dwarf opened her eyes wide as she looked to him.

"Who?" She asked with false innocence. Daridar growled, stepping closer to the dwarf.

"You had better tell us what we want to know," she said in a low and threatening voice; "or I will ask you these questions, privately!" Daridar had leaned in close to the female with her last words and, she was glaring. The dwarf looked at her, then to Melsikan as Isabella came up behind her husband. Kris and Besaline came from the room. "Do you want to talk with me in private?" Daridar roared at the dwarf, leaning in even closer, her face flushed red and her fists clenched, and half raised. The female showed her terror of the thought of what Daridar might do without witnesses and began to talk, loudly.

"I brought them in the hidden door," she screeched, trying to back from Daridar's enraged face.

"Where is this door?" Melsikan asked, placing his hand on Daridar's shoulder, gently pulling her from the other dwarf.

"I will show you, I swear I will," the dwarf squeaked. Melsikan nodded.

"Do so now," he told her. The dwarf turned, or tried to.

"Bind her hands and then let her lead us," Melsikan told the ones holding her. They nodded and followed his orders. "Now show us this door," Melsikan told her when she was bound. She turned and started walking. The guards stayed to her side, as the rest followed.

Brando woke Corlaar and several others' when he returned to the barn. They gathered at the center table, still rubbing the recently found sleep from their eyes. "Brendo has been captured," he announced. They all looked to each other and then to him.

"What are we to do to get her free?" Corlaar asked with the dedication of a true protector. Brando smiled.

"We will free her, if she has not already freed herself, when we have captured the castle," he told them all softly. They looked to him in confusion. "I had thought that the defenses would be ready for an attempt like this and had given Brendo her instructions, in case she was captured." Again, the others' looked to each other. "She and, the four with her, are to be the third leg of our attack," Brando told them with a smile.

The dwarf led them to the hidden door. Melsikan examined it completely, inside and out. He posted several hidden guards to watch the inside and had the outer patrols, the ones closest to the castle, to include surveillance of it in their patrols, but not to make it obvious that they were doing so. He and those with him then joined Zachia and all of the commanders, in the throne room. When all were seated and quiet had settled, he told them what he planned.

———

Brendo sat on the hard mattress that covered the even harder slatted bed, in her cell. She scowled as the door was locked by the guards. She waited until the guards had left her alone and her scowl turned to a small grin as she pulled the active amulet from her pants. It had been hidden in a place that was doubted would be searched. Her smile grew as she placed the chain around her neck and hid the amulet under the shirt she wore, knowing the four soldiers that had come with her, were doing the same thing. She allowed herself a quiet chuckle as she thought of what they were going to do when her brother launched his attack.

———

Neither Brando's commanders, nor the commanders of the forces of the castle, had gotten much sleep after their meetings, but both sides woke to the morning sun with a purpose. Brando's forces began the gathering of the remainder of the individual four armies, around the castle. Most of those armies were already in place, or very close to their positions. The commanders and the squad leaders were the last to arrive. Corlaar, who was to lead the fifth group and were going to enter the castle through the secret door, was reviewing the drawings of the castle layout.

In the castle, Werelaran, who was in charge of the wolves and werewolves inside of the castle, was giving his final instructions to his troops. Most of those forces went to the cavern that Kris had first brought Isabella to, waiting for the alert as to where in the castle they were to travel. The rest maintained their patrols in the tunnels. The humans and the races inside the castle doubled their patrols of the castle and the watches on the ramparts of the castle. The fairy folk and imps were busier than ever carrying messages and aiding the patrols, inside and outside of the castle. Grrale, the leader of the wolf and werewolf forces who patrolled outside the perimeter of the castle, again told his troops what to watch for, and to be at maximum alert to any build up of people. The Natharian's, who had been patrolling as individuals, now did so in groups of three. The police and the Mayors guards of Namsia, with the ogres and those from Ventoria, increased the number and weaponry of their patrols around the castle. A short time after the sun reaching its highest point in the sky, both sides were in position and finishing their preparations for the coming assault.

Zachia, Emma, Melsikan, Isabella, Kris, Alan, and Jennifer, stood in the center of the highest tower, watching the preparations of the castle forces. "You have planned well Melsikan," Zachia said as he slowly turned, looking from the many windows around the room.

"There's one thing that still bothers me," Melsikan said as he too looked from the windows. Zachia and the others' looked to him. He turned to face them. "Brendo didn't seem all that surprised at her capture," he told them. There were exchanged looks by all there and suddenly Emma looked to Zachia.

"Wasn't it said that Brando and those who had come with him to Neponia, had stolen the deactivated Power Stones from Nepolia and her people?" she asked him. Zachia nodded his answer. "What if Brando had thought that Brendo would be captured and had given her and those with her, the deactivated stones and they had hidden the active stones that they had gotten from Nepolia, on them, where they wouldn't be found?" Zachia looked to Melsikan and they both ran from the tower, heading for the cells of Brendo and the four soldiers. Alan chased after them.

Brando gathered the six soldiers who had come with him and his sister to Nepolia's castle and he talked earnestly to them, separate from the rest. Shortly, he and the six joined the others' studying the castle layout. When they all thought they had what they needed, Brando took Corlaar aside and they plotted the final assault through the hidden door. It was mid afternoon when Corlaar told his troops what they were going to do. There were many smiling faces among those who felt the sureness of their victory.

Even though Brendo had slept fitfully, when her breakfast was brought, she woke with a definite feeling of readiness. She picked up the tray that had been slid through the small opening at the bottom of the door and went to her bed, pretending to eat as the guard who had brought the tray, sneered at her, and then left. Once alone again, she set the tray aside, and with her eyes, slowly and carefully explored the room that held her cell. Hers was one of the two cells in this room, and the thick stone walls of the room, had but two doors. She ignored the one the guard had entered and left through, and concentrated of the other, heavy metal door. She called out to the soldiers who had come with her and received no answer. She smiled as she brought the amulet from beneath her shirt and began her incantation. The door trembled and then slowly and silently, opened. She turned to her cell door and repeated her spell, and it too swung open. She almost laughed as she walked from the cell and through the other door. She stopped and looked down the dark hallway, which curved away from her. She called again to her troops and was rewarded with a feint answer. She started for the sound, her grin growing with each step.

Alan caught up with Zachia and Melsikan just before they got to the guards room. The two guards came to attention when the three entered. Zachia pointed to the door. "Open it," he commanded. One of the guards pulled a large key ring that held three keys, from his coat pocket and opened the door. Zachia cautiously lead the three through the door. He stopped and looked to the empty cell and the open door, opposite of the one he had come through. He turned to the guard. "Is there another way into this cell block?" he asked and the guard nodded and told him the way. Zachia turned to Melsikan. "You and Alan get there as quickly as you can. I will count to thirty and that should give you enough time," he told him. The two nodded and started to run for the other entrance. "Be careful. She is powerful, and she heading for her troops!" Zachia called after them. Melsikan waved his hand. They were quickly out of sight. Zachia turned to the guard. "Send a message to put all in this section on alert," he ordered. The guard saluted and left the room. Zachia turned back to the other door and began his count. When he reached thirty, he started into the hallway, following Brendo.

Melsikan and Alan burst into the second guard room and caught the two there, napping. The guards tried to make excuses, but Melsikan waved their words aside, pointing to the door leading to the cell block, speaking to the one closest to him.

"Open it and then go and get any soldiers you can find. Brendo has escaped and she has a Power Stone," he ordered. The two guards stared at him in disbelief. "Move!" Melsikan roared at them and they did. Melsikan and Alan entered the door and Melsikan turned back to the remaining guard. "Relock it and don't let anyone, but us or Zachia, through it," he ordered. The guard saluted and relocked the door while the other went for help. The two turned back to the hallway that faced them and started forward. They had not traveled far when they heard an echoing call from Brendo, and the answering call from her soldiers. They shared a quick glance and started to move quicker, trying to be as quiet as they could.

———

Zachia had been moving as quickly as he dared. He had traveled a distance when he heard the same echoing call from Brendo that Melsikan and Alan had heard, and the answer of her soldiers. He started to trot and hoped that Melsikan and Alan were coming the other way. The next call from Brendo stopped him completely, for it sounded as though the woman was just ahead. He eased forward cautiously. He followed the curved hallway and almost walked up on Brendo, who was stopped, her hand raised and pointing at a cell door. Quickly, one of the soldiers came out and they went to the next door and Brendo repeated her actions. It was while Brendo was opening the fourth door that Zachia saw Melsikan and Alan walk into sight, from the other side. One of the soldiers cried out and the five lifted their hands to cast blast spells at the same time that Melsikan and Alan did. The five never got the chance to send their spells as Zachia put an immobilization spell on the five. Both Melsikan and Alan looked to Zachia with relief, as they walked to the frozen five. Zachia smiled as he removed the amulet from Brendo. Melsikan and Alan laughed as they removed the amulets from the soldiers.

"Cut that kind of close, didn't we?" Alan asked as he and Melsikan came near Zachia. Zachia smiled again with his nod.

"Now what do we do with them?" Melsikan asked, pointing to Brendo and the soldiers. Zachia chuckled.

"Alan, would you go and get some of the guards to help move them back to their cells?" he asked. Alan nodded as he turned back the way he had come. "I've got to call Neponia and find out if there is some safe way to destroy these," Zachia said holding up the Power Stones that had been taken from the five. Melsikan nodded with lifted brows.

Zachia, Melsikan, and Alan, returned to the command room, where the others' had already gathered. Melsikan went to the grouped commanders as Zachia called to his sister, Michele, about the captured stones. She told him that Neponities said that he should spell the stones to her and that the Mearlies could deactivate them easily. Zachia nodded, with a silent sigh and spelled the stones to the Queen. "Zachia," Melsikan called to him. Zachia went to the group, Emma joining him there. "The rebels are doing little to hide their gatherings," Melsikan told the Overseer. Zachia looked to him and then to the commanders. They nodded their agreement. "We are receiving reports of four large groups massing, around, yet still a distance from the castle," Melsikan told him, pointing to four places on the map of the area around the castle. Zachia looked at the map, thinking.

"The fairy folk said that he was planning a three phase attack," Emma whispered, standing beside Zachia. Zachia looked to her. "These four placements are but one." Zachia nodded as a small grin came to him. He looked to Melsikan and the commanders.

"It is probable that Brendo and her troops were to be part of one of those phases," he said softly; "which would probably include some coming through the hidden door in the castle wall." They all nodded.

"That's only two, what can he plot as the third?" Emma asked, her voice still hushed, as she looked to her husband. He looked to her, then to each of those around the map on the table, and then around the large room itself. Some of those commanders actually shrugged. Zachia almost smiled when he spoke.

"I think that Brando will come after the leaders of our forces, directly," he told all of them. Brows lifted. "I think he plans to spell himself and a small band, to attack this command center, to disrupt whatever orders that would come from here. He plans to destroy the leaders, hoping that those who would follow those orders would not be able to coordinate efficiently enough, to stop the main attack from these four armies!" Melsikan was actually smiling for real, when he spoke.

"Then I think it best that it not be the commanders he meets, but a force that he would not expect," Melsikan said. Zachia nodded, as did Emma, as they too smiled.

"Remember, you must find Brendo as quickly as possible," Brando told Corlaar. "She is aware of my plans and she will direct you and your troops, to your responsibilities." Corlaar nodded as he grinned at Brando. "If for any reason, that you are unable to find her, you are to come to the throne room and join me in the defeat of the commanders. We will destroy the very heart of those who would take our right to rule from us. And so, we will destroy all of those who would deny us our proper rule!" Corlaar could not stop his laughter at the thought of the defeat of those of the Realm. He led his forces towards the castle, to be ready when the attack was signaled. Brando went and sat, relaxing. He could not stop his pleasure as his thoughts went to his future success and when he would take his place as ruler of all Bandarson!

<hr />

As Zachia, Emma, Melsikan, Isabella, and the commanders, plotted about how this new idea should be handled, Corlaar and his troops found their place of waiting, near the door that would lead them to their success. The rest of the Namsia forces were creating lines of defense against the four large armies that were massing. Many, with a greater magical power began to create a wide and deep ditch, in a semicircle, out from the rear of the castle. The ditch was to slow, or at best, stop any who would attack from the rear. Others began building low, double walls. These walls, which wound through the streets of the city, formed a semicircle around the front of the castle. The walls, separated by the width of the streets they followed, were just over chest high, and were meant to slow any attackers, yet not inhibit the sending of blast spells by the defenders. The dragons, some of which would carry riders of magical power and some who would carry riders who carried reflectors, gathered and studied the maps of the two different areas around the castle. Eagles and Bats gathered in another area, going over maps themselves, as to where the bags of sleeping potion, were to be dropped and, when. Werelaran and the wolves inside the castle gathered and they again went over the layout of the tunnels, so that they could quickly travel where there might be battles. Alan gathered the troops that would be the ones to defend the secret door, stopping any that would try to enter, with sword and spell. Grrale, met with all those leaders who were part of the outside defenses. They reviewed the plans of how they were to battle. Fairy folk and imps were very busy carrying messages from one group to another, as the sun started its slow fall to the horizon.

CHAPTER FOURTEEN

Zachia looked to Melsikan and they both gave a small nod. They turned from each other and went to places that had been decided they must be, but each looked to a window as they passed and saw the suns first touching with the horizon. They both felt the tensions of a coming horror.

Brendo had been ordered back from the cell door as the guard prepared to shove her supper plate through the small opening at the bottom of the door. The guard watched her as he slid the plate. His words taunted her. He laughed as he told her that she was defeated and that she, and her rebellious brother, were to pay the price for their traitorous acts. She showed no outward reaction to his taunting. The guard began to stand, but had to use his hand on the floor, to push himself from his crouched position. Brendo moved as a striking snake, quickly grabbing the guard's neck, snapping it as she spun his body. She reached into the coat pocket she had seen the guard place the keys and pulled them free as she dropped the body. She quickly slipped the key into the cell door and opened it. Not a sound had been made, so the guard in the other room did not know of Brendo's escape. She snuck to the door that the guard had left open when he had entered and looked into the room beyond. She saw the other guard at the desk, his head dropping and lifting as he fought sleep. She was grinning as she closed her hands on his neck and broke it, easily. She then locked the outer door and returned to the room that held her cell, locking the door behind her. She crossed to the door that led to the cells that held her troops and opening it, she passed into the hallway. She relocked the door and then sprinted down the hall.

———

Brando looked to the west and watched the sun as it collided with the horizon and he smiled. That was the signal for his armies to begin their attack on the castle. He felt an increase in his heart beat and an excitement, for what was to be his taking of power from the Realm and those who would follow it. He looked to the six who sat in the barn with him. His smile grew, as did theirs. "Be prepared, we attack soon!" he told them loudly and they cheered for their coming success!

———

Zachia arrived in the south west tower at the same time as Melsikan reached the north east one. Emma was already in the south east tower, as Isabella was in the northwest one. They each looked to charging armies, still a long way from the castle. They each saw the eighty eagles, twenty per charging army, take flight from the trees. They were heading straight towards the charging armies. They watched as the eagles neared the armies and began to drop their bags of sleeping potion. They did not miss and many of the charging people suddenly fell to the ground, asleep. Those in towers cringed, as those who had been put to sleep, were trampled by those following them. The four in the towers, sent messages to the commanders to begin the next part of their defense, as the armies were now approaching the walls and ditch.

Those of greater magical powers began launching blast spells at the attackers. Those spells were meant more as a warning than a threat, as they were still too far from the attackers to have much of an effect, but it didn't slow the attackers. Then they found the double walls, and the wide and deep ditch. Many of the front lines tumbled into the ditch, as those who faced the walls, were shoved over them, being impaled by the spiked tips. This managed to slow the rest, but not for long. Quickly, styles and bridges were brought, as the rebels had seen the walls and ditch being made, and they had prepared for them both. The charge continued, as the styles and bridges were placed. Some of the rebels, who had a stronger magical power, sent their spells at the defenders, covering the crossings. That is when the bats made their first run with their bags of sleeping potion. There were many that started across the styles and bridges, but didn't make it all the way, before sleep came to them. Then the dragons arrived. They were unable to flame the styles directly, as they were too close to the houses that sided the streets, but could those who had reached the streets, between the styles. The dragons coming to the rear of the castle, started to flame the bridges. Unfortunately, the attacking forces had planned for this as well and it would seem that they had plated the wooden bridges with some kind of metal and the flames did not succeed as well as hoped. The attackers kept coming!

Corlaar and his troops charged the door in the wall. They had been waiting for the armies to attract most of the defenders attentions. They expected some troops to be there to fight them off, but when they entered the door, most of those first through the door, were hit with arrows and blast spells and bodies quickly filled the doorway. This had also been planned for and those coming behind the first ones, used the bodies of their fallen comrades as shields and pushed their way into the castle, casting their own spells around the bodies they carried.

Alan, the one in charge of this section, received word that the rebels had gotten inside of the castle, through the secret door. He sent reinforcements, as he notified Zachia and Melsikan of his status. No one had yet learned that Brendo and, the four she had brought, had found their freedom.

Brendo and her four had surprised the guards, at the other end of the cell block. They killed them and locked all the doors, throwing the keys through the grated window of the outer door, back into the guard's room. She knew what she was to do. She hoped that she was not too late.

The five ran for the area that held the secret door, hearing the battle long before they came to it. The defending troops were not expecting an attack from the rear, so Brendo and her four managed to kill many of the defenders, by surprise. She walked to Corlaar, smiling. He returned her smile, but there was concern in his eyes, as he held the wound to his left arm he had received from a sword of one of the defenders. Brendo looked to the wound and then to his eyes. "Can you still fight?" she asked him. He nodded with his words.

"Yes, what are we to do now?" he replied, handing Brendo a power stone amulet. One with medical skills came to him and bandaged his wound as Brendo told him what must be done. He nodded to her orders and divided their remaining troops. Corlaar and the limited number of his troops headed for the throne room, to give Brando a rear guard. Brendo began her assault on the interior troops that patrolled the outer regions of the castle. Alan had anticipated the possibility of a possible break though and had alerted Werelaran and the wolves in the tunnels, to spread out, over the exterior hallways and be prepared for the attacking forces. Brendo received a surprise as she tried to defeat the defending forces. She died as she sent a blast spell at some of the defenders. Three huge wolves and one werewolf landed on her at the same time. She did manage one scream before she died. The surviving troops with her, quickly surrendered.

Brando had been counting slowly and when he reached two hundred, he stood. The troops with him stood as well. They were grinning at him as he nodded to them. He made the movements with his hands and a portal open. They all charged into the throne room, roaring, expecting to surprise the commanders. Corlaar was almost to the throne room when he heard Brando's roar as he and those with him, charged into the room. He came to a sudden halt as he and the ones with him, heard the roars of Brando's troops, change to screams as they charged into the blast spells that met them. The defenders had been told to try and not kill Brando, but capture him and keep him guarded until Zachia and Melsikan could question him. Unfortunately, the adrenalin rush of battle overcame some of the defenders and Brando died with his troops. Word was quickly passed of that death.

<hr />

By now, the attacking armies were meeting the first line of defense. Minor magical power, swords and spears and staffs, challenged the defenders. The attackers yelled and roared at those they saw as the true enemy of Bandarson. The rebels had seen the creatures, on their patrols around the castle, but had no real idea of the power of the Natharian's, the Ventorians and the ogres, not to mention the wolves, trolls, eagles and dragons from the air, nor the determination of the Mayors guards and police of Namsia. They really hadn't considered the soldiers of the Realm and their magical powers, who came pouring out of the castle, joining in the battle. Despite being vastly outnumbered by the rebel's armies, the defenders of Namsia began to drive the rebels back.

The vast number of rebels created more of a problem for themselves than they had expected. There was no room for them to fight effectively. As the opposing forces blended, there were wounded and killed on both sides, but the rebels losses were rapidly becoming many, many, times greater. As the fighting raged, becoming more and more one sided, all around the castle, those in the back of the rebel's armies, who had not even reached the fight yet, began to see what was happening and they turned and ran, depleting the attacker's numbers radically. The direction of the battle moved rapidly to the defenders advantage. Many of the rebels, who had been in the first onslaught, began to surrender and that momentum grew at an astounding rate. Quicker than many had thought possible, all was quiet and the battle was over. Surviving rebels were herded into groups and guarded. Healers tended to the wounded as much as they could. The dead were grouped in one area, divided as to rebel, or soldier of Namsia, or Realm. From the moment of the rebels beginning attack, when the sun had first touched the horizon, until the rebels were defeated, had taken a little over an hour.

CHAPTER FIFTEEN

When the sun had finally again returned to Namsia, Zachia, Emma, Melsikan, Isabella, Kris, Daridar, and Parsony sat at the table in the throne room, sharing coffee, listening to, or reading, the varied reports that were coming in at an amazing rate. There was sadness that was shared in the tired eyes of each, when they would occasionally glance to another. Very few of Namsia had slept that night. None of those at the table, nor those who brought the reports, the guardians of the captured rebels, the healers and their assistants, or the morticians, had slept at all. What was to be done with the rebels and what was to be done about the physical damage done to the city of Namsia had become the main topic of discussion.

"There are too many to imprison," Parsony said to all present, as he looked around the table. Daridar growled, but nodded her agreement with the others.

"To say nothing of the costs for rebuilding," she muttered. Zachia managed a small, tired grin.

"I suggest that the rebels bear the brunt of those costs, "he told Daridar. She looked to him, confused.

"I think that you and your government should impose a fine upon them. Some to pay in monies, some to pay with part of their harvest, or stock sales and all should make payments with their labors, for the cities repairs." Zachia explained to her. "You will have to implement a department of finance to control the records of payments and such, but that is the only possible solution I see." Daridar slowly nodded her head, as she thought. She turned to Parsony.

"I also suggest," Melsikan said, interrupting Daridar's thoughts; "that you form a defensive army of your own, to watch for any others that would think of rebellion in the future." All those at the table, nodded their agreement. Daridar looked to each and began to nod herself. She looked to Parsony.

"Would you take the position of General of that army?" she asked, in her official voice. He smiled as he nodded.

"Yes Mayor, I would be honored to lead your army of defense," he told her. Tired grins tried to show their approval. Zachia looked to Melsikan, Isabella, and Kris.

"It is time that you all return to your families," he told them. Melsikan began to say something, but Isabella grabbed his arm, hard, and jerked it. Kris laughed out loud at her friends actions.

"We are more than ready to do that Zachia, very more than ready," she said earnestly, as she looked into Melsikan's eyes. He looked at her with surprise at first, but that quickly changed to a grin and a nod. He looked to Zachia and Emma.

"It would seem Overseer," he said in a soft voice; "that my wife is again, quite correct!" They all laughed, as they all nodded. An hour later, the three disappeared from Namsia and appeared behind their homes, in Zentler. The entire town had known of what had happened and the three were welcome home, as heroes. With their return, the children settled from their separations of the adults, though Benjamin stayed more to himself than even before.

During the next twenty four hours, those of the Realm, Ventoria, Weretoran, and Natharia, were returned to their Domains

Zachia, Emma, Tarson, who had come with Zachia, to command the troops from the Realm, and Prelilian, who had come to be with her husband, after the battle was over, stayed in Namsia for over two weeks. Tarson worked with Parsony, on starting and training of the Namsia Guard. That was what Parsony named those who chose to defend Namsia, City and domain.

Daridar, with Zachia and Emma's help, named the head of the cities treasury as Director of Finance and worked with the Council members on what the fairest fines to be levied would be. All of the captured rebels names and livelihood had been recorded and then those rebels were released. They were all warned of what would be if they tried to repeat their actions and told they would be financially responsible for whatever costs came from their actions. Many of these rebels gladly shared the names of those of their cause, who had run away, for they did not want to pay the runners fines. Those who had fled the battle were found and told the same as those who had been captured.

Finally, almost three weeks after the rebellions end, Zachia was satisfied that those of Namsia could continue on their own, Zachia, Emma, Tarson, and Prelilian, returned to the Realm. Glornina, and the Overseers children, welcomed them home, with tears of pride and joy! Both Zachia and Emma saw the resolute look in their son's eyes. They knew that their battles with those who would try to take what they had not earned, was not over. Mike reminded them regularly!

The talkers, seers and sensitive's, of Somora's small empire, had been relaying the events of the battle in Namsia, to Somora. When they reported that the revolution seemed over, he called his General to him. They met in Somora's office. Somora began to outline his plans for the future efforts of his spies, the Gargoyles and Gaspilarians and, what part the Listamans would be involved in. "I do not trust the Listamans," Hantopan said to Somora. Somora grinned widely as he faced his General.

"Neither do I, but they have the ferocity we will need to cause the worries the Domains of Rightful Magic must feel," Somora told him, going to his chair behind his desk. As Hantopan sat in the chair, in front of Somora's desk,

Somora was thinking of all of the possibilities of how the Listamans could be used, to wreak a deadly havoc on the Domains of Rightful magic. Hantopan felt a chill of fear wash over him as he looked to the deadly smile of his King.

CHARACTORS

Human

<u>Alan</u>- magical powers, high- husband of Jennifer

<u>Ava</u>- magical powers, very, very, high- daughter of Isabella and Melsikan-

<u>Baldor</u>- magical powers, med- spy in Overseer's palace, for Somora

<u>Barkoor</u>- [Namsia]magical powers, med- henchman for Brando

<u>Beling</u>- [Namsia]magical powers, med-illegitimate son of Porkligor- chief of police for Namsia City

<u>Bella</u>- {Isabella}- magical powers, high- daughter of Marcus and Penelopy- younger sister of Giorgio

<u>Ben</u>- magical powers, med[Dremlor]- spy for Somora- husband of Terressa- father of Benjamin

<u>Benilon</u>- [Namsia]magical powers, med[talker]- daughter of Pelinon

<u>Benjamin</u>- magical powers, high- son of Ben and Terressa

<u>Bortenon</u>- magical powers, med[sensitive/seer]- works for Somora

<u>Brando</u>- magical powers, high- son of Brandaro and Cenlinas- twin brother of Brendo- leader of rebels on Namsia

<u>Braxton</u>- magical powers, med[sensitive, seer]- husband of Glorian

<u>Brendo</u>- magical powers, med- daughter of Brandaro and Cenlinas- twin sister of Brando

<u>Calitoran</u>- [Neponia]magical powers, low- advisor to Nepolia

<u>Carl</u>- no magical powers- husband of Kris- father of Nathan and Geebee

<u>Carla</u>- magical powers, very high[talker]- wife of Edward- mother of Barrett and Karrie

<u>Carsanac</u>- [Neponia]magical powers, med- Chosen Mate of Nepanities-

<u>Cartland</u>- magical powers, high[shape shifter]- son of Quansloe and Hannah[Plain]- son of Megan and Darren- husband of Xanaleria

Cartope- [Neponia]magical powers, high- leader of Dark City refugees to Neponia- daughter of Castope- wife of Ralsanac- mother of Nepopea- grandmother of Seastaria

Cenlinas- [Namsia]no magical powers- mother of Brando and Brendo

Corlaar- [Namsia]magical powers, low- second in command of rebels of Namsia

Crandon- magical powers, high- grandson of Brei, Crondasa, Candy, Paul- son of Crodena and Farsel- husband of Pentilian- father of Jarsona and Paolaria

Crendoran- magical powers, high- grandson of Elamson, Ferlinos, Renoria, Crandora- son of Gerpinos and Vandora- husband of Michele- father of Mearlanor, Dafnorian, Ramnarson

Croldena- magical powers, high- grandson of Crendosa, Maelie, Cindy, George- son of Xanadelis and Peter- husband of Meladiana- father of Creldora and Aaralyn

Depelia- [Nepolia]magical powers, high- second strongest of power in Southern Section of Neponia

Dolores- magical powers, high[Dremlor]- spy in Zentler, Mayor's office, for Somora

Dospora- magical powers high[Dremlor]- comate of Somora

Edward- magical powers, high- Keeper of Magic for the North West Domain- grandson of Narisha, Brandon, Brei, Crondasa- son of Quoslon and Xanalenor- husband of Carla- father of Barrett and Karrie

Emma- magical powers, very, very, high- older sister of Cartland- wife of Zachia- becomes Mistress of the Realm

Gabriella{GeeBee}- magical powers, very, very, high[seer, talker]- daughter of Carl and Kris- younger sister of Nathan

Giorgio- magical powers, low- son of Marcus and Penelopy- older brother of Bella

Glorian- magical powers, very, very, high[talker]- daughter of Namson and Glornina- younger sister of Zachia- older sister of Michele

Glornina- magical powers, very high- granddaughter of Tyrus, Heather, Trayton and Chrystal- daughter of Sonilon and Ventia- wife of Namson- mother of Zachia, Glorian, Michele

Gordon- magical powers, med- mayor of the town Zentler- husband of Xanaporia- father of Isabella, Barttel, and Xanaleria

Isabella- magical powers, high- daughter of Gordon and Ava- wife of Melsikan- mother of Ava[young]

Jarsalon- magical powers, high- Keeper of Magic of Dolaris- grandson of Jardan, Dana, Tommy, Carmon- son of Jardilan and Marge- husband of Quentoria- father of Quentia and Jarponer

Jennifer- magical powers, very high[talker]- daughter of Morsley and Penny- wife of Alan

Kris- no magical powers- saves Isabella from Brandaro- best friend of Isabella- wife of Carl- mother of Nathan and GeeBee

Marcus- no magical powers- husband of Penelopy- father of Giorgio

Melsikan-magical powers, very, very, high- husband of Isabella- father of Ava

Mesetere- magical powers, high[Dremlor]- daughter of Mestilia- sent as spy to the Realm

Mestilia- magical powers, high[Dremlor][talker]- strongest talker for Somora- mother of Mesetere

Michele- magical powers, very high- granddaughter of Sonilon, Ventia, Elamson, Ferlinos- daughter of Namson and Glornina- youngest sister of Zachia and Glorian- wife of Crendoran- mother of Mearlanor, Dafnorian, Ramnarson

Namson- magical powers, ultra high- overseer of the Realm- husband of Glornina- father of Zachia, Glorian, and Michele

Nathan- magical powers, med[latent]- son of Kris and Carl- older brother of GeeBee

Nepanities- [Neponia]magical powers, high- daughter of Neponities- mate of Carsanac

Nepelia- [Neponia]magical powers, high- Queen of Northern Section- mother of Nepeslia

Nepeslia-[Neponia]magical powers, high- daughter of Queen Nepelia

Nepolia- Neponia]magical powers, med- Queen of Southern Section- tries to make a pact with Bandarson

Neponities- [Neponia] magical powers, high- Queen of Central Section- mother of Nepanities

Nepopea- [Neponia] magical powers, high- daughter of Cartope and Ralsanac

Paolaria- magical powers, high[invisibility]- daughter of Crandon and Pentilian- wife of Karlten

Parsony-[Namsia] magical powers, low- head of Daridar's guard-

Pelinon- [Namsia]magical powers, med- seamstress for Nepolia- mother of Benilon

Pelinoria- magical powers, very high[invisibility]- wife of Morgan

Penelopy- magical powers, low[latent]- daughter of Sophia- wife of Marcus- mother of Giorgio and Bella

Perilia- magical powers, med[Dremlor]- comate of Somora

Prelilian- magical powers, very high- wife of Tarson

Seastaria- [Neponia]magical powers, high[seer]- granddaughter of Cartope and Ralsanac- daughter of Nepopea

Somora-[Dremlor] magical powers, high- leader of Marauders- seeks to control all rightful magic- mate of Perilia and Dospora

Tarson- magical powers, high- general of Realm Armies- husband of Prelilian

Terressa- magical powers, med[powerful talker]-husband of Ben- mother of Benjamin

Ventia- magical powers, high- daughter of Edward and Carla

Xanaleria- magical powers, very high-daughter of Gordon and Xanaporia- wife of Cartland

Xanaporia- magical powers, very high- wife of Gordon- mother of Xanaleria

Zachia- magical powers, ultra high- son of Namson and Glornina- husband of Emma- becomes Overseer when Namson killed

Elf

<u>Pelidora</u>- Magical powers, med- nurse/ healer for Overseer's palace

Fairy Folk

<u>Tremliteen</u>- magical powers, high- messenger for Overseer

Wingless

<u>Drandysee</u>- Magical powers, med- Elder of the Guardians

Troll

Wolf

<u>Crrale</u>- magical powers, low- son of Grrale and Terryle- mate of Serryle

<u>Grrale</u>- magical powers, low- leader of the Realm wolf pack- mate of Terryle- sire of Crrale

<u>Serryle</u>- magical powers, low- mate of Crrale

<u>Terryle</u>- magical powers, low- mate of Grrale

Dragon

<u>Cartile</u>- magical powers, low- leader of the Realm dragons- mate of Jastile- father of Chartile and Semitile

Jastile- magical powers, low- mate of Cartile- mother of Semitile

Merlintile- magical powers, med- mate of Semitile- becomes leader of Realm dragons with Cartile's death

Semitile- magical powers, med- daughter of Cartile and Jastile- mate of Merlintile

Natharian

Balsarlan- magical powers, low- leader of the Natharian tribe in the Realm- mate of Slirous- father of Belserlan

Belserlan- magical powers, low- 1st son of Balsarlan and Slirous- mate of Salirous- friend of Zachia- goes to Natharia as representative for Realm

Bistalan- magical powers, low- starts revolt against father Bleudarn- killed by Pastilan's forces

Blautdarn- magical powers, low- 4th son of Bleudarn- becomes ruler with defeat of revolution

Bleudarn- magical powers, low- Ruler of Natharia

Blirous- magical powers, med[talker]- 1st daughter of Bleudarn

Bremtilan- magical powers, low- eldest council member- is killed when he tells Bistalan he will be defeated

Castilan- magical powers, low- aide to Bistalan

Daralan- magical powers, low- aide to Pastilan

Dasilan- magical powers, low- leader of resistance fighters, against Bistalan and Pastilan

Pastilan- magical powers, low- spy for Somora- kills Bistalan to take rule of Natharia

Salirous- magical powers, low- mate of Belserlan

Slirous- magical powers, med[talker]- mate of Balsarlan

Dwarf

Daridar- Mayor of Namsia

Mearlie

Weltizorn- magical powers, low- old leader of the Northern Section Mearlies

Wenzorn- magical powers, low- leader of the Central Section Mearlies

Weslizorn- magical powers, low- leader of the Northern Section Mearlies

Wespozorn- magical powers, low- leader of the Southern Section Mearlies

Gargoyle {Gargoylia}

Garator- magical powers, med[winged]- ruler of Gargoylia

Garpilar- magical powers, low[winged]- misshapen henchman for Garplasar- leader of Gaspilarians

Garplasar- magical powers, high[winged]- most powerful of wizards in Gargoylia

Garpartor- magical powers low[wingless]- mate of Gorsentor- father of Garteltor and Gorastor

Garsendar- magical powers, low[wingless]- one of the six Gargoyles that live in Weretoran- male gargoyle that Cartland copies

Garteltor- magical powers, low[wingless- son of Gorsentor and Garpartor- older brother of Gorastor- leads attack on Garator's castle

Gorastor- magical powers, low[wingless]- daughter of Gorsentor and Garpartor- younger sister of Garteltor- leads revolt of slaves in Garator's castle

Gorpeelia- magical powers, low[wingless]- becomes friend of Gorastor- helps in revolt of slaves of Garator

Gorsentor- magical powers, low[wingless]- spy for Weretilon- wife of Garpartor- mother of Garteltor and Gorastor

Werewolf {Weretoran}

Peritor- magical powers, low- winged Weriron and messenger for Weretilon

<u>Werelaran</u>- magical powers, med- King of Weretoran-husband of Wereselon- father of Wereperan and Werenesilon

<u>Werementran</u>- magical powers, med- council member

<u>Weresanran</u>- magical powers, med- General of the Weretorian armies

<u>Wereselon</u>- magical powers, med- Queen of Weretoran-wife of Werelaran- mother of Wereperan and Werenesilon

<u>Weretilon</u>- magical powers, high- most powerful witch of Weretoran

<u>Weriron</u>- magical powers, low- messengers for Weretoran-females winged, males wingless

Listamans

<u>Liaganost</u>- magical powers, high- second in command to Lianost- mate of Liorpanora

<u>Lianost</u>- magical powers, high- leader of the prides of Listaman- mate of Liornora

<u>Liornora</u>- magical powers, high- mate of Lianost

<u>Liorpanora</u>- magical powers, high- mate of Liaganost